Night Magic

Night Magic

JENNA BLACK

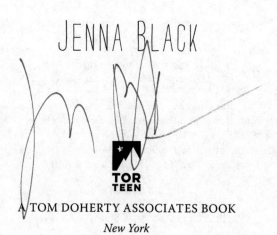

TOR TEEN

A TOM DOHERTY ASSOCIATES BOOK

New York

This is a work of fiction. All of the characters, organizations, and events portrayed in this novel are either products of the author's imagination or are used fictitiously.

NIGHT MAGIC

Copyright © 2017 by Jenna Black

All rights reserved.

A Tor Teen Book
Published by Tom Doherty Associates
175 Fifth Avenue
New York, NY 10010

www.tor-forge.com

Tor® is a registered trademark of Macmillan Publishing Group, LLC.

The Library of Congress Cataloging-in-Publication Data is available upon request.

ISBN 978-0-7653-8006-7 (hardcover)
ISBN 978-1-4668-7177-9 (e-book)

Our books may be purchased in bulk for promotional, educational, or business use. Please contact your local bookseller or the Macmillan Corporate and Premium Sales Department at 1-800-221-7945, extension 5442, or by e-mail at MacmillanSpecialMarkets@macmillan.com.

First Edition: May 2017

Printed in the United States of America

0 9 8 7 6 5 4 3 2 1

Night Magic

CHAPTER ONE

I was trapped in a quarantined city that went foaming-at-the-mouth crazy every night. My house was trashed so badly it was unlivable. My father was dead. I'd shot and killed my best friend.

And I was having the best time of my life.

I walked down the streets of Center City, Philadelphia, on a beautifully brisk winter night hand in hand with the hottest guy I'd ever seen and couldn't stop smiling.

Aleric grinned at me, his green eyes glittering in the darkness. The power was on—you could tell from the lighted windows all around—but the streetlamps turned into gallows every night, so the city didn't have the ambient glow I was used to. I loved the air of intimacy the darkness added.

"Are you wondering now why you resisted for so long?" Aleric asked.

"Stop being so smug." I punched him in the arm with my free hand. He laughed, letting go of my hand and putting his arm around my shoulders. I slipped my own arm around his waist, sidling closer until our hips were touching and we were forced to time our steps to each other. I rested my cheek against the buttery soft leather of his jacket, inhaling its delicious scent.

Just yesterday, I'd been almost suicidally miserable. I'd

blamed myself for the darkness that had descended on the city, for all the deaths that darkness had brought, for all the suffering. I'd even blamed myself for the death of my father, though with my new, clearer viewpoint it was hard to remember why. Any idiot could see that it wasn't my fault. Well, any idiot except the non-Nightstruck me, that is.

I'd slipped away during the night intending to kill Piper, but I never really expected to succeed. I wasn't depressed enough to take my own life, but I'd been in a bad-enough state that taking a suicidal risk had seemed like a good idea. Piper and Aleric had known that, had counted on it to lure me out into the night.

In the end, it had all been a giant trick, designed to weaken my psyche and make me susceptible to the lure of becoming Nightstruck. Turns out all it takes to become Nightstruck is to be outside during the Transition from night to day. If you're weak and vulnerable, the lure of the night magic will call to you and you'll be swept away to . . . well, wherever the Nightstruck disappeared to during the day. Even being Nightstruck myself, I wasn't sure I understood exactly what happened to us when daylight hit.

I'd desperately tried to avoid becoming Nightstruck, tried to get inside before the dawn Transition occurred, but I hadn't made it.

Thank God! It was hard to imagine why I'd fought something so wonderful. All that pain and guilt and grief . . . Gone, in the blink of an eye.

I rubbed my cheek against Aleric's leather jacket again, enjoying the decadent texture. Then I looked down at myself and frowned. I was wearing the same clothes I'd worn yesterday, obviously. I couldn't go back to my house and get a change of clothes, seeing as Piper and her Nightstruck friends had destroyed everything I owned. It was too cold for me to be terribly rank yet, but I still felt kind of scuzzy. Not to mention that my nice warm puffer coat was hideously ugly, made even more so in contrast to Aleric's gorgeous black leather jacket.

"I need some new clothes," I said, then frowned. "But I can't exactly go shopping, can I?" Aside from the fact that I had no money, all the city's stores were closed and locked up tight by sunset.

Aleric snorted. "You'll never have to shop again. Anything you want is yours for the taking."

"Well yeah, I know, but all the stores are closed, and the ones that didn't have good security have been stripped bare by now." When the city had first gone mad, packs of the Nightstruck had roamed around breaking into stores and houses willy-nilly. Those without good enough security measures had long since been picked clean, and the rest were virtual fortresses at night.

Aleric shrugged. "That may be a problem for the more run-of-the-mill Nightstruck, but you're different. I'm the king of this city and you are my queen."

He whistled loudly. A group of Nightstruck who'd been hanging out on someone's front stoop passing around a bottle of booze snapped to attention at the sound, then hurried to gather around us when Aleric beckoned with his free hand. The Nightstruck stared at him attentively, like a pack of devoted dogs, but he didn't speak. I gave him a quizzical look, but he just winked at me.

We must have stood there for like five minutes, the Nightstruck never taking their green eyes off Aleric, never speaking, barely even twitching. He was the center of their universe, and I had the vague sense that the old me would have been completely creeped out by the way they were looking at him.

"What are we waiting for?" I finally couldn't help asking. The temperature was dropping, and warm though my ugly puffer coat might be, I was starting to shiver.

"Patience, Becket," Aleric said with another of his smug smiles.

"I'm Nightstruck, idiot," I told him. "Patience is not one of my virtues." It felt just a little strange to talk to this virtual stranger, this guy I'd once considered my enemy, as if we were the best of friends. The old me had always been shy and tongue-tied, carefully thinking about every word that left my mouth. All that had changed, and I felt absolutely no discomfort about calling this powerful, dangerous person an idiot.

Aleric seemed more amused by my rudeness than irritated, and a moment later I heard the metallic clang of something approaching. Something four-footed, by the sound of it.

Most of the city's statues came to life at night, transformed from their daylight selves into nightmare constructs that would happily prey on any non-Nightstruck person who dared set foot outside. I figured that since we were only a few blocks away from Rittenhouse Square, the approaching footsteps came from one of those statues, and it turned out I was right.

I'd had some nasty run-ins with Billy, the bronze goat statue from the square, but what turned the corner now was about ten times more terrifying. I was pretty sure that during the day, it was a snarling lion that was as dangerous-looking as Billy was harmless, but the night had given it a serious makeover. Its mane consisted of a mass of writhing, hissing metal snakes, and its tail had turned into a scorpion-like stinger. And as if that wasn't bad enough, it also had a set of finger-sized mandibles that looked very much like a spider's. Being Nightstruck, I was supposedly immune to the terror of the city's constructs, but this one gave me a serious case of the shivers.

The mutant lion sauntered right up to Aleric, the other Night-struck moving quickly aside to let it by. Guess I wasn't the only one who thought the creature was scary. Aleric, however, reached out to pet the damn thing's head, heedless of the snakes and the constantly moving mandibles. I shuddered and slipped out from under Aleric's arm when the lion made a low thrum-ming sound that I supposed was a purr and butted its head—very gently—against his chest.

"Leo here would be happy to take us shopping," Aleric said. "Wouldn't you, Leo?"

Leo made a whuff of what was probably agreement. Aleric reached for my hand, but I shied away. I'm not one of those girls who runs screaming at the very thought of a snake, but I had no interest in getting closer to that writhing, hissing mass on Leo's head, and the spider jaws made my stomach turn.

Aleric laughed at me but made a little shooing motion with his hand. "Back off and give us a little room. There's a good kitty."

Leo stepped back by maybe about ten inches. He was still way closer than I liked, but I didn't want Aleric thinking I was a wuss, and I knew that the construct wouldn't hurt me. I gritted my teeth and stepped forward to take Aleric's hand. One of the snakes in Leo's mane lunged at me. I squeaked and tried to jump back, but Aleric held me fast and the snake's fangs snapped together about six inches from my nose.

"Relax, Becks," Aleric said. "He's just playing with you."

Playing. Right.

I was more relieved than I could say when Aleric gave my hand a little tug and we started walking down the street again. The Nightstruck fell in behind us like an untidy army, and Leo walked beside us, his metal claws clanking against the pave-ment with each step.

Our little parade made its way over to Walnut Street, one of the more fashionable shopping areas of the city. Many of the windows were boarded up, the stores having been early victims to the marauding Nightstruck before anyone knew they needed extra protection. The rest were covered by metal doors or grilles. At least, I'm sure they were metal doors or grilles during the day. At night, they looked like age-yellowed bones or rocklike scales or swarms of small metal bugs. Unlike most of the changes that took place during the night, these were actually semi-helpful, making the stores even harder to get into than they would be if the window coverings were mere grilles.

The first store Aleric stopped in front of was a small boutique that sold ridiculous fur and leather goods, the kind of place where you could buy a pair of mittens for twenty-five hundred dollars. In other words, a store I had never set foot in and had never really aspired to set foot in. It looked even less inviting now, thanks to what had once been a set of bars but had become frothy tentacles reminiscent of a giant jellyfish.

"How about we start here?" Aleric suggested, gesturing to his little army.

Like obedient and highly stupid zombies, the Nightstruck waded in, grabbing handfuls of tentacles and tugging them aside. Ordinarily, the constructs ignored the Nightstruck as if they didn't exist, but apparently these tentacles didn't appreciate being under attack. The Nightstruck screamed as the tentacles wrapped around them and started squeezing. Some seemed to have sharp edges that drew blood, and some seemed to crush bones with the force of their grip.

The tentacles were so busy crushing the life out of the Nightstruck that they left an opening through which we could see the store's front window. Leo squeezed himself into that opening. One of the Nightstruck freed an arm and tried to grab hold of Leo's mane, screaming for help. Leo casually turned his head and bit the poor guy's hand off, the spider jaws eagerly shoving that hand down his gullet as blood fountained and the screams reached a new height.

I watched all this happen with a kind of appalled fascination. These people were dying for me, screaming in fear and pain. I thought it was kind of a waste—surely there would have been some other way to get inside without getting people killed—but I didn't feel particularly bad about it. I certainly didn't feel any need to try to help them. If they were so blind stupid that they walked into a mass of killer tentacles just because Aleric told them to, then it was their own damn fault they were dying.

It was an interesting feeling, watching those people die and not being overcome with horror and guilt. I wasn't completely unmoved by their deaths, and I would have saved them if I could. At least, I'm pretty sure I would have. But it was obviously point-less to try, because if all of them weren't enough to take on the tentacles, what the heck could *I* do? And realizing I couldn't help but could only get myself hurt made it surprisingly easy to just stand there and watch.

"You didn't have to kill anyone to prove your point," I told Aleric as Leo head-butted the front window and shattered the glass.

"But how else could I prove that I *would* kill for you?"

I had no answer for that. Aleric gestured for me to go through the hole Leo had created in the window, and I saw no reason not to do so. The hole was big enough that I didn't even have to worry about being sliced by stray shards. The floor crunched beneath my feet. The Nightstruck weren't screaming anymore.

I expected Aleric to follow, but he remained standing on the sidewalk, looking in at me through the broken glass.

"Aren't you coming?" I asked.

He gave me a lopsided smile and raised his eyebrows. It took me a moment to remember that he was more like the constructs than like the Nightstruck. The Nightstruck were human—at least something very like human—but Aleric and the constructs were creatures created by magic, and for whatever reason, they couldn't seem to enter buildings.

I turned away and groped at the wall until I found a light switch. I flicked it on and found I was standing next to a mannequin that was wearing a black knee-length mink coat. I reached out to stroke the sleeve, and it was possibly the softest thing I'd ever touched. Without meaning to, I sank my fingers into the fur, luxuriating in the feel of it.

Even if I could have afforded it, I would never have chosen to wear a fur coat of any kind before I'd been Nightstruck. I recoiled every time I saw a human being wearing fur, overcome with pity for all the animals who had died to make said human being feel important. I wondered how many cute little weasels had been slaughtered for the sake of this coat, but I realized it didn't matter. They were already dead, and me refusing to touch a coat made of their pelts wouldn't bring them back.

"Try it on," Aleric suggested.

I hesitated. It was one thing to pet and admire the coat, another to actually put it on. "It's a little much, don't you think?"

Aleric rolled his eyes. "That's your old self talking. You can have whatever you want. If you want a mink coat, take a mink coat. If you'd like to wear evening gowns every night, be my guest. You make the rules."

I bit my lip and shivered. My parents were such sticklers they wouldn't even buy me a crappy used car because they thought it would spoil me. The thought of just taking what I wanted—no working for it, no begging my parents, no disapproving looks—was so intoxicating I felt almost dizzy with it.

"At least try it on," Aleric urged. "See how it feels."

14

"I guess there's no harm in that," I muttered under my breath. I stripped off my puffer coat, dropping it to the floor, then carefully slid the mink off the mannequin's shoulders and put it on.

"Oh my God," I moaned as I clutched the lapels closed then tied the belt. The coat was like a mink bathrobe, and aside from being so wonderfully soft, it was about ten times warmer than what I'd been wearing. It also weighed about ten times as much, but that was a price I was more than willing to pay.

Thinking of price, I checked the tag that was attached to the belt—and almost choked on my own tongue.

"This thing costs almost *nineteen thousand dollars*!" I screeched. My mind could barely encompass the idea of wearing something that cost more than some brand new cars.

Aleric gestured for me to come closer, and I did. He reached out like he wanted to touch the fur, and I leaned forward through the broken window so his hand didn't have to cross the threshold to touch me. But instead of admiring the coat, he yanked off the price tag and smiled at me. "Tonight, for you, it's free."

I laughed with pure delight as I realized he was right, then hurried back into the store to a full-length mirror to get a good look at myself.

I let out an involuntary gasp when I saw a pair of bright green eyes staring out of my face. It shouldn't have surprised me. All the Nightstruck had unnaturally green eyes. But the face I saw in that mirror was not the one I thought of as mine.

I told myself to pretend I was wearing green contacts and shook off the strangeness. The coat looked absolutely fabulous, like it was *made* for me. The rest of me, though . . .

I tugged off the knit hat I had pulled down over my ears and searched the store until I found a white chinchilla hat that was so soft it almost made the coat feel scratchy. The white hat looked a bit weird with the black coat, but I loved it too much to resist it. It wasn't like Aleric or the Nightstruck were going to look down on me for my poor fashion sense.

A little more shopping, and I found the perfect pair of shearling boots to keep my feet warm during the long winter night. I was by now sweltering inside the store—the heater was doing its best to counter the arctic blast coming through the front window—but I wasn't about to take my wonderful new furs off. I looked at myself in the mirror one more time and frowned at the cheap skinny jeans that peeked out between the hem of the coat and the tops of the boots.

"I need new jeans," I declared. "Something with a little pizazz. And doesn't come from someplace like Target."

"I can make that happen for you," Aleric said.

I had no doubt he could.

CHAPTER TWO

After about three hours of what Aleric termed *shopping*—otherwise known as looting—my feet were killing me. Under my fur coat, I was wearing a brand-new pair of $350 jeans, a gorgeous cashmere sweater, and brand-new silk underwear. I'd never owned a matching bra and panty set before, much less in designer silk. I'd also picked up a Prada handbag I didn't have much need for, as well as several other outfits that I would probably never wear. Leo continued to accompany us. He helped us get into the shops I wanted, then served as pack mule when I came out. If you've never seen the snakes in a metal lion's mane carrying shopping bags, you're missing out.

"What am I going to do with all this stuff?" I asked as we left what I declared our last stop of the night. "I'm basically homeless."

Aleric made a tsking sound. "Do you have any idea how many empty homes there are in Philadelphia right now? You can have any one of them you want. Hell, you can have a different one for each night."

Yet again, Aleric was saying things that should have bothered me, reminding me how many people had died since the madness began and how many people had been Nightstruck and had therefore abandoned their previous lives. Instead, I just found it convenient.

"Is there somewhere close?" I asked. "I am past ready to get off my feet."

He took me to a fashionable little old house on Delancy Street. He promised me the place was vacant, its owner dead for three days now. I was still half convinced we'd run into a family member or someone else who might take exception to us occupying the place, but no one came running or yelled when Leo broke down the door for us. Even in my furs, the warm air that wafted out of the house felt inviting, and I entered eagerly, expecting Aleric to be right behind me.

But when I turned to thank him for such a wonderful night, he was still standing in the doorway, Leo hovering at his side.

"I can't cross the threshold," he reminded me.

That was the second time in one night I'd forgotten he wasn't human. I wondered how long it would take that fact to sink into my head. I looked around at the elegant home I was invading, wondering what I was supposed to do with the rest of the night. I wasn't even remotely sleepy, and though my legs were tired and I was happy to be out of the cold, I was filled with so much energy that there was no way I was just going to sit and veg on someone's couch. Especially not all by myself.

I pouted at Aleric. "It's no fun without you." I had disliked and distrusted Aleric since the first moment I'd met him, and yet tonight he'd been great company. I wasn't interested in going our separate ways.

"Tell you what," Aleric suggested. "Why don't you raid the fridge, see if there's anything good. The owner hasn't been dead all that long, so it's not like stuff should be rotting yet. Then look around, see if there's anything you want, and come back out. I'll be waiting for you right here."

It still didn't sound like much fun. Not compared to breaking into designer boutiques and trying on clothes and shoes I never could have dreamed of affording. But my stomach was rumbling, and I had to get food from somewhere. It wasn't like we could just waltz into a restaurant and order dinner.

"All right," I said. "I'll be out soon."

I found the kitchen and discovered that my late and unwilling host had been a junk food addict. The fridge contained a cornucopia of leftover Chinese food as well as what was left of some kind of gourmet pizza that had artichokes on it. The walls and the ceiling above me were making me feel claustrophobic. I didn't feel like taking the time to heat anything up, and cold artichoke pizza sounded disgusting. Instead, I raided the pantry, where I found several unopened bags of chips as well as a box of chocolate-chip cookies that were just a little bit stale. There was also a box of S'mores Pop-Tarts. I shoved a couple packets of Pop-Tarts into my pocket for later, then grabbed a handful of cookies and a bag of chips. One more trip to the fridge netted me a can of Coke and a three-quarters-full bottle of white wine that was probably super expensive.

I couldn't stand being inside any longer, so with bulging pockets—and probably with smears of chocolate on my face from shoving down a couple of the cookies—I made my way back to the front door, where Aleric was waiting just as he'd promised. He smiled at my food choices.

"I see you're going for the gourmet dinner option," he teased.

I gave him a haughty look. "I have a couple of the basic food groups covered. Chips and cookies are food groups, aren't they? Besides, are you going to tell me I can't have dessert unless I eat my veggies?"

He grinned. "Of course not. I'm also not going to tell you you can't drink that wine until you're twenty-one."

I'd had much more extensive brushes with rebellion that night, but somehow the idea that I could eat chocolate-chip cookies for dinner and wash them down with wine—and not care that it wasn't good for me or even legal—filled me with delight. I let out a little whoop and threw my arms around Aleric. I probably crushed half the chips in the bag I was holding.

"Being Nightstruck is the best thing that ever happened to me!" I declared as Aleric hugged me back and I inhaled the scent of his jacket again. "Thank you so much. And I'm sorry I was so . . . difficult about it."

If I'd just stopped fighting it, I could have been Nightstruck ages ago. Maybe then my father would still be alive, since the only reason Piper had killed him was to make me so miserable I'd be vulnerable to the temptations of the night.

I braced for the wave of guilt that should have followed that thought, but it didn't come. My father had been the police commissioner. While he was hardly a patrol officer, he was very much the kind of man who would throw himself into danger if he thought someone needed saving. A hero. Which meant even if Piper hadn't killed him to get to me, he probably would have gotten himself killed going out into the night to rescue people. It was in his nature.

Don't get me wrong. I still wished he weren't dead. But my emotions felt strangely distant, and very safe. Nothing could devastate me now, nothing could kill my buoyant mood.

"I know you're tired of walking," Aleric said, still holding me. "How about we make for Rittenhouse Square and have ourselves a little picnic? If you feel you can't make it that far, I'm sure Leo here would be happy to give you a ride." He patted Leo's head, heedless of the hissing snakes.

"Um, I'm good." No way was I getting on that creature's back and riding him like a horse. Even if it weren't for the snakes and the scorpion tail, he was made of bronze, which would make for a very hard and very cold seat. Besides, the square was only a few blocks away.

Rittenhouse Square is a great place for a picnic on a warm and sunny day. I wasn't sure how great it would be in the wee hours of a frigid winter's night, but I was game to find out. Especially with Aleric and that bottle of wine keeping me company.

Since Aleric couldn't cross the thresholds of stores, he ordered another pack of Nightstruck to bring us a blanket for our picnic. I don't know where they got it from, and I didn't ask. He laid the blanket down on a patch of grass, and I emptied my pockets. I wasn't sure I would feel much like eating with Leo hovering so near—even being in his presence for hours had not yet warmed me to him—so I was relieved when he wandered off. He was still carrying all my packages when he did, but since I didn't know what I would do with my ill-gotten gains anyway, I decided that was no great loss.

Aleric's Nightstruck brought us a slew of super-soft pillows to help insulate and protect us from the frozen ground, and they also thoughtfully provided wineglasses. We tore into the chips and cookies, then split a packet of Pop-Tarts. I quickly discovered that wine does not go well with cookies or Pop-Tarts. I'm sure that technically it doesn't go all that well with chips, either, but at least it didn't taste gross.

The wine added a lovely buzz to my already cheerful mood, and between the alcohol and the mink coat, I was pleasantly warm. Aleric's playful flirting didn't hurt, either.

I'd been in an odd sort of relationship with Luke, Piper's exboyfriend. Well, sort of ex. The two of them were still officially going out when Piper became Nightstruck and they lost interest in each other. I'd had a crush on Luke for forever, but I'd always figured he was out of my league. We seemed to have developed some mutual attraction, though there were too many extenuating circumstances for me to consider him my boyfriend.

Luke was out of my league, but someone like Aleric ordinarily wouldn't even know my league existed. He was seriously the hottest guy I'd ever seen in real life. Like, if I'd seen him on TV walking down the red carpet with some supermodel on his arm, I wouldn't have been the least bit surprised. To have him flirting with me was more intoxicating than the wine.

My more sensible side was dormant, but not dead. I knew that Aleric was only interested in me because I was the one who'd opened the doorway between our worlds. He was a construct created by the alchemy of my blood mixing with magic, and that created a bond between us that had nothing to do with any true emotional connection or friendship. If it weren't for the blood bond, there was no way he'd be spending his whole night showing me a good time. He wouldn't even have noticed me, much less flirted with me.

Strangely, knowing all that didn't make it any less fun. I didn't have a whole lot of experience with flirting, myself, but I tried my best to keep up. It helped that I was no longer self-conscious or embarrassed when I said something stupid. Instead of blushing and stammering and trying to take my words back, I just zipped right on ahead.

And time zipped right on by, too. When we were finished with the wine, and I was hoping we could maybe take this flirting thing to the next level, the blackness of night was more like a deep navy blue.

"Dawn is coming," Aleric said, taking my hand.

I remembered the previous dawn, when I'd tried so desperately to escape the Transition. I remembered watching the dawn light spread, the city changing back into its daylight self inch by inch. And after that . . . I remembered nothing, until I was suddenly walking down the street with Aleric.

"What happens to us at dawn?" I asked.

From all accounts, the Nightstruck were gone by the time the sun came out, but to my knowledge, no one knew where they went. You'd think becoming Nightstruck myself would have solved the mystery, but though I strained to remember where I'd been during the hours of the day, I couldn't scrape up the tiniest hint.

"Don't be afraid," Aleric said, tugging me to my feet.

The city was beginning to change, the light progressing steadily toward us.

"I'm not afraid," I told him, and it was true. It should have bothered me not to know where I'd been for hours on end, but it was more a source of curiosity than an actual fear. "I just want to know what happens to us."

Aleric gave me an enigmatic smile. Maybe he was about to answer my question—he'd been pretty good about answering questions all night—but before he had a chance, the dawn light reached us.

On my second full night as one of the Nightstruck, I got falling-down drunk for the first—and possibly the last—time of my life. Aleric had some of his people raid a liquor store for us. We sat in Rittenhouse Square for another picnic, and the Nightstruck soon arrived with a shopping cart full of assorted liquors. They'd kindly thrown in a variety of mixers and glasses as well. Aleric made me drink after drink. Many of them, I only took one sip of. Turns out I'm a picky drinker. Who knew?

I fell dangerously in love with chocolate vodka. It felt a little like battery acid going down, burning all the way to my stomach, but that rich, chocolaty aftertaste was to die for, so I kept drinking it even as the ground turned unsteady beneath me and my limbs started to feel floaty and strange, like they belonged to someone else.

"I've never had a hangover before," I slurred to Aleric as I took another warming sip of pure vodka. "Guess I'm all for new experiences tonight." I'd also never drunk so much I felt like hurling before, and based on the sheer volume of alcohol I'd consumed, that was how I feared this night would end.

"You won't have to suffer through a hangover," Aleric said. I knew he was referring to the fact that I wouldn't be waking up in the morning after having overindulged, and that reminded me that he had never answered my question the night before about what happened to us during the daytime. I once again had no idea where I'd been since we'd disappeared from the square last night.

However, I was feeling too mellow and fuzzy-headed to tackle such a difficult question, so I let it go and drank some more. Sometime later, the Nightstruck brought us a wireless speaker along with a cell phone. The phone obviously belonged to someone who had an unholy love of music, because there were about a million songs loaded onto it. I tried to find a playlist I liked, but my vision was all swoony from the booze, and I doubt my fingers could have hit the right buttons even if I could have focused my eyes enough to read.

Aleric snatched the phone from my hand, and soon music was blasting from the speaker. It was heavy metal, which wasn't my favorite, but with the bass turned up the beat vibrated through my body and added to the dreamy pleasure of the booze.

"Let's dance," Aleric said, tugging me to my feet.

All around us, the Nightstruck were moving to the music, bodies writhing and whirling, hips gyrating as they abandoned themselves to the beat. Under the best of circumstances, I dance with all the grace and ease of Frankenstein's monster. Since I was under the influence and thought standing up was a pretty tough challenge, I figured I was taking my own life in my hands by making any attempt to dance. However, I knew Aleric wouldn't laugh at my clumsiness, wouldn't make fun of me or judge me or grade me. And probably if one of the Nightstruck dared do any of the above, he or she would be dead in seconds, thanks to my knight in shining armor. So I danced.

Okay, maybe saying I danced is a little . . . generous. I made it to my feet and moved my arms and legs around in some approximation of the beat. I tried to twirl once, and it would have turned into a face-plant if Aleric hadn't grabbed me and held me up.

Once he grabbed me, he didn't let go. The music was still heavy metal, the lyrics—when I could understand them through the screaming—nasty and offensive, but I was content to wrap my arms around Aleric's neck and slow dance with him. He put a hand against the small of my back, pulled me close so that my breasts were squashed against his chest and I could feel his whole body pressed up against mine. Tonight, he was wearing some musky aftershave that blended deliciously with the scent of his jacket. I buried my head in his shoulder and inhaled deeply. We were dancing so slowly we were practically standing still, and yet I felt the earth tipping and swaying under my feet.

"I am so drunk," I murmured against his chest. I'd kind of liked the sensation when it had first set in, but by now the wooziness and lack of balance was getting old. I guess becoming Nightstruck hadn't swept away my control-freak nature. Thank goodness I wouldn't have a hangover, and thank goodness I didn't feel like puking. At least not yet. But I decided then and there that I'd be a little bit more careful about my alcohol consumption in the future.

Aleric's hands had somehow found their way to my butt, his fingers squeezing hard enough I could feel them through the thickness of the mink I still wore. The touch was meant to be sensual, but at that precise moment a wave of dizziness hit me. All I could think about was trying to stay upright as I clung to Aleric's neck and ordered my knees to firm up. If he'd been hoping to get me drunk so he could get into my pants, he'd chosen the wrong strategy.

Aleric lowered me down onto our nest of pillows, and the world steadied, though not by much. He lay on top of me, and one of his legs found its way between mine. I could feel the warmth of his breath on my face, smell the anise scent of the Sambuca he'd been drinking. I liked the scent of anise, but a single sip of Sambuca had threatened to come back up immediately, and that sensory memory made my stomach turn over. He tried to kiss me, but I turned my head, afraid I would puke if I tasted his mouth.

"Never drink Sambuca again," I ordered him, afraid he'd be angry with me for turning him down. I wanted to kiss him, wanted to do far *more* than kiss him, but not when I felt like this.

Far from being annoyed, Aleric laughed lightly and brushed a stray lock of hair out of my face. "Your wish is my command, my queen," he said and winked at me. His body was still pressed against mine, warm and inviting, and I loved the feel of him. It never even occurred to me to feel self-conscious about being outside and in full view of about a dozen Nightstruck who were still dancing to the music. Of course, considering how much crotch-grabbing, twerking, and stripper-strutting was going on around me, I suppose we fit right in.

"I've had a great time tonight," I told him, still a little worried I'd offended him. I felt like I lost a little piece of myself as I looked up into those green eyes of his.

"I know," he said. "And I promise there will be many more good times to come. Sorry about the Sambuca. I'm still learning my way around what you like and don't like."

My nose wrinkled, because he was still really close to me and I couldn't help taking in that anise scent. My stomach felt wobbly and unsure. I wondered how long we had before dawn would take me away from all this. It was abundantly clear that if it didn't come soon, I would have to suffer the consequences of my overindulgence—which was just wrong. Being Nightstruck was supposed to mean I didn't have to suffer consequences, didn't have to *think* about consequences.

"I don't want to be sick," I said, even as I grew more certain I soon would be.

"Just close your eyes," Aleric advised me, "and it will all go away."

Despite my skepticism, I did as I was told.

And the next thing I knew, I was standing on the corner of a street, my hand clasped with Aleric's, my mind clear and my body steady.

CHAPTER THREE

*W*hat did you do to me?" I asked Aleric, giving him a world-class glare. I couldn't deny that being Night-struck had changed some things about me, but I was still basically the same person I'd been before, and that person had been very fond of being in control. The thought that I could go from lying in the square with Aleric on top of me to walking down the street by his side without any memory of what had happened in between was unnerving to say the least.

"You were starting to feel unwell," he reminded me. "You didn't want to be sick, so I made sure you weren't."

I stopped walking and hugged the mink coat around me. It still felt decadently soft to my fingers. I shivered in a chill that had nothing to do with the cold. "But *how*?"

"I took you home early, that's all." His brows drew together in an expression somewhere between concern and confusion. "It's no big deal. We only had a couple of hours left before dawn anyway. You didn't miss much."

I took a step back from him. I didn't think he'd meant any harm by what he'd done, but I don't like people making decisions for me, and I certainly don't like having a couple of hours of my life erased from existence. Bad enough that the daylight hours were already lost to me.

"What do you mean, *home*? I don't have a home anymore, and even if I did, it wouldn't be . . . wherever you took me."

His lips pressed together with impatience. "There's no reason to be so difficult about this. Next time, I'll let you barf your guts out, okay? The night and the city are ours for the taking, so why waste that time arguing?"

He reached for my arm, but I twitched out of reach. Piper had once told me that being Nightstruck didn't mean you couldn't get angry anymore, and here was proof positive that she was right. My fingers curled into fists, and my shoulders were so tight and tense I could have worn them as earrings. Aleric was looking pretty pissed off himself, his eyes narrowed and his lips turning white. The rest of the Nightstruck asked how high when Aleric ordered them to jump, but—thank God—I felt no burning compulsion to do whatever he told me to do. He didn't seem to know how to interact with a girl who had a will of her own.

He took a deep breath and smoothed the heavy crease that had formed between his brows as his sensual lips eased into a smile. "Come now, Becks," he wheedled, "it was an innocent mistake. I assumed you would prefer not to be sick. You even *said* you didn't want to be. I took you at your word. I promise I'll be more careful in the future."

He was right, of course. I *had* told I didn't want to be sick. Was it his fault he had taken that as permission to steal a couple hours of my life? He had, after all, given me exactly what I'd asked for.

But tonight I didn't feel like being mollified. Especially when Aleric had once again completely ignored my question about what happened to me during the day. I hated having that huge blank space in my memory, hated the idea that those hours were disappearing from my life, hated the idea that as the year progressed, there would be more and more hours missing as the days became longer. The only thing I truly missed from my old life was having twenty-four hours in my day.

Aleric reached for me again, and again I avoided his grasp. It had not escaped me that so far, he had not left my side even for a moment since I'd become Nightstruck. I wondered if he was worried that I'd go running back to my old life if he wasn't constantly monitoring me.

Not that that was possible, at least not as far as I knew. I had never heard of one of the Nightstruck being restored before. Piper had seemed to come back to herself, the Nightstruck green of her eyes fading away, but that was only because she was dying. I was pissed off at Aleric and unhappy about my missing hours, but not enough to die for a chance to go back to normal.

Anyway, normal sucked for me. I wasn't having a great time right this moment, but I felt far better than I had when I'd been mourning the loss of my dad and fearing for the lives of everyone else I cared for. If I had to trade a few hours of my life every day to have this blissful relief, then it was so worth it. But Aleric needed to learn that I wasn't his bitch and that I would not tolerate him making decisions for me.

"I think that tonight, I'd like some time to myself," I told him.

Aleric rolled his eyes like this was the most ridiculous thing he'd ever heard. "Don't you think it's a little childish to go off in a huff because I did *exactly what you wanted me to do*?"

Once upon a time, I'd been scared to death of Aleric. If I had any good sense left, I'd be scared of him now. He was used to getting everything he wanted all the time, and he didn't seem to be enjoying this new experience of being denied. I'd never seen him be violent, but I had no doubt that he had it in him, and I'd certainly seen his careless disregard for the lives of the other Nightstruck. I also had no idea just what kind of power he held over me. Was it possible I had a will of my own only because he let me?

But despite all these quite sensible reasons why I should have been scared of him, I just wasn't. Becoming Nightstruck had made my grief and guilt retreat to a dark corner of my mind where I could see they existed but couldn't really access them. It now appeared fear was keeping them company in that corner.

"I'm not going off in a huff," I said. "I just want to spend some time by myself. You've been stuck to me like glue my every conscious moment for the last couple of nights, and I'm ready for a break."

Aleric's eyes glittered, and he took a menacing step toward me. I took a step back to keep out of his reach, but I still felt nothing more than a vague unease. Nothing close to fear, despite my logical mind telling me this guy could be super hazardous to my health if he wanted to be. Maybe I was just convinced he didn't want to be.

Aleric stopped himself with a little jerk. I could still see the anger and frustration hovering about him in a little dark cloud, but he spoke in a conspicuously reasonable tone. "Very well. Have it your way. See how much fun you can have all by yourself. When you decide I was right all along, just call for me. It doesn't matter where you are, I promise I'll come."

He turned his back on me and walked away. But I couldn't help wondering just how much freedom he was really giving me. After all, the easiest way to make sure he could always come when I called was to never let me out of his sight. So even after he disappeared from view, I felt like he was just around the corner, watching me. And maybe he was.

* * *

I was determined to have a good time without Aleric, to prove to him that I didn't need him. I was still my own person, just like I always had been. I had never been and never would be the kind of girl who needs a male around to validate her existence.

The problem was that wandering around the city streets alone at night in the cold was a hard thing to make into fun. I thought about trying to break into some more stores for another shopping trip, but even if I could have gotten in somewhere without the help of Leo and Aleric and his sacrificial Night-struck army, I didn't think it would be all that exciting a second time. And, okay, it wouldn't be that much fun alone, either.

I shoved my hands deeper into the pockets of my coat as I walked down Chestnut Street, trying to think of something to do. Maybe I didn't need some guy to make my life worthwhile, but I guess I wasn't really made to be a loner. Within half an hour, I was bored out of my skull. Also cold. Also hungry.

But Aleric wasn't going to get the best of me that easily. No way in hell I was going to call for him, even if it meant wandering the city aimlessly until dawn swept me away again.

When I finally realized there was a reason why the Night-struck traveled in packs, I felt like a moron for not having thought of that before. Just because I didn't want to hang out with Aleric all night didn't mean I had to be alone.

I fell in with the first pack I came across, tagging along at the tail end without waiting for anyone's invitation. No one seemed to mind, though they didn't go out of their way to be friendly, either. There were three men and two women other than me, and they were all high or drunk or both. Both of the women were dressed like stereotypical hookers, in high heels that made my ankles hurt in sympathy. It was too cold out for bare legs, but that didn't seem to have discouraged them from wearing microminiskirts. They both walked with an exaggerated hip sway that the men seemed to enjoy.

One of the men was okay-looking, or might have been without all the tattoos on his neck. Nothing against tattoos or anything, but these looked like they'd been drawn by a five-year-old. A *blind* five-year-old. The other two men had scraggly beards and mustaches and smelled like they spent a lot of their time under bridges. I quickly decided that these were not my type of people and veered away. One of the gross men voiced a protest and started describing the things he would do to me if I hung around. In his twisted mind, I think it was an invitation rather than a threat, but I hurried away anyway and was relieved not to be chased. I reminded myself that the Nightstruck didn't prey on each other—and that Aleric would likely kill anyone who dared lay hands on me.

After a little while, I found another pack, this one made up of mostly teens. They seemed boisterous and happy, all talking at once and laughing as they passed around a bottle. A girl with dreadlocks held the bottle out to me and beckoned me to join them. She looked friendly enough, and the guys in this group were a little more clean-cut, so I figured why not? I took the bottle and checked to make sure it wasn't Sambuca before taking a swig. It was vodka—regrettably not the chocolate kind—and though I didn't exactly love it, I had no trouble getting it down.

Generally, the packs I'd run across seemed to be wandering aimlessly, just waiting for something to pique their interest. However, there seemed to be some focus and purpose to this group. They were drinking, but not drunk, and I soon picked up on a sense of low-level excitement.

"Where are we going?" I asked the girl in dreadlocks.

She smiled at me and pointed at one of the guys. "You see Damien over there? His girlfriend dumped him, and we're going to help him mend his broken heart."

I frowned. "I didn't think the Nightstruck got their hearts broken."

The girl sniffed. "The bitch broke his heart *before* he was Nightstruck. Now we're going to teach her a lesson."

The others chorused agreement as Damien threw back his head and howled. They all laughed and punched each other in the shoulder or gave each other high fives. I doubted any of them had ever met Damien before tonight, and there was certainly no reason why they should be taking revenge on the girl who dumped him.

But an awful lot of the Nightstruck seemed to find crap like that fun. Piper and her skeevy friends had had a great time torturing my dad to death before my eyes. I searched for that spark of malice inside myself, wondering why the idea of terrifying and hurting some girl I didn't know held no appeal to me. I tried to imagine myself whooping it up as these Nightstruck did . . . whatever it was they were planning to do, and the image just wouldn't come to me.

I'd expected to become a wholly different person when I was Nightstruck, but that wasn't at all what seemed to have happened. As far as I could tell, I was the same old Becket, minus the guilt, the grief, and the insecurity. I might be angry with Aleric and concerned about where those missing hours of my life were going to, but I was still incredibly glad I'd finally given in. If I'd known then that I wouldn't become some cackling sadist, I never would have fought it so hard.

Of course the old Becket probably would have felt honor-bound to try to stop this pack from tormenting Damien's ex, but that Becket had been absurdly idealistic. I was one person, and

34

if I had any supernatural powers, I had yet to see any sign of them. There would be absolutely nothing I could do to stop my Nightstruck companions from doing anything they wanted to do, and I certainly knew better than to try to talk them out of it. Maybe you think I was being cold and uncaring, but I think I was just being smart and rational when I let myself fall a little behind the group, then turned the corner and walked away when I had a chance.

The reality was I would not find any great fun and entertainment by hanging out with a pack of Nightstruck. They just didn't have the same definition of fun as I did. But being alone still sucked, and I was far too stubborn to call for Aleric.

I didn't consciously plan to do it, but after a few minutes of being completely lost in thoughts that circled pointlessly through my brain, I snapped out of it and realized my feet were taking me back toward my old house. Not that there was anything left there for me. Piper and the Nightstruck had broken, torn, spray-painted, and/or peed on everything I owned, so there was no good reason to go back there.

But of course it wasn't really my house my feet were leading me toward. No, they were leading me to the house across the courtyard from where I used to live. The house where Luke lived, and where I'd been making my home ever since Piper left me effectively homeless.

The lights were on inside, though they were barely visible behind the mouthlike openings the windows had become when the sun went down. Those mouths came complete with vicious fangs that were no doubt ready to chomp down on anyone who came too close. I kept a respectful distance from those fangs—they were decorative bars during the daytime—as I peeked through the first-floor window.

There was a sudden and ferocious bark, and I leapt back in

surprise as suddenly a familiar form threw itself against the window, claws scrabbling against the glass. I had never been on the receiving end of one of Bob's tirades before, and I completely understood why people were generally terrified of him.

"It's just me, Bob," I yelled, but I doubted he could hear me over the sound of his own barking and snarling. It was a good thing for me he was inside and I was out, because he seemed about ready to tear my throat out. I felt a mild twinge of regret that my own dog wanted to tear me apart, and the fur of my mink coat suddenly didn't seem as soft or desirable. I wanted my dog curled up beside me on a couch as I dug my fingers into his ruff. But Bob could obviously tell I was Nightstruck, and he hated the Nightstruck and the constructs with all the fury a trained attack dog can muster.

When Bob had been defending me from the terrible things that roamed the night, he'd been so mindless with fury he'd ripped his poor paws apart trying to claw his way out. I was glad to find I still cared about his well-being enough to back away from the window in hopes that he would quiet down.

"I love you, too, Bob," I whispered, but the love I had once felt for him was strangely muted. Yes, I would have loved for him to greet me with a wagging tail and happy eyes, and I would have liked to give him a little scratch behind the ears, but I wasn't heartbroken or anything. Only mildly regretful in a way I knew would fade the moment he was out of my sight.

Bob's barking had drawn the attention of the house's other inhabitant, and when Luke grabbed Bob's collar and dragged him away from the window, my heart did a little flip-flop in my chest. I'm not sure if what I'd felt for Luke before I'd been Nightstruck could technically count as love, but it had at least been close. Close enough that my last act before being taken by the night was to text him with an embarrassing *Luv U*. Not my finest moment.

Luke glanced out the window, but I'm guessing all he saw was his own reflection as he looked out from his lighted house to the dark street. I could hear Bob carrying on still. I knew I should give the poor guy a break—it couldn't be good for him to get this worked up—but I couldn't force my feet to move. Not while Luke stood in that window.

Secure in the knowledge that he couldn't see me, I stared to my heart's content, drinking in the sight of him. For years, he'd been my ideal of masculine perfection, the boy I'd always wanted but thought was too good for me. He had the perfect lean, athletic build, beautifully warm hazel eyes, and a decadent baritone voice that made my insides melt no matter what he was saying. The time we'd spent together in the last few weeks had proven that his appeal went far beyond his good looks. He was loyal, and brave, and kind. And he was an awesome kisser. Maybe Aleric was the hotter of the two in a bad-boy kind of way, but Luke still pushed my buttons.

Of course he had to hate my guts now. He and Piper had been well on their way to breaking up before she'd been Nightstruck, but in a sense she'd still officially been his girlfriend when I killed her. He might not have liked what Piper turned into, but he was way too loyal to have anything to do with her murderer.

The lights went off inside the house. It took me a second to realize Luke had turned them off so he could see out the window, see what had gotten Bob all riled up. He blinked a couple of times as his eyes adjusted to the darkness. I could tell when he spotted me, because his entire body went still.

Our eyes met through that closed window, and I felt a distinct pang of longing in my chest. I'd thought the daylight hours were the only part of my previous life I missed. Turned out I was wrong. The joy of being Nightstruck was that I could have anything I wanted—except, it turned out, the thing I wanted most.

Piper had told Luke and me that he was not vulnerable to the charms of the night, that it wasn't possible for him to be Nightstruck. I wondered if she'd known that for a fact, or if she'd just been parroting something Aleric had told her. I supposedly hadn't been vulnerable, either, at least not until Aleric goaded me into killing Piper for all the wrong reasons. Maybe I could do to Luke what Piper had done to me, weaken his defenses so that he could be Nightstruck, too. My life would be perfect then.

Luke slid the window open, and I felt like I might faint in shock when I saw he had a gun—and was pointing it right at me.

"Get out of here, Becket." He had to yell to make himself heard over Bob. "I don't want to shoot you, but I will if I have to."

That was bravado speaking, and we both knew it. Luke was a total novice with guns, and though I couldn't see clearly in the darkness, I figured the one he was holding was my dad's old backup piece. Which meant Luke had gone through my things after I'd disappeared, which kinda pissed me off.

I almost taunted him, almost said something monumentally stupid like, "You're not going to shoot me." You know, the kind of thing that always gets you killed in the movies. But though I didn't believe he would shoot, there was no reason to be dumb about it.

I raised my hands so he could see I was unarmed. "I'm not here to hurt anyone," I yelled. "I just . . . wanted to check on you. See if you're all right."

Luke snorted in disdain. "Yeah, right. Tell me another one."

After everything he'd been through, Luke had every right to be suspicious and distrust my motives. That didn't mean I had to like having the guy I was at least halfway in love with pointing a gun at me and looking at me like I was some kind of disgusting creature he'd just as soon kill. Never mind that he was right. I couldn't have told you exactly why I'd shown up on his doorstep, only it hadn't been to check on him.

"I'm not like Piper," I tried. "I haven't changed that much. I may be Nightstruck, but I'm still me."

"The Becket I knew wouldn't strut around in a fur coat, and she wouldn't act like some Peeping Tom looking in my windows. Get out of here. I'm serious."

His words didn't exactly hurt, but they didn't make me feel good, either. "Stop pounding your chest like some gorilla. We both know I'll leave when I feel like leaving and not a moment before." I crossed my arms over my chest and gave him my best stubborn glare. I noticed his arms were starting to quiver just a little from the strain of holding that gun pointed at me for so long. It wasn't that heavy, so I figured the quivering meant he was holding on to it way too hard. Either that, or he was freezing from standing at the open window.

I don't know what I'd been hoping to accomplish by coming to Luke's house. Maybe I'd been hoping for nothing more than a quick stolen peek. If it was more than that, I obviously wasn't going to get it, but I was far too contrary to leave just because Luke told me to. Also, the fact that Luke had opened the window and was still standing there talking to me told me there was at least part of him that wasn't in so much of a hurry to get rid of me.

Luke shook his head and lowered the gun. There were too many shadows for me to get a good look at his expression, but I knew it wasn't a happy one. He had loved Piper, and he had at least liked me a lot, and now both of us were lost to him. I imagined that felt pretty crappy. Maybe his defenses were already well on their way to weakening enough to become Nightstruck. If I could just push him a little further, maybe he could be like me, no longer burdened with grief or pain.

For the first time, I understood why Piper had worked so hard to bring me over. How could I feel this free and not want to share that feeling with those I cared about?

"It really isn't so bad, being Nightstruck," I said. "I haven't turned into some psycho killer or anything. I'm not about to forgive Piper for how she went about showing me the light, so to speak, but I see now that it really was the best thing for me."

The gun rose again, and I realized belatedly that bringing up the girlfriend I had murdered in cold blood had been just a tad insensitive.

"You come near me or my mom or my cousin, and I swear I will shoot you. I'm not going to let you hurt them."

Once again I put my hands up in a gesture of harmlessness. "I would never do that, Luke. I told you, I haven't changed the way Piper did. I want you to come out and join me, but I would never hurt anyone to make that happen." Luke's mom had taken me in when my dad had died, and I still felt grateful for her kindness. Just as I felt grateful for the kindness of Luke's cousin, Marlene, who had made cheering me up her personal mission over Thanksgiving, and who had revealed that Luke had always had a secret crush on me—just like I'd had on him. Maybe if the two of us hadn't been too chicken to admit we liked each other, we wouldn't be in this situation right now.

"I don't believe you," Luke said flatly. "If I had any sense, I'd shoot you now and put us both out of our misery."

There was a hoarse, scratchy sound to his voice that worried me. Everyone has their breaking point, and it sounded like Luke was getting close to his. Was it possible he would pull that trigger after all? I never would have thought myself capable of shooting my best friend, but when I'd thought she was a danger to everyone else I cared about, I'd killed her just the same. If Luke was having those same thoughts . . .

Arguing with Luke wasn't going to get me anywhere, and since I couldn't honestly say why I'd come to his house in the first place, there was no good reason not to make a strategic retreat.

"Take good care of Bob," I said as I began backing away. "And tell your mom I'm really grateful for everything she did for me. I'm sorry I ran off like I did. You both deserved better from me, but it was the only way I could see to keep you safe from Piper."

I don't know if Luke would have answered me or not, because I turned and ran for the nearest corner as fast as I could.

I wasn't entirely surprised to find Aleric waiting there for me, lurking in the shadows.

CHAPTER FOUR

For the next several nights, I contented myself hanging out with Aleric. There was no point in mooning over Luke, after all. He clearly wanted nothing to do with me. Like everything else, he was a part of my past, best left behind. At least that was what I tried to tell myself.

"Do you ever miss your past life?" I asked a young Nightstruck named Shelley one night. We were having another impromptu party in the square, and she was trying to teach me how to dance—futilely. I looked like a mannequin undergoing electric shock therapy as I tried to copy her graceful, sinuous moves. But at least I wasn't self-conscious about it. If someone didn't like the way I danced, screw them!

Shelley looked at me like I'd grown a second head. "Are you kidding me? My life was shit. What is there to miss?"

I shrugged. "I don't know. Weren't there any people . . . ?" I let the question trail off. I hadn't met a Nightstruck yet who showed any signs of sentimentality. Piper had seemed to miss me when she'd been Nightstruck—that was why she claimed she was working so hard to get me to join her—but I think she missed me like a child missed its favorite toy. It wasn't sentiment so much as possessiveness.

"People suck," Shelley said. "The minute you care about someone, they stab you in the back. It's so much better and easier not to give a damn." She grinned at me. "If I could snap my fingers and put you back where you were, would you want me to?"

"No way," I said with a shudder. I missed Luke, and I didn't think I was just being a possessive baby, but I didn't come close to missing him enough to go back to my old life.

"So forget about it and let's dance!"

I tried to take her advice. I had never admitted it to anyone before, but I actually kind of love to dance. I'm just so bad at it that I was ordinarily too uncomfortable to do it much in public. It felt great not to care what anyone thought, to just let myself do whatever I felt like and not worry if I looked clumsy. Especially once I got a little alcohol in me. I was more careful with my intake this time, enjoying the nice, mild buzz that still left me feeling in control of myself.

What's not to love about partying all night long? When dawn came along, I was nearly giddy with the joy of dancing, and my last thought was I couldn't wait for night to fall so I could do it all again.

And we *did* do it all again, the next night and the night after that. Aleric danced and flirted with me, always trying to get me to drink more than I wanted. When we danced together, his hands were always on me, and my pulse always sped with something other than pure exertion. I kept thinking that any moment now we were going to have ourselves a world-class make-out session. One that might well end with our clothes coming off.

There was no question what my body wanted, and most of my mind was completely on board with that. I was a modern woman, and thanks to being Nightstruck I had no inhibitions. If I wanted to throw myself into Aleric's arms and start kissing him senseless, there was no reason not to do it. But something kept holding me back. Maybe the same something that kept him from making the first move himself.

So here's the thing: I spent my every waking hour with Aleric, and he was seriously hot and sexy, but when you came right down to it, I wasn't sure I really trusted him. The night when he'd taken me "home" before dawn had made it clear how much power Aleric had over me, and just because he didn't make a habit of exercising that power didn't mean he *wouldn't*. It was by his choice that I had become Nightstruck, and I didn't think he was spending so much time with me only because he was so into me he couldn't resist. His constant presence sometimes made him feel more like a stalker or a prison guard than a fun date, and that somewhat lessened his appeal.

Every other Nightstruck I had met obeyed Aleric's orders without question. I couldn't help remembering our first night together, when Aleric had sent several Nightstruck straight to their deaths so we could get into the shop where I'd gotten my coat. They'd screamed for help when the shop's tentacles got hold of them, but they'd nonetheless walked right up and let themselves be taken.

Did Aleric have that same kind of power over me? If he told me to jump off a bridge, would I do it? I felt like I had free will, but maybe that was just an illusion, one Aleric was giving me for his own purposes.

On our third consecutive night of partying in the square, I kept a careful watch on Aleric, waiting for him to be distracted. It happened at least once a night. The Nightstruck all seemed to find Aleric alluring, and whenever a particularly pretty girl came into his orbit, he took notice. Maybe he was trying to make me jealous, but I didn't think so. The Nightstruck viewpoint was that you could have whatever you wanted whenever you wanted it—and that included people. There would be no such thing as exclusivity, even if I did decide to take another step with Aleric.

It took a couple of hours, but eventually Aleric was properly distracted and I slipped away from the party. I wanted to see if Aleric would let me go or if he would come after me the moment he realized I was missing. I had to know just how much freedom I had.

I went to Luke's, of course. Where else would I go when everyone else who really mattered to me was either dead or trapped outside the quarantine the government had imposed on the city?

As before, it was Bob who noticed me first. He greeted me with a chorus of barks and snarls and bared teeth, keeping it up until Luke dragged him away and, by the sound of it, shut him into another room.

I was prepared for Luke to greet me at gunpoint this time, but I still felt a little pang when I saw the muzzle of that gun pointed at me. I put my hands up and stood still as Luke took one hand off the gun to open the window.

"I thought I told you to get out of here," Luke said, putting his second hand back on the gun. He had the shooter's stance down, and if I didn't know he'd never held a gun until recently, I'd have thought he was an experienced shooter.

"I'll go away in a few minutes," I promised him. "Maybe less than that, depending on how Aleric reacts when he finds I'm gone." I had no doubt he could find me, just as I had no doubt he would be pissed that I'd slipped away. The question was *how* pissed, and what would he do about it?

"So you're hanging out with Aleric these days?" Luke made a face ugly enough to see even in the dim light.

"I don't have a whole lot of choice. He rarely lets me out of his sight. I don't know why he's being so clingy, but every once in a while I need a breath of fresh air. I'm sorry to bother you, but . . . I don't know where else to go."

Luke looked perplexed. I knew I wasn't acting like a typical Nightstruck, and I hoped that would help convince him that I wasn't like the rest of them. I decided to press my advantage.

"Thanks for taking care of Bob," I said, giving him a tremulous smile. "And thank your mom for me, too. It's really nice of her to let him stay when she's allergic."

The gun was steadily lowering, though I felt sure he was ready to take aim again at the slightest provocation.

"I didn't think the Nightstruck were capable of being grateful," Luke said. "I've certainly never heard of one saying thank you for anything."

"I told you I haven't changed as much as Piper did. I still feel like me—only better."

"So do you feel bad about your dad being dead?"

"Yes," I lied easily. Though in a way it wasn't that much of a lie. When I thought about my dad—like now, for instance—I felt a mild twinge. Nothing strong enough to call grief, or even sadness, but it was *something*. Of course being Nightstruck meant I rarely let thoughts of my dad enter my head, and when they did, it was easy to chase them away again. Very different from how it had been before, when unpleasant thoughts had stuck to me like gum in my hair.

"Uh-huh. You sound real torn up about it."

The gun was pointing at the ground now, so I let my hands lower slowly to my sides. I kept them splayed open and slightly away from my body so Luke could see I wasn't reaching for a weapon.

"I'm not in unbearable mortal pain anymore," I said. "Are you really going to tell me that's a bad thing?"

46

"Yeah, Becket, I am. When someone you love dies, it's supposed to hurt. It sucks, but it's part of being human."

"So are you sobbing into your pillow every night because Piper's dead? Assuming you really did love her, which I think you did."

Luke frowned at me. "She's not dead. She lost a lot of blood, and it was touch and go for a while, but the doctors say she's out of the woods now."

My mouth dropped open, and I stood there staring like a moron. I'd been sure I'd killed her, sure there was no way she could survive when I was forced to run away and leave her bleeding out in the middle of Rittenhouse Square. I waited for a giddy rush of joy and relief, but it didn't come. I should have been ecstatic to discover I hadn't actually murdered my best friend in cold blood, and yet I felt nothing but surprise.

"If you could see your face right now," Luke said, "you'd understand that you've changed a lot more than you think."

Right. Luke had been expecting to see that joy and relief I should have felt, and I hadn't thought to fake it. It was too late to put on a show now—he'd never believe me. So I was honest with him instead.

"I know I've changed," I admitted. "All I'm saying is that I'm not going to go around killing people just to get my way. I still have a moral compass." Although that compass no longer pointed toward true north. "Have you seen Piper since . . . ?"

"Since you shot her?" Luke finished for me with a noticeable edge in his voice.

"I shot her because I thought she was going to hurt you and your mom and the rest of your family just to get to me. It was the lesser of two evils."

"You shot her and left her for dead!"

Call me crazy, but I was detecting some hard feelings here.

47

I suppose it was only natural, but it was also completely unfair. "I was pretty sure *I* was going to be the one who got killed in the end, but I went after her anyway because it was the only way to protect you and your mom. How about giving me a little credit for risking my life for you?"

Luke shook his head at me. "The real Becket would never ask me to thank her for almost murdering my girlfriend."

A spike of jealousy came out of nowhere, surprising me. "Don't you mean *ex*-girlfriend? Or are you the kind of guy who makes out with your girlfriend's best friend while you're still dating?"

I could see from the flare of anger in his eyes that I'd put my foot in it. Nothing like trying to win a guy over by calling him a cheater. Though of course that begged the question of *why* I was trying to win Luke over. He was out of my reach, and even if I never set a foot wrong and recited beautiful love poetry till I turned blue in the face, he would never be interested in me now.

"If I had any sense," Luke growled, brandishing the gun once more, "I'd shoot you just like you shot Piper. Maybe that would bring you back to yourself like it did Piper."

I held up my hands in alarm and took a hasty step backward. "Don't do it," I warned. "I don't know how I would have lived with myself if I hadn't become Nightstruck, and that option isn't open to you." Plus going back to my old self was about as appealing as diving into a pool of acid. Why would I put myself through that kind of pain if I didn't have to?

There was a breathless moment when I almost thought he was really going to do it. There was a pit of cold fire in the middle of my belly. At first, I thought that meant I was afraid, but as the cold heat spread through me and my body began to hum with it, I realized it wasn't fear; it was fury.

How dare this self-righteous asshole threaten to kill me? He had no right to be angry with me, not when I'd risked my life for him, not when everything I was now was a direct result of trying to protect him and his family. He should be getting down on his goddamn knees and *thanking* me.

I stared down the muzzle of that gun and found that I wasn't a bit afraid. I didn't know the limits of Aleric's magic, but it seemed possible he'd be able to save me even if I got shot. He hadn't saved Piper, but then again he hadn't *cared* about Piper—and Piper wasn't the one who'd given him his spark of life.

I took a step toward that window. I'm not sure what I was planning to do. Even without a gun in the mix, I couldn't have hurt Luke if I tried. He was a big, powerful, athletic guy, and I was no ninja warrior. But the rage in my gut propelled me forward, demanded I take action. Make Luke see what a mistake it was to insult me and be so ungrateful.

Luke pointed the gun at the pavement a few feet to my left and pulled the trigger.

The shot was a shocking boom in the quiet of the night. Chips of pavement flew up, a couple of them pattering against the leg of my jeans. In the window, Luke was panting, his eyes too wide as if he was as surprised as I was. Bob started barking again, as did several other dogs in the neighborhood, but these days no one was about to peek out their windows to see what was happening.

"Don't come any closer, Becket," Luke said. There was a grim set to his jaw, and though I had a feeling he'd frightened himself by shooting, he looked ready to do it again if he needed to. "I won't point at the street next time."

Rage still pounded in my veins, still urged me to teach Luke the kind of lesson he would never forget. It was a palpable force inside me, and it took all my willpower not to lunge forward and take my chances.

Luckily for me, I still had a scrap of common sense left, and I didn't want to die. Not when my life was worth living again.

"I hope you and Piper have a nice life together." I sneered at him, then turned my back and marched briskly away.

CHAPTER FIVE

I wasn't surprised when I found Aleric waiting for me just around the corner from Luke's house. The old me would have been embarrassed and worried about just how much of that conversation he'd overheard. The new me was too furious to care.

"Don't say a word," I growled at Aleric.

"I wasn't going to."

I braced myself for him to make some obnoxious, gloating comment anyway, but he merely fell into step beside me in silence. My face glowed with fury-fueled heat, my fists and jaw clenched so hard they ached. I seriously considered throwing a punch at Aleric just to vent some of my rage.

Luke had *shot* at me! After everything I'd done for him, everything I'd sacrificed to try to protect him and his family. What an asshole. I was well rid of him, and he was damn lucky I wasn't as vindictive as your average Nightstruck.

I was too angry to stay still, and I marched down the sidewalk with no destination in mind, moving just for the sake of moving. I kept expecting Aleric to say something snarky and cutting, but he walked by my side in silence. I suspected he was enjoying the spectacle of me losing my temper, but at least he wasn't rubbing it in.

After a couple of blocks, the anger lost some of its intensity, and I slowed down to a more normal pace. I kept walking, though, in no mood to stop in case Aleric would take that as an invitation to start a conversation.

My seemingly aimless wandering eventually took us to the Art Museum and the giant Fairmount Park, where there are a lot of wooded areas and scenic lookouts. There's a gorgeous row of boathouses that look out over the Schuylkill River, and it wasn't until I reached the sidewalk that wended past them that I realized that, of course, they too had changed with the night. Instead of being festooned with colorful lights that reflected on the river's surface, they were choked by some kind of vine, with terrifyingly sharp thorns. When we got close enough to make out details in the darkness, I saw that those vines were made out of plastic and metal—and they were wiggling and squirming.

"Getting too close would be a bad idea," Aleric said with a hint of humor in his voice.

I couldn't help shuddering. Maybe someday I'd get used to the constructs of the night and they wouldn't freak me out anymore, but I wasn't there yet. I almost asked Aleric why I seemed to be the only Nightstruck who was bothered by them, but instinct told me he wouldn't answer. I didn't know what he had against answering innocuous questions, but only an idiot wouldn't have picked up on it by now. I'd had enough frustration already, and though walking had taken the edge off my anger, I was well aware it wouldn't take much to bring it right back up to the surface again.

"It was a lot prettier out here with the lights on the boathouses," I commented instead as we continued strolling along the side of the river.

Aleric took my hand and gave it a squeeze, closing some of

the distance between us. "And is it the scenery we came here for?" he asked.

We passed the last of the grotesque boathouses and came upon a patch of . . . Well, I'd call them woods, except I'm not sure something counted as a wood when you could see both ends of it without having to turn your head. It was more a patch of trees surrounding a moss-covered outcropping of rock. Aleric had been following my lead up until now, but he gave my hand a little tug and led me toward the darkness at the base of the rock. It probably would have been pitch black in there if it weren't for the full moon hanging high and bright in the sky.

"Let's have a rest," Aleric suggested.

I considered protesting, but my legs were pretty tired, and so far Aleric had been surprisingly quiet and sensitive. Besides, he was the closest thing I had to a friend these days, and I needed a friend right now.

The temperature had risen above freezing for the first time in a while, and the ground for once wasn't frozen solid as the two of us took advantage of a cozy alcove in the rock to sit down. The alcove was small enough that we had to put our arms around each other to fit. I let out a soft little groan, not having realized how much my feet hurt until I finally got off them. We had walked for miles tonight, and the energy I'd drawn from my earlier anger was long gone.

I still didn't fully trust Aleric, but I had to admit it felt nice sitting next to him like that, absorbing the warmth of his body. I rested my head against his shoulder with a little sigh. Unlike Luke, he would never judge me, never look down his nose at me. He would never reject me.

"I can give you so much more than Luke ever could," Aleric said softly. I wondered if he'd been reading my mind. "I will make you queen of this city, and I'll expect nothing from you in return. There is nothing from your old life you need, not anymore."

He cupped my cheek in his hand, turning my face toward his. I fell into his green gaze, my heart pattering against my breastbone. He leaned in for a kiss, and I saw no reason not to give it to him. His lips were deliciously warm and soft, and when his tongue slipped into my mouth I thought I would melt on the spot.

My whole body flushed with heat, and I clung to Aleric's shoulders, feeling like the world was bucking beneath me. I couldn't get enough of his kiss. My hands twined in his hair, and I made embarrassing little mewling sounds of need. Before I had any idea what was happening, I found myself lying on my back on the cold ground, my mink coat having somehow come open. But I wasn't cold. I was on fire.

Aleric was on top of me, his hips resting between my legs, both holding me down and warming me. His tongue thrust aggressively into my mouth, and my back arched with pleasure. I was so drunk on the heat and the pleasure that I couldn't be bothered to notice mundane details. I had no idea how the cashmere sweater I was wearing beneath the coat ended up gaping open, nor did I know how Aleric's hand had found its way under my bra. I only knew that his touch felt *amazing*, that my whole body burned for him.

I'd never felt anything remotely like the wild abandon that came over me. My little make-out sessions with Luke had been great, but I'd been far too self-conscious and inexperienced to enjoy them fully. Not to mention that they'd never gone beyond some really nice kissing. Nothing like what I was experiencing now.

The need was utterly overpowering, and there was no room in my head for anything like higher reasoning. No room for caution, no room for questioning Aleric's motives, no room for restraint. When he started tugging on the zipper of my jeans, it never even occurred to me to protest or ask him to slow down. I was caught in a vicious undertow that inexorably dragged me under. And I went willingly, heedlessly chasing the pleasure that Aleric's touch promised.

There was very little pain, and it was quickly obliterated by the warmth and magic of Aleric's body. I stared into his electric eyes and gasped for breath as I clung to him. He made my blood sing and my heart dance. I forgot I'd ever been angry with him, forgot my feelings for Luke, forgot . . . everything.

After sleeping with Aleric, I expected to feel fundamentally different. Giving up her virginity is supposed to be this huge deal in a girl's life, a rite of passage that instantly changes her from a girl to a woman. I didn't expect the earth to shake or for a choir of angels to start singing or anything like that, but I didn't expect *nothing,* either.

Don't get me wrong: the sex was great, and I thoroughly enjoyed myself. As I cuddled in Aleric's arms in the breathless aftermath, I was thankful I was no longer burdened with the ridiculous self-denial that would have kept me from enjoying his body before I became Nightstruck. But I was strangely disappointed to realize that losing my virginity just wasn't that big a deal.

"Have fun?" Aleric asked with one of his patented smug grins.

I laughed and rolled my eyes as I wriggled my way back into my clothing—it was too chilly out to sit around half naked. Something was stuck to the side of my leg, and I brushed it away before pulling my pants up. I frowned when I looked down and saw the foil packet that had been plastered against me.

"You used protection?" I said incredulously. Aleric wasn't human, so I seriously doubted he could make me pregnant or give me a disease. Even if he could, he was hardly a paragon of responsibility, and I wouldn't have expected him to care.

He flashed me another of his careless grins. "I was being a gentleman."

I snorted.

"All right, I was being proactive. I thought you might start to worry and ruin the mood. Turns out, I needn't have bothered."

If I hadn't just had my bell rung in the most pleasant of ways, I might have pressed a little harder, because neither of his answers quite made sense to me. How could he possibly think I would worry about such petty details when I was Nightstruck? But asking him more questions just seemed like too much work. I felt all mellow and melty and wonderful, and I didn't want to risk getting into a fight over nothing.

Fully clothed, I settled back into Aleric's arms and sighed contentedly. My life had never been better, and I was determined that from now on, I was going to leave the past—and my doubts—behind and enjoy every moment of being free.

I ended up falling asleep in Aleric's arms. Which was nice and all, except I slept all the way up to Transition and didn't come to myself again until the next night. Aleric and I were in Rittenhouse Square, and I blinked and shivered as I realized I had another of those day-long blank spots in my memory.

"I'm never going to get used to that," I muttered under my breath.

"Say what?" Aleric asked with an inquiring raise of his brow.

"The last I thing I remember was falling asleep in Fairmount

Park. And now here I am sitting in the square, wide awake as if no time has passed at all. It's freaky."

He shrugged. Empathy and compassion were hardly among his strong suits. "You'll get used to it. And all you're missing is a few hours you'd spend sleeping anyway. What's the big deal?"

Maybe he was right and it wasn't a big deal. But I still didn't like it. "I thought being Nightstruck was about being able to do whatever I want. Well what if I want to stay up all night . . . day . . . whatever? I can't do that now because for me, day doesn't even exist anymore." I stuck out my lower lip in what I'm afraid was probably a childishly pouty expression.

The corner of Aleric's mouth twitched upward, as if he were about to smile, but he schooled his expression so fast I'd never have noticed if I weren't peering at his face so closely. I didn't think I'd said anything remotely funny, so the almost-smile puzzled me.

"It doesn't have to be this way," he said, taking both my hands in his and regarding me gravely.

His hands felt warm and strong around mine, and looking up into his jewel-green eyes gave me a pleasant shiver. My heart rate kicked up a notch, and I thought he was going to chase my cares away by seducing me. It would be only a temporary solution—I was way too stubborn to drop the subject no matter how long the interruption lasted—but I was sure to enjoy the attempt.

"You can only be in Philadelphia during the night," he continued.

An arrow of disappointment shot through me as I realized this wasn't the start of a seduction after all. "No kidding? Really? I hadn't figured that out yet."

He narrowed his eyes at me, and his hands tightened their

grip to an almost painful level before he caught himself and let up. I doubted he was surprised that I talked back to him in ways that none of the other Nightstruck dared, but it wasn't his favorite thing about me. Which was tough, because I'd spent most of my life biting back sarcastic comments and one of the best things about being Nightstruck was being able to give voice to my true feelings.

"Do you want to hear what I have to say or don't you?" he asked in a tight voice that said he was still irritated.

I cocked my head to the side. "I don't know. Do I?"

"Yes."

"All right, then talk." I smiled sweetly at him. He returned the smile, but it looked a little forced. I was not following whatever script he'd put together in his mind. I took an admittedly perverse pleasure in annoying him.

"What if I told you we could stop the Transition from happening for part of the city? Like, say, this part." He swept his arm in a circle to indicate the square.

I gave him a puzzled frown. "What do you mean? That it would, like, stay night here all day long?"

His lips curled with satisfaction. "That's exactly what I mean."

"How would we do that?"

"We would create a gateway, and I could bring a Night Maker through it."

Aleric had mentioned Night Makers before, but I had no clue what a Night Maker was. I made a keep-talking gesture with my hand instead of asking the obvious question.

"The Night Makers are the authors of the magic that comes into the city at night. If I bring one into the square, it will bring its own little pocket of night with it. If you don't want to go away during the day, then all you'll have to do is make sure you're in the square by Transition time. Simple."

Like anything was really simple where Aleric was concerned. "Uh-huh. And what exactly happens to the square?"

"Nothing, really. It just stays in its nighttime form. Which of course means it's advisable for day folk to stay out."

That didn't sound so bad. Even being Nightstruck, I knew that the night magic was not a good thing and that letting more of it into the city was something the old me would never have considered doing. But I really hated the fact that I seemed to cease to exist during the day, and letting one square block of the city—a pretty, but otherwise useless square block at that—be swallowed by the night seemed like a small price to pay. But even Nightstruck me knew better than to take Aleric entirely at his word.

"So these Night Makers . . . They don't move around?"

He shook his head. "They wouldn't in this world. They'd be tethered to the gateway they entered through." He held up both his hands in a gesture of innocence. "I'm not trying to trick you here, Becks. I'm just trying to give you what you want."

The two were not mutually exclusive, but I refrained from pointing that out. There was no denying I wanted what he was selling, and I found myself reluctant to look too closely into the gift horse's mouth.

"So I noticed you said we would create a gateway," I said instead. "What would I have to do?"

I thought I saw a flare of satisfaction in his eyes—one that almost, but not quite, gave me second thoughts.

"The same thing you did to bring the magic into the city in the first place."

Even Nightstruck, I still looked back on the time I'd started all this mess with a shiver of dread. I remembered picking up the boneless heap of faux-baby that had felt so utterly wrong, and I remembered the hidden pin pricking my finger and drawing

59

my blood. I didn't think it was the picking-up-a-baby part Aleric was referring to.

"You mean I have to stick myself," I said, curling my fingers in protectively. I had a strong preference for keeping my blood inside me, where it belonged.

Aleric made what I guessed was supposed to be an apologetic face. He wasn't very good at it. "I'm afraid we'd need more than a single drop to make a gate big enough for a Night Maker."

No, he hadn't been trying to trick me. He'd just been trying to get my hopes up before revealing the major catch. I crossed my arms over my chest and resisted the urge to take a step back from him. It was a disconcerting thing to discover my boyfriend—or whatever the hell Aleric was—wanted my blood. I realized with another chill that it would also be ridiculously easy for him to take it from me.

"Relax," Aleric said. "If it were as easy as grabbing you and bleeding you by force, the whole city would be covered with Night Makers by now."

I scowled at him. "That's supposed to make me feel better? Nice to know you'd happily bleed me dry if you could. So romantic."

"You know what I mean," he said, rolling his eyes in exasperation.

What it meant was that the only reason he was hanging around with me was because he wanted my blood. I had never flattered myself that he was somehow wildly in love with me—at least I think I hadn't—but I'd thought he had at least a little fondness for me. Old me would have been heartbroken, or at least badly hurt. New me was just pissed off.

"Yeah, I know what you mean, and if you think that makes it better you're delusional."

It looked like Aleric was holding on to his patience by a thread.

A thin one at that. "I meant that I'm not going to force you to do anything. I can use your blood—freely given—to make a gate and let a Night Maker through. If you'd rather things keep on the way they have been, then that's your decision."

I gave myself a mental kick in the butt. Aleric's motives didn't much matter in the grand scheme of things. It wasn't like I was looking for a soul mate or anything. What he was offering was a pretty straightforward deal. Give a little blood, and I could go back to having twenty-four hours in my day. I can't say I liked it. But I wanted what he was offering too badly to refuse.

CHAPTER SIX

Aleric cleared the Nightstruck and the constructs from the square so we could have it all to ourselves. Then he led me to the very center and pulled a wicked-looking switchblade from the pocket of his leather jacket. I gave him a sidelong look.

"You carry a switchblade around with you?" It wasn't like he was in need of it for self-defense. The constructs and the Nightstruck worshipped the ground he walked on, and since he hadn't died when I'd shot him point blank, that seemed to suggest he was invulnerable.

"You never know when one might come in handy," he said, extending the blade with a wicked *snick* and holding it out to me.

I swallowed hard. In other words, he'd been carrying it around so he had it ready the moment he talked me into doing this. I suddenly wondered if this weren't all some big illusion, meant to trick me into spilling my own blood for his use. Maybe I didn't have to have complete blackouts during the daylight hours and that was just some magic Aleric was performing on me so I'd want to do his bidding.

Deciding it didn't matter, I took a deep breath and reached for the knife. Trick or not, I wasn't getting those hours of my day back unless I did as Aleric wanted and drew some blood.

The blade glinted in the moonlight. The hilt was of some dull gray metal that felt cold and heavy in my palm, and I found my hand was shaking. I wasn't sure I could go through with it.

"We need more than a pinprick," Aleric said, "but we don't need buckets. Just make a small cut in the center of your palm. The knife is so sharp it will hardly hurt at all." His voice had gone low and seductive, as if he were urging me to give him a kiss rather than cut myself.

I knew the part about how it would "hardly hurt at all" was bullshit. I didn't care how sharp the knife was: this was going to suck. But I wanted those missing hours back, and if I had to endure a little pain to get them, I was just going to have to deal with it.

Biting my lip and wincing in anticipation, I poked the tip of the knife into the center of my palm and gave it a little flick. For half a second, I thought I'd been too timid and hadn't broken the skin. And then the fierce stinging started, and a thin line of blood welled from the cut. Aleric took the knife from my unresisting hand, retracting the blade and sticking it back in his pocket. I stood motionless, my hand cupped as I stared at the thickening red line.

I felt light-headed and faintly queasy, but I couldn't seem to stop myself from staring at the blood. In hindsight, I don't think it was really that much, but at the time it looked to me like I'd gashed myself open to the bone.

Aleric took my wrist and turned my hand over so that the blood dropped to the pavement. I swayed on my feet as the fat drops splattered down. My pulse was fluttering erratically, and I doubted I had a hint of color in my cheeks. My stomach gave an unhappy lurch.

If Aleric noticed my distress, he paid no attention to it, his eyes instead focused on the constellation of drops that collected at our feet. My blood shone almost black in the moonlight, and I told myself those were just spatters of ink, nothing to be concerned about at all. As I watched, the blood changed somehow, the color going from almost black to true black. Like ink for real, only no light reflected off it at all.

And then the drops started to spread. And rise.

"You might want to back up," Aleric said, but he didn't have to tell me twice.

I didn't realize just how sick and shaky I was feeling until I tried to take that first step back, and my knees buckled. I would have gone down if Aleric hadn't caught me. The blackness continued to grow, and he half-carried me backward, keeping us about a foot or two from the edge of the darkness.

Once when I was a kid, my mom and dad and I went to visit a show cave. The tour guide led us inside, telling us all about how the cave was formed. I remembered it being beautiful and almost alien. When we entered the heart of the cave, we stopped for the guide to do his spiel—and he turned the lights off. I think I was about five years old at the time, and I had never been so terrified in my entire life. The guide was showing us something you never see in everyday life: the true absence of light. And you realized the darkest darkness you'd ever experienced before was nothing compared to what it was like when it was really and truly *dark*.

The darkness that was emerging from the splatter of blood I'd spilled was like the darkness in that cave. It seemed to absorb all light around it, and I felt something like a strange gravitational pull trying to suck me in. It was like a freaking black hole had suddenly formed in the square, and it wanted to eat me.

I let out a frantic sound somewhere between a bleat and a squeak and tried to speed up my retreat. My heart was beating so hard I could hardly breathe, and my eyes were in danger of bugging out of my head. It wasn't just how that darkness *looked* that had me so freaked out, it was how it *felt*. Wrong. So, so wrong.

And it was of my own making.

My vision went gray around the edges. I was vaguely aware of Aleric laughing at my reaction. A model of compassion he was not, but I was too close to passing out to let him know what I thought of him.

I think the only thing that kept me conscious was the fear that if I passed out, Aleric would let the darkness touch me. I couldn't imagine anything I wanted less than to come into contact with it. Hell, just *looking* at it made everything in my body want to rebel.

I forced my eyes shut, then turned away and ran blindly. I would have run smack into a tree if Aleric hadn't reached out to stop me. I started to struggle, thinking he was going to make me look at the darkness again, but he scooped me up into his arms.

"Just keep your eyes closed," he advised me. "I'll get you to where you can't see the Night Maker anymore."

A shudder racked my body, and I buried my face against his shoulder. I was no longer sure having a few more hours in my day was worth the price I had paid.

The first thing I noticed when I woke up was that my head was pounding. I squinched my eyes more tightly shut and curled in around myself. The ground was unpleasantly hard beneath me, and my body felt chilled and achy. I had to find somewhere more comfortable to sleep. Groaning, I turned onto my back and slitted my eyes open.

I was looking up at a clear blue sky, dotted with fluffy white clouds. The sun was shining merrily, and I should have felt its warmth on my face. But I didn't.

I closed my eyes again and breathed deep, wanting nothing more than to go back to sleep. Maybe when I woke up next, my head wouldn't hurt, and I wouldn't feel so groggy. My brain was so fogged I had almost drifted back to sleep before I fully registered what I'd seen: the sun shining in a blue sky. Something I thought I'd never see again.

Like magic, I was suddenly wide awake, sitting up so fast I practically gave myself whiplash. I blinked and rubbed my eyes, sure the sun and the blue sky would disappear like a mirage, and for a moment I thought that was exactly what happened.

I was sitting on a blanket on the ground in Rittenhouse Square. All around me was the familiar darkness that had now become my whole life. Music was pounding from a wireless speaker, but there was nobody dancing. The Nightstruck were scattered all around me, most of them sleeping in positions that looked terribly uncomfortable. A few of them were sitting around staring into space, empty bottles and burnt-out butts providing an explanation for the spaced-out look.

I glanced over at one of the nearby park benches and saw that it was still in its nighttime form: rows of wicked sharp teeth just waiting to snap down on anyone or anything stupid enough to get too close. Then I looked up at the sky.

I hadn't been imagining it or dreaming it. There was definitely blue sky up there. And clouds. And the sun.

But somewhere between the sky and the square, that sunlight seemed to disappear. Not a single ray penetrated into the square, where it was still dark as night.

A wave of dread rolled over me, and I remembered what I'd done last night, remembered that blackness growing and spreading in the middle of the square. I shuddered and wrapped my arms around myself, more relieved than I could say that I saw no sign of that blackness—the Night Maker—now. I had no doubt it was still there, lurking in the center of the square, but I was heartily glad not to have to look at it. I took another look up at the sky to remind myself why I'd done it, and though the sunlight didn't reach down far enough to warm my face, it warmed my spirit.

Last night had been terrifying and sickening, but it was over now and I had my days back. That was a big win in my book.

You've changed more than you think, Luke's voice whispered in my head, and for the first time I wondered if he was right. I still felt like myself, still felt like the Becket I remembered being before—with a few notable and pleasant exceptions. But the me of before would not have been okay with what I'd done last night. I hadn't killed or even hurt anyone, but there was no mistaking the evil that emanated from the Night Maker, and I had let it into our world for purely selfish reasons.

I probed my conscience in search of guilt, but there was none to be found. I let out a sigh of relief and thanked my lucky stars that I was Nightstruck.

CHAPTER SEVEN

My life settled into a comfortable new routine. My nights were wild and full of an excess I never would have dreamed I'd enjoy in my earlier life. There was a party in the square every night, and now that I'd given Aleric what he wanted, he went out of his way to show me a good time. As long as I stayed away from the center of the square, I could almost pretend everything was normal, and I mostly forgot about the malevolent, light-absorbing darkness that squatted there.

Days were mostly for sleeping, although I didn't need as much sleep as I had in my pre-Nightstruck days. I spent at least part of each day sitting at one of the square's entrances. It was like looking out of a window, watching people go by, being reminded of what life was like for those who weren't Nightstruck. People gave the square a wide berth. They had to know that the Nightstruck and the constructs couldn't get out—there was no other way to explain why we all stayed inside during the day—but I guessed they preferred not to see the unnatural patch of night. I couldn't blame them, though I wished someone would come close enough to talk to me just to pass the time.

I had tried making friends with my fellow Nightstruck, but

I had yet to meet one who was good friendship material. The night took only the cruel and the selfish, and they weren't the kind of people I wanted to hang out with, at least not beyond the most casual acquaintance. Since the night had taken me, I guess that meant I was more selfish than I liked to think, although Piper and Aleric had had to work awfully hard to get me into a vulnerable state of mind. But I was different enough from the rest of the Nightstruck that I just couldn't relate.

I'm making it sound like I was lonely and miserable, but of course I wasn't. I was merely aware that I wanted things the rest of the Nightstruck didn't care about, and that therefore—unlike them, and contrary to what Aleric kept telling me—I *couldn't* actually have everything I wanted after all.

Luke's house wasn't far from the square, so I wasn't entirely surprised when one day I saw him walking by on the far side of Walnut Street. Some pedestrians were wary enough of the square that they'd go out of their way to avoid walking by even on the far side of the street, and long before he saw me, Luke was casting anxious glances at the giant, spiky fence that surrounded the square. I wondered what our patch of night looked like to those who walked by during the day. It had to be a pretty weird sight.

Because it was dark inside the square, I wasn't sure if Luke would see me. Hell, I wasn't sure if I *wanted* Luke to see me. After all, the last time we'd talked, he'd actually *shot* at me. If I'd had any sense at all, I'd have forgotten all about him. I certainly wouldn't have forgiven him. And yet even now, when we lived in separate worlds and there was no hope we could ever be friends, much less a couple, I was drawn to him in a visceral way I couldn't deny.

Slowly, I stood up, my limbs stiff from sitting on the cold

ground for so long. One thing I would readily admit I missed was central heating. We had fires in the square every night, but even with those and even with my coat, I was always cold.

The movement drew Luke's attention, and he came to a stop across the street, staring at me as if not sure if I was really there. I waved at him and smiled. He just stood there and stared, unsmiling, until I dropped my hand back to my side and let my own smile fade. I figured he'd eventually get tired of giving me that cold stare and would walk away, but instead he waited for a break in the traffic—not that he had to wait long, since even people in cars tended to avoid the square—and crossed the street.

He came to stand a few feet from the entrance to the square, almost within touching distance of me. The darkness behind me made him visibly nervous, especially when Billy the goat trotted by on his clawed metal hooves. Luke had been with me when Billy killed my father, so I wouldn't have blamed him if he'd changed his mind and crossed back to the other side of the street.

"He can't get out of the square," I assured Luke. "Nothing can get out of here during the day."

"Even you?" he asked, cocking his head to one side.

"Even me." I demonstrated by walking to the very limit of the square, at which point I was suddenly and inexorably stopped. I gave him a wry grin. "I'd love to know how the government is explaining that it's always night in Rittenhouse Square these days. Is the leading theory still some kind of mass hallucination?"

The theories that had been bandied about by the press—back when I had access to the Internet and actually had some clue what was going on in the world—were sometimes downright hysterical, but unless things had changed since I'd been Night-

70

struck, the government was still treating it as if the entire city had some crazy communicable disease that caused hallucinations. That was why they'd quarantined the city and I hadn't been able to go to Boston to live with my mom after my dad died.

"That's still the party line," Luke confirmed, rolling his eyes. "I don't know how they think so many people are having the *same* hallucination, but they're sticking to their story. And of course no one can get a photograph of this." He indicated the square with a sweeping gesture of his arm.

"What do the photos look like?" I asked, genuinely curious.

"It looks like Rittenhouse Square, only filled with hundreds of homeless people sleeping on the grass."

I nodded, unsurprised. For whatever reason, the changes that took over the city at night were impossible to capture on film or video, which was why the government claimed we were all sick and hallucinating.

"Rumor has it this happened because there's something called a Night Maker in the square," Luke said. "Is it true?"

"Yeah." I hoped the rumor didn't include the news that I had brought that Night Maker into the world, but Luke would probably not be talking to me at all if he knew that part. "It's super creepy. It's like there's a big black hole in the center of the square. On the plus side, I don't . . . disappear during the day, or whatever it is that happens to the Nightstruck."

His eyebrows shot up. "You don't know?"

I shook my head. "I don't know if I'm unconscious or what, but I don't remember anything about the days before the Night Maker came."

"Piper said the same thing, but I thought that was her way of saying she didn't want to talk about it."

"You've seen Piper?"

Luke nodded, his expression grim and haunted. "She's out of the hospital now, convalescing at home."

"How . . . is she?"

His expression had already clued me in that she wasn't doing too great, so I wasn't surprised that he shook his head. "She's not doing so well. I mean, physically she's going to be okay, but . . ." His voice trailed off, and he cleared his throat. He was silent for a moment before he continued more firmly. "She wanted me to tell you she was sorry. For everything."

I snorted. There was no apology big enough to cover everything she had done to me. Being Nightstruck had changed her in ways she couldn't have imagined before she let it happen, but the fact would always remain that she *had* let it happen. I'd been taken against my will, tricked by Aleric and Piper, and I'd tried desperately to get inside before the dawn struck and did whatever it had done to me. Piper had gone willingly, and for that I would never, ever forgive her.

"Feel free to tell her what she can do with her apology," I said with a curl of my lip.

"She's not expecting you to forgive her," Luke said. "She just thought she should tell you anyway."

"What about you? Do you forgive her?"

Luke frowned in thought. He and Piper had been dating for months before she was Nightstruck, but it seemed to me their relationship had already been starting to go downhill. Piper tended to go through boyfriends like potato chips, and I'd gotten the feeling he was losing patience with some of her less than considerate behavior.

"I don't know," Luke admitted. "She wasn't in her right mind when she said and did all those terrible things, so I feel like I *should* forgive her." He shrugged. "But I'm not sure I can."

"Good," I said with a firm nod. "She doesn't deserve you. She never did."

That was not something the old me would ever have said. I might have *thought* it, but I never, ever would have put it into words. Being able to say what I was thinking—without worrying about whether it hurt someone's feelings or pissed them off—was such a great relief I couldn't imagine how I'd survived all those years of self-censorship.

Luke gave me a disapproving look, and I thought I was about to get a lecture about what a bitch I was being. Luckily, he kept his opinion to himself.

"Her parents have her seeing a shrink," he said. "Doesn't sound like it's helping much. They're so afraid she's going to run away and get herself Nightstruck again that they're keeping her under twenty-four-hour supervision. They even lock her in her room at night."

"My heart bleeds for her." Of course Piper would want to run off again. The reason the night had taken her in the first place was that deep down she was so self-absorbed she sometimes forgot other people mattered. So why wouldn't she want to be Nightstruck once more, even though she knew exactly what kind of creature it would turn her into? Her own comfort was far more important to her than the lives of the people she would kill or hurt when her stunted conscience went bye-bye again.

Luke shook his head. "I miss you. The real you, I mean."

"This *is* the real me," I insisted. "You just don't want to accept it."

"I'm going to get you back," he continued, as if I hadn't spoken. "I don't know how yet, but I'm going to do it."

"Newsflash for you: I'm perfectly happy where I am. There is no way in hell I want to go back to what I was before. So ditch the shining armor and get off your noble white horse. This princess does not need saving."

It would have been the perfect time to turn my back and stride back into the depths of the square with my head held high. I certainly intended it to be a parting shot. And yet somehow my feet seemed rooted to the pavement. I just couldn't walk away when there was still a possibility Luke would keep talking to me.

From the look in his eyes, I'd say Luke was seriously considering walking away himself. I don't suppose I was much of a joy to talk to, and it wasn't like we had anything worthwhile to say to each other. But apparently he was just as reluctant to walk away as I was, because he just kept standing there, gnashing his teeth and not saying anything.

"There you are!" said a voice from behind me, and both Luke and I jumped about a mile in the air.

I looked over my shoulder, and Aleric seemed to materialize out of the darkness, though I quickly realized he was merely walking out from beneath the deepest shadow of a tree. I wondered how long he'd been listening in. I didn't believe for a moment he had announced himself the moment he arrived.

"I've been looking all over for you," Aleric said, smiling pleasantly. An unwholesome glitter in his eyes told me the pleasantness was an act. The Nightstruck might not be possessive of each other, but Aleric was not Nightstruck, had never been human, and I was definitely getting a testosterone-fueled jealousy vibe from him.

Luke had gotten over his surprise, the look on his face now frozen into a combination of wariness and loathing. His right hand had ostentatiously disappeared into his coat pocket. It might have been a bluff, but even if he was carrying a gun, we had already seen proof that it was useless against Aleric. I'd shot him multiple times once before, and the bullets had passed harmlessly through. Luke had seen it happen.

"I'm sure you've been searching for hours, this square being so huge and all," I said to Aleric. I tried to make my voice light and flippant, but my instincts were telling me having these two anywhere near each other could be a recipe for disaster. I wondered what it meant that even Nightstruck, I was at least mildly worried about Luke's safety.

Aleric looked Luke up and down with a curl of his lip. "Why don't you come on in and have a proper visit?" he mocked, making a sweeping gesture of invitation. Hidden in the shadows behind him, Leo was crouched and ready to spring, just in case Luke was stupid enough to accept the invitation. Which of course he wasn't.

"We were having a perfectly pleasant conversation just as we are," Luke said. "Until you showed up, that is."

I stifled an urge to laugh. Luke had a very generous interpretation of "a perfectly pleasant conversation."

Aleric *did* laugh, the sound full of sharp edges and holding no sign of genuine humor. He came up beside me and put a possessive arm around my shoulders. No doubt about it: he was jealous. I mentally scribbled a memo to myself to put some thought into how I could use that to my advantage.

I tried to shrug Aleric's arm off, but his fingers dug in tight enough to hurt. I declined to put up too much of a struggle. I probably couldn't have gotten Aleric to let go anyway, and if Luke thought Aleric was hurting me, he might lose some of the good sense that was keeping him firmly outside the square's borders.

"I'm sure you were having a lovely talk," Aleric said. "You two have so much in common these days."

"You're being a dick," I told Aleric crisply. I gave him a world-class glare, but he wasn't even looking at me, his eyes locked with Luke's.

"If the Night Maker chooses to move in this direction," Aleric said to Luke, "the patch of night will move with it. All it would take was a few feet, and suddenly you'd be in my reach."

Behind him, Leo snarled and stalked out of the shadows so that Luke could get a good look at him. Anyone in their right mind would take a few steps backward if they caught sight of Leo. Luke was in his right mind.

For a few seconds, Luke couldn't seem to tear his eyes away from the monstrosity that was Leo. I couldn't blame him, seeing as Leo *still* gave me the creeps after all this time.

"Night Makers are very possessive of their territory and reluctant to move it," Aleric said. "However, since Becket and I are the ones who brought this one here, it owes us a debt of gratitude. I can probably persuade it to move over the few feet I need."

Luke's horrified look shifted from Leo to me.

Crap. I'd had no intention of letting Luke know I had anything to do with the arrival of the Night Maker. I might not have killed anyone myself, but I knew people had been killed in the square because they dared to venture in during the day. They were idiots, and one could say it was an example of survival of the fittest, but it wasn't too much of a stretch to lay those deaths squarely on my shoulders.

I considered explaining all these perfectly logical reasons why Luke shouldn't blame me for what had happened, but I knew none of them would convince him. Aleric had known it, too, which was why he'd opened his big mouth in the first place. The guy was pretty much the center of my world these days, but sometimes he could be a colossal pain in my ass.

"He's bluffing," I said, although I knew perfectly well it wasn't

Aleric's threat that was causing Luke to back away. "If he could persuade the Night Maker to move, he'd have done it already." Besides, he'd told me the Night Maker was tethered to the gate through which it had come, and I saw no reason not to believe him.

Aleric had done exactly what he'd set out to do. Luke was no longer interested in anything I had to say. He shook his head at me in disbelief, his face twisted into a grimace of pure disgust. Then he turned his back and hurried away, crossing the street without even looking to see if any cars were coming. He was in that much of a hurry to put distance between us.

So much for my would-be knight in shining armor.

CHAPTER EIGHT

Thanks to the industrious thieving of his minions, Aleric and I now had a large tent set up on the grass. We even had furniture, including a luxurious featherbed and a leather sofa so soft it was like sitting on taffy—without all the stickiness. It was a comfortable little space, for the most part, except for the constant bone-chilling cold. We'd tried setting up a space heater, taking advantage of the electricity that had once powered the square's lights, but of course the city had shut the electricity off.

It wasn't quite sunset yet, but I was wide awake and restless, pacing the tent like a trapped animal. Glad as I was to have my days back, being trapped in the square all day was driving me crazy, even when I spent much of that time sleeping. It didn't help that ever since Luke had come by, Aleric had been watching me—or having me watched—twenty-four/seven. Even on the rare occasions when he let me out of his sight, there always seemed to be some construct lurking in the shadows.

Aleric was lounging naked in the bed, watching me hungrily. It seemed I was constantly pissed off with him these days—and he with me—but I saw no reason why our little arguments should stop me from enjoying the pleasures of having a hot guy in my bed. He and I got on much better when we weren't talking, if you know what I mean.

"Any chance you'll let me have some time to myself tonight?" I asked.

He gave me a look of wide-eyed innocence. "What do you mean?"

"Stick to looking menacing," I advised him. "You're much better at menacing than innocent."

I was rewarded by a quick narrowing of his eyes, though he banished the expression almost before I could see it. He sat up straight, wrapping the covers around his hips. If it'd been me, I'd have been freezing with that naked torso, but Aleric never showed any sign of feeling the cold.

"You can have as much time to yourself as you want," he said curtly. "I'm not keeping you prisoner."

"It's not time to myself if I have Leo or Billy or some other construct breathing down my neck," I retorted. "What are you afraid I'm going to do if you're not watching? Run off with Luke and get married?"

He rolled his eyes at me, but something in his body language told me that Luke was indeed the reason behind the extra scrutiny. I didn't understand how Aleric could possibly be jealous of Luke. It was *Aleric* whose bed I shared, and Luke wanted nothing to do with me. Then again, human emotions are rarely logical, so I guess it was no great surprise Aleric's weren't, either.

"I'm looking out for your safety," he said, not very convincingly.

"Seriously?" I said. "That's your story? Who the hell do you think is going to mess with me?"

"I can think of one person," he snapped in response, eyes flashing in annoyance.

It wasn't hard to guess who he meant. "Luke would never hurt me!" The denial came quickly enough to my lips, but fast on its heels came the memory of Luke pointing my own gun at me, of him shooting it in my general direction. I still honestly couldn't believe Luke could shoot me, but maybe now that he knew I was responsible for the presence of the Night Maker, his attitude toward me would have hardened even more.

"He already has," Aleric fired back. "You should be having the time of your life being Nightstruck, and instead you're pining for some vanilla Boy Scout who can't stand the sight of you."

I flinched. I was hardly Luke's favorite person right now, but it wasn't as bad as all that. At least, I thought it wasn't. Still, Aleric's barb had sunk in pretty deep, and I didn't have a quick rejoinder.

He reached for me, and I let him take my hands and pull me toward him. I felt the intensity of his eyes on me, though I couldn't meet his gaze.

"I'm sorry this has been so hard on you," he said, and he let go of one of my hands to brush his fingers gently over my cheek. The touch made me shiver. "Our trap was meant to catch a different sort of person altogether. It would have called to anyone nearby who had the proclivity to become Nightstruck. It's only bad luck that you were there and that you were too strong a person to let your fear hold you back."

This unexpected kindness took some of the sting out of his earlier words. It had been obvious to me from the beginning that I wasn't quite like the rest of the Nightstruck, that I wasn't quite as . . . free. I was happy with my current life, and I had no wish to go back to what I'd been like before. But there did seem to me some tiny piece of me that was still stuck in the past. Otherwise, why would I still care what Luke thought of me?

"I have an idea," Aleric said, a note of sly cunning entering his voice. "Something that may help you get the most out of being Nightstruck."

"Oh? What do you have in mind?"

Annoyingly, Aleric decided he wanted his "treat" to be a secret. He said he needed a little time to set it up, so he left me to fend for myself for the first few hours of the night. Unfortunately, I had to fend for myself with Leo on my heels. I tried to think of somewhere I could go where he couldn't follow, but the only idea that came to my mind was to go inside somewhere, over a threshold that the constructs couldn't cross. But it wasn't like people were leaving their doors open these days, and if I wanted to get inside somewhere, I'd need Leo's help to break me in. And unless I found somewhere that had a back exit I could escape through, he'd be waiting for me right by the entrance.

In the end, I decided it was all too much trouble for not enough gain. The nightly party was well under way in the square, and though I had actually grown a little bored with partying, at least in the midst of the crowd I could try to pretend that I wasn't being watched.

It was probably around three in the morning when Aleric returned to the square. As usual, an entourage of Nightstruck followed in his wake, but I could tell something was up by the brightness in their eyes and the almost palpable aura of energy and excitement that emanated from them. I had dipped into the stash of chocolate vodka we kept in our tent, and I was pleasantly tipsy. Enough so that I'd been dancing almost nonstop for the last hour, reveling in the warmth and buzz though my legs were getting tired and my hair was plastered to my face with sweat.

I stopped dancing and stepped away from the crowd when I saw Aleric approaching. I had dumped my coat on the grass after the first dance, the movement and the booze keeping me toasty warm, but now I shivered as a chill breeze tried to freeze the sweat on my face. I quickly found my coat—a little worse for wear—and slipped it on.

Aleric came to a stop about an arm's length away from me. His eyes gleamed in the moonlight, and his lips were curved into a cat-who-ate-the-canary smile. Whatever surprise he'd arranged for me, he sure was proud of himself.

Behind him, his Nightstruck groupies fanned out in a semi-circle. They were practically bouncing with anticipation, barely able to contain their excitement. I resisted the urge to ask what was going on. Aleric was sure to tell me anyway. I was both excited about what Aleric had in store for me, and a little wary. I'd already established that I wasn't like the other Nightstruck, that I shared very few interests with them. It was hard to imagine something they found so exciting would be something I'd like.

I waited for Aleric's explanation, but he was apparently in no hurry. Grinning like mad, he indicated the row of Nightstruck behind him with a sweep of his arm.

"See anyone you know?" he asked.

Frowning, I examined the ragged group more closely, looking from face to eager face. There was no one I recognized, and I turned to Aleric to tell him so.

"Look more closely," he insisted before a word left my mouth.

I scanned quickly over the group once again, and once again failed to recognize anyone, at least beyond a vague awareness that I'd seen a couple of them hanging around the square once in a while. I wondered if Aleric was playing some kind of mind game with me. I wouldn't put it past him.

I was about to turn away once again when something stirred

somewhere in the back of my brain, and my eyes locked onto one of the waiting Nightstruck. He was a total stranger to me, and yet . . .

I stared more closely. He was skinny as hell, his elbows and knees sticking out sharply, his cheekbones forming dramatic shadows on his face. His eyes were Nightstruck green, sunken deep into bruise-colored sockets, and his hair and beard—both of which were filthy—were a whitish blond. When I'd first seen him, I'd thought he was about thirty—and a hard thirty at that—but now that I was really taking him in, I realized that he was about my age.

With a shock that drained the blood from my face, I finally thought to imagine that face with eyes of ice blue instead of green. And I knew exactly who he was.

"Stuart," I whispered.

When I was in middle school, I was very shy and got exceptionally good grades. This combination of traits was like an evil catnip for the school bullies, and I'd been picked on mercilessly. Stuart Caufield was the boy who in sixth grade dubbed me "Becky the Brain," and that hated and hateful nickname had stuck to me like glue until my parents finally decided they wouldn't be spoiling me or turning me into a snob if they sent me to a private school.

It was no surprise that rotten kid had turned into just the kind of rotten teen who would be Nightstruck. He'd pulled every bully stunt you could imagine on me, from coining the nickname, to hitting me—and then insisting to the credulous teacher that I fell—to stealing my lunch money, to trying to trick me into thinking an older boy "liked" me. He was the bane of my existence for many years, and was absolutely the last person I ever wanted to see again.

Though come to think of it, it was kind of nice to see how

skeevy he looked. He'd thought he was quite the stud when I knew him, and his blond-haired, blue-eyed good looks had won him many an admiring glance. Now he looked like a dirty, homeless junkie, and I had no doubts that if he pushed up his sleeves, there'd be track marks. Couldn't have happened to a nicer guy, I thought with just a touch of satisfaction.

I curled my lip in distaste and gave Stuart my best sneer. "Looks like you've moved up in the world," I said. "Been sleeping in a Dumpster lately?"

Stuart broke from the crowd of Nightstruck and came toward me. Despite how awful he looked, he hadn't lost the swagger in his stride, and he sure could look down his nose with the best of them.

"Aleric told me you wanted a piece of this," he said, going for the ever-so-classy crotch-grab.

"Ew, gross!" I said, jerking my eyes away and glaring at Aleric, who grinned and shrugged.

"If I'd told him why I was really bringing him to you," Aleric said, "it would have spoiled the surprise."

"Huh?" I said in reply, and heard a similar sound fall from Stuart's lips.

Aleric just smiled mysteriously. But I noticed the loose semicircle of Nightstruck had gotten tighter, filling in the space Stuart had vacated and forming a human wall behind him. And I also noticed the rest of the Nightstruck in the square had started drifting toward us.

The air was suddenly charged with electricity, and I remembered how excited the small pack of Nightstruck had been when they'd approached. Stuart might have been excited by what Aleric had told him was going to happen when we met up, but public sex was hardly a cause for excitement for the rest of the Nightstruck. Hell, there were virtual orgies going on in the square at all hours of the day and night, and no one would care about having an audience.

The music went silent, and I could hear the excited murmuring of the crowd as they gathered closer, forming a large circle all the way around Stuart, with Aleric and me standing side by side in the front row.

"What the hell?" Stuart asked in alarm, turning a quick circle and finding himself surrounded. When his eyes locked on Aleric's, they were wide enough that I could see the whites all around the shocking green.

"You're tonight's entertainment," Aleric announced.

I'd seen Nightstruck throw themselves into harm's way at Aleric's command without showing the slightest hint of fear or reluctance, but Stuart was clearly terrified. His breath steamed in the cold air, coming in frantic puffs.

"You can't!" he choked out. "You can't hurt me. I'm Nightstruck."

Aleric laughed long and loud, and the rest of the crowd joined in. I wasn't amused enough to laugh, but I did smile. I'd already seen how carelessly Aleric could throw away the lives of the Nightstruck, and it would never have occurred to me to think that he *couldn't* hurt them just because he generally chose not to. What cause would he have to hurt people who asked "how high" when he told them to jump?

Heavy metallic footsteps clanked against the pavement, and the crowd of onlookers parted as Leo lumbered forward into the circle. Stuart's eyes almost bugged out of his head, and he backed away until he reached the wall of Nightstruck behind him. One of them gave him a hard shove in the back, sending him sprawling on his face right at Leo's feet.

"Are you feeling any great and generous urge to hug it out with your old pal?" Aleric asked me.

I bit my lip, looking at the pathetic figure cowering at Leo's feet. He'd tormented me day after day, year after year, and though I didn't consider myself a hateful person, I did indeed hate him. The old me probably would have felt sorry for him now. His life had obviously gone to shit since I'd last seen him. Although now that he was Nightstruck, I didn't suppose he was too unhappy with how his life had turned out.

My conscience wasn't completely dead. I knew without question that no matter how cruel Stuart had been to me, he didn't deserve a playdate with Leo. But I wasn't going to heroically run into that circle and throw myself over him to protect him.

"I'd never get the stink out if I so much as shook his hand," I said. "So no, not hugging."

"Glad to hear it," Aleric said with a satisfied smile.

One of the snakes on Leo's head darted out and sank its metal fangs into the meat of Stuart's shoulder. He let out a shriek of pain and pulled away, the fangs ripping through flesh and sleeve as he freed himself and charged toward the wall of observers.

Someone started chanting Leo's name, and other voices soon followed suit. Heat flooded my body, and my breaths came short as my heart rate skyrocketed. Stuart was shoved back into the circle once more, and this time it was Leo's scorpion tail that struck, impaling Stuart's thigh with a thud I could feel through the pavement beneath my feet. His scream could have shattered lightbulbs if there were any around.

"If it gets too much for you," Aleric said, "let me know, and I'll put a stop to it."

My fingers curled at my sides, nails digging into my palms. Leo gave Stuart an almost playful swat with his paw, his claws leaving bloody furrows.

This is wrong, I thought to myself. *You should tell him to stop.*

I opened my mouth, meaning to tell Aleric that that was

enough, that I was satisfied Stuart had paid for everything he'd done to me. But no sound came out, and I couldn't tear my eyes away as Leo bit clean through Stuart's ankle. The circle was already slick with blood that steamed in the cold air, and the metallic scent of it made my nose wrinkle.

Okay, it was hard to deny that this was wrong. But *I* wasn't the one hurting Stuart. And it wasn't like this had been my idea. It was all Aleric's doing. Besides, just because Aleric said he would put a stop to it if I asked didn't mean he would actually do it. And even if he did, Stuart had lost a lot of blood already and wasn't going to get any medical attention. He was already dead.

I never got fully into the spirit of the thing, never joined the chanting, never cheered or jeered or applauded. But my blood hummed with excitement, and I couldn't have torn my eyes away from the spectacle if I'd tried. Stuart might not technically *deserve* what was happening to him—not based on what he'd done to me as a child at least—but it sure was satisfying to know how deeply he was paying for all the pain and misery he'd caused me.

Becky the Brain, frightened and shy and goddamn weak, would have saved him. Nightstruck Becket didn't even try.

CHAPTER NINE

Some of the luster had worn off being Nightstruck. Aleric's moodiness and the fact that I couldn't turn around without bumping into him were grating on my nerves, as was the constant vigilance of Leo and Billy. Try having a scorpion-tailed, snake-headed, spider-jawed lion breathing down your neck every night and see how you like it.

Even the parties were getting old, though I still sometimes lost myself to the music and the dancing. But it wasn't as exciting as it had been in the beginning. Aleric offered to track down some of the rest of the bullies who'd tormented me in middle school. However, although I didn't feel *bad* about what I'd let happen to Stuart, I didn't feel particularly good about it, either. Not enough to do it again at least.

Being Nightstruck was a little like living on a diet of potato chips and ice cream. I love potato chips and ice cream, but every once in a while I craved a good, solid meal.

"You're still holding back," Aleric told me when I declined his generous offer to find another bully to "play" with. "Until you give up the last vestiges of your past, you'll never be truly free."

"By *last vestiges of your past* you mean Luke, right?"

I was rewarded by an unmistakable flare of jealousy in his eyes. I hadn't seen Luke in over a week, and we hadn't exactly parted on good terms, but Aleric was still obviously touchy about his "rival." Despite his heated denial.

"I wasn't talking about your Boy Scout," he said with a sneer. "You can't give up what you don't have."

"Ouch," I said with an exaggerated wince that was only partly fake. I wasn't sitting around pining away for Luke or anything, but I would have greatly preferred it if he didn't hate my guts. I sneaked a glance toward the center of the square, where the Night Maker crouched in its veil of darkness. I still couldn't bring myself to get within sight of it. I didn't regret bringing it into the square and regaining the missing hours of my days, but I did wish Aleric hadn't told Luke I was responsible.

"I'm serious, Becks," Aleric said, the rancor now gone from his voice as he took both my hands in his. "This life still isn't quite natural to you. But it could be if you let it."

I looked into his eyes and wished it could be that easy. "I'm trying," I told him. "I watched you torture someone to death and didn't say a word. What more do you want from me?"

"I want you to fully embrace your new life. I want you to reach out and *take* what you want." His lips turned up in a sexy smile. "But first you have to figure out what that is."

My heart gave a very pleasant little flutter. I might not know what I wanted in the long run, but I certainly knew what I wanted at the moment. Aleric was still holding my hands, and I gave him a little tug.

"How about if I start off by taking you?" I suggested.

Not surprisingly, Aleric had no objection.

Afterward, I lay drowsing contentedly in Aleric's arms and tried to remember why I'd ever thought I had cause to complain. He stroked my sweat-dampened hair, and I cuddled close to him, feeling warm and free and sated. My life was pretty damn spectacular, and I wouldn't trade it for anything.

"I've been thinking it might be nice for you to have a house," Aleric said out of the blue.

I pulled a little away from him and propped my head on my hand. "A house?" I asked, frowning at the thought of it. We had occasionally "borrowed" someone's house during the night, but I always felt weird about it. Not because it was "wrong" to trespass, but because I found little comfort in a house that wasn't mine. I was much more comfortable in our tent in the square, even though it was tiny and missing many of the creature comforts.

"I think you might enjoy having a place to call your own. I can have my Nightstruck go clean out your old place and refurnish it for you one of these nights."

I raised my eyebrows at him. "You'd let me have my house back even though you and your constructs could never go inside?" I should have known right then that there was a catch. Aleric wasn't about to let me have my privacy without getting something out of it.

"I want you to be happy."

I believed he meant it, though I was sure his motive was more complex than that. And I wasn't sure how I felt about the house I'd grown up in. Though it would be nice to have better shelter than a tent—especially on rainy or snowy nights. "I'm not sure it would feel much like a place of my own if I had to make sure to clear out of it every morning."

As soon as the words left my mouth, I understood what Aleric was *really* suggesting, and I sat bolt upright in bed, clutching the blankets protectively to my chest. "You're talking about summoning another Night Maker!" I said in my most accusatory voice.

"Of course. We wouldn't have to summon him right in front of your house. We'll make sure he's well out of sight of your windows but close enough that your house will be within his territory."

"My house and all the other houses on my block," I whispered.

"Naturally. But it's not as if anyone there matters to you, right?" There was an almost teasing lilt to his voice, like he was daring me to contradict him.

What would happen to all those houses and to all the people inside them if daylight never came? Most importantly, what would happen to Luke and Dr. Gilliam and Bob?

To be perfectly honest with you, I didn't much care. I could give Luke a warning in advance so he could get himself and his mom and Bob out of harm's way before we brought the Night Maker through. It wasn't conscience or empathy that made me hesitate. It was the memory of how the sight of the Night Maker had made me feel. It was the only time since I'd been Night-struck that I actually felt afraid, and that was an experience I was happy to do without. Not to mention that cutting myself *hurt*, and I wasn't eager to do it again.

"Let me think about it a bit," I told Aleric.

He shook his head but didn't argue. He probably thought I was hesitating because of Luke. If I'd thought denying it would have helped, I might at least have tried. But Aleric's potentially hurt feelings didn't trouble me enough for me to make the effort.

I thought about Aleric's proposition a lot over the next couple days and nights but couldn't seem to make up my mind. I loved the idea of having my house back—especially after Aleric spontaneously sent his Nightstruck to clean it up and stock it with the stolen loot I'd collected and never used. But every time I imagined the ordeal of summoning another Night Maker, I chickened out.

"We can put a blindfold on you," Aleric suggested. "Out of sight, out of mind, right?"

That's the philosophy I'd adopted with the Night Maker I'd already helped bring into this world, but I didn't think it would work in this instance.

I suspected I would eventually summon the nerve, and that meant I would have to warn Luke—preferably without Aleric breathing down my neck while I did.

I stole a cell phone from one of the Nightstruck. She'd conveniently left it in the pocket of the coat she'd tossed off when she and one of the guys started going at it with no concern for privacy. I couldn't get used to the way the Nightstruck never seemed to care who was watching when they were having sex, and despite having lost almost all my inhibitions, I still generally preferred to look away. This once, I decided to take advantage of their distraction, and I doubt either one of them even knew I was there when I reached into the coat pocket and snatched the phone.

As a general rule, the Nightstruck have no need for phones, but some of them still carried the ones they'd had before they were Nightstruck, and sometimes they stole them from their victims just because they could. The phone I took from the coat pocket was definitely one of the latter, based on its contents. The girl I'd taken it from was nowhere near old enough to have photos of her grandkids on her phone.

I was proud of my little bit of thievery. Aleric and his spies had eyes on me pretty much twenty-four/seven, but they were at their least vigilant during the nightly parties. After all, Luke couldn't come to me at night, and I couldn't leave the party without being noticed, so there was no need to be super para-noid. I doubted they'd considered the possibility that I'd steal a phone and text.

I settled myself into an especially dark corner and tried not to look too furtive as I turned the phone's brightness down until it was barely visible and then sent Luke a quick text.

meet me @ entrance 2morrow? need 2 talk

He wouldn't recognize the number, of course, but he would have no trouble figuring out it was me. Whether he'd be willing to talk to me or not was a whole other question. And let's not even discuss the question of just what there was for us to talk about. If I told him I was going to summon another Night Maker and park it on our block, it wouldn't exactly go over very well. It would be much more sensible to shoot him an e-mail and then ditch the phone so I didn't have to see his reply. But if I *did* summon the Night Maker and chase Luke from his home, then I might never see him again, and that I didn't want.

I set the phone in my lap, putting my arms around my knees to hide its faint glow. I tried not to stare at it, tried not to act weird and suspicious enough to make anyone watching me cu-rious, but it was hard. I willed Luke to answer me, but as the minutes ticked by, the phone went to sleep and stayed there. Which was an answer in its own way, though one I found my-self reluctant to accept. I gave it one more try, though it's hard to be persuasive when texting.

i'll b there @ 2, see u

I wasn't shocked when he didn't answer that one, either. I'd have tried a third time, except I didn't think it had any better chance of succeeding. Besides, the more I texted, the better chance someone was going to see me doing it and wonder what I was up to.

I turned the phone off and shoved it deep into the pocket of my coat. Luke would either show up, or he wouldn't. If he was there waiting for me when I slipped away, we might have as much as five minutes to talk before Aleric showed up. We'd likely have to live with being watched and listened to by Billy or Leo, but I wasn't sure if they were capable of relaying our conversation to Aleric, and it probably didn't matter anyway.

Even if Luke showed up, the conversation was bound to go about as well as our previous ones. It was a stupid plan—if you could even call something a plan when I couldn't tell you what I hoped to accomplish or why I was doing it. Maybe I was hoping Luke could talk me out of summoning the Night Maker, and his arguments would help counter some of Aleric's persuasions. Or maybe I was doing exactly what Aleric kept accusing me of and clinging to the past.

Aleric was rarely around during the day. I don't know exactly where he was, but my best guess was he was hanging out in Night Maker Central, wherever that was. Another dimension maybe? Who knew, but I guess it was a more exciting place than Rittenhouse Square during the day, when lack of sleep and too much drink invariably caught up with the Nightstruck.

I'd have said this worked to my advantage, if it weren't for the vigilance of Billy and Leo, although even the two of them seemed somehow bored during the day. If nightmare constructs made up of metal and magic can get bored.

I peeked out from Aleric's and my tent at just before two o'clock the next afternoon and saw no sign of my watcher du jour. Either they had grown complacent because I so rarely left the tent during the day lately, or they were watching from the distance. I peered into the shadows, but despite the bright sunlight I could clearly see when I looked up at the sky, it was dark as a cloudless night in the square and I couldn't see very far into the distance.

I shrugged. It probably didn't even matter if I was being watched, because Luke probably wasn't going to show up. And even if he did, it wasn't like we were going to be talking about top-secret plans. Aleric would not be surprised to learn I planned to warn Luke before summoning a Night Maker in his backyard.

I had myself so convinced he wouldn't show up that I stopped in my tracks and blinked when I got close enough to the Walnut Street entrance to see Luke standing there. I'm not gonna lie: Luke was nice to look at. He didn't have Aleric's bad-boy vibe—the vibe I'd never found all that attractive, at least not until I'd been Nightstruck—but I felt a predictable punch of desire whenever I saw him.

I wished he were a little less wholesome. If he had some character flaw the night's magic could exploit, he could be with me here in the square every day. It sure would have been nice to have a friend, an ally, a lover, who was *not* Aleric. But Luke was way too selfless and kind to be vulnerable, and even in my current state I knew I didn't really want him any other way. If he were Nightstruck, he'd be just as good-looking, but all the other things I loved about him would go away.

I got over my surprise quickly enough and hurried toward him. I still had no clue what I was planning to say to him—how do you tell someone you're thinking of permanently shrouding his home in malevolent night?—but it was hard to care too much when all I wanted to do was throw myself into Luke's arms.

Judging by the look on his face, throwing his arms around me wasn't the first item on Luke's agenda. His arms were crossed over his chest, and he looked both grim and worried, though I wasn't sure why.

"You got my text," I said inanely as I approached.

"I did," he confirmed. His posture didn't soften, and I noticed him scanning the darkness behind me. Keeping an eye out for Aleric and the constructs, I suppose. "What was it you wanted to talk about?"

In the old days, I'd had an embarrassing tendency to turn into a gibbering idiot in Luke's presence. I couldn't just launch into a conversation about summoning a Night Maker—not if I wanted Luke to stand still and listen to me. But it was hard to think of how to start, and the old me would have blushed and stammered and generally made it obvious that I had nothing of any value to say. Being Nightstruck had changed all that, and I wasn't even mildly worried that I might make myself look stupid as I made up a bogus explanation for why I'd wanted to talk.

"Aleric says my dad is still alive." It was a total lie—Aleric had told me no such thing—but I knew it would keep Luke talking, at least for a while.

The look on Luke's face softened, and his voice came out gentle as he said, "You and I both know that's a lie. There was no way he lived through that."

"I was sure Piper couldn't survive after I shot her." Luke winced at the reminder, and I realized I probably could have been a little less blunt—and a little more remorseful-sounding—about it.

Then again, Luke knew I didn't feel bad about it, so what was the point of pretending?

"She *wouldn't* have survived if she hadn't gotten lucky," he said. "From what I hear, her heart stopped a couple of times on the way to the hospital. But I don't think there's any chance your dad could have survived even if he'd gotten immediate medical attention." He frowned as if he'd just caught up with the conversation. "Wait a minute. Why do you even care?"

Oops. He was right, and if Aleric had told me my dad was alive, I'd have been happy to hear it, but wouldn't exactly be dwelling on it. Nor would I feel the need to tell Luke about it. But I was committed to the story by now, so I stuck with it.

"I just do," I said. "I mean, I'm not going to start weeping and pulling my hair out or anything, but I would prefer it if he was alive."

Luke nodded. "Piper was right, then."

"About what?"

"She said you weren't really suited for the night. She said you probably weren't as Nightstruck as the other Nightstruck."

She was probably right, though I wondered if she'd have felt the same way if she'd seen what I let happen to Stuart. "I'm still a creature of the night now," I said, putting my hand against the invisible barrier that kept me trapped in the darkness. "I know that if I hadn't been Nightstruck, I wouldn't want to be here. But I *was* Nightstruck, and even if I'm not as suited to it as the rest, the last thing I'd want to do was go back to how I was before."

It was true. I wasn't on some kind of continuous high like most of my fellow Nightstruck, and Aleric was getting on my last nerve, but my life was a hell of a lot better here and now than it had been before. I would never admit it out loud, and I planned to hold a grudge against Piper until the day I died, but I was glad she'd helped Aleric trick me.

Luke startled me by reaching out and wrapping his strong fingers around my wrist. I tried to pull away, but he didn't let go.

"Stop it!" I said, jerking my hand back. "You're not safe inside the square." I pointedly stared at his hand, which had crossed into the square's perpetual night. I hadn't seen or heard any constructs following me, but by crossing the plane, Luke had apparently triggered some kind of alarm. There was a chorus of growls and howls and hisses from the darkness behind me.

Instead of letting go, Luke reached over the border to grab my other arm.

"What are you doing?" I shouted, once again jerking backward. Not that I had any hope of freeing myself. Luke was way stronger than me. "You're likely to lose any body part that's on this side of the border."

Luke didn't answer me. His eyes practically glowed with intensity, and his chin was set at a determined angle. He pulled on my wrists, hard, and I slammed into the invisible barrier. The impact knocked my breath away, and I could only gape at Luke.

"Sorry," he said. "But I talked this over with Piper, and she thinks it might work, so it's worth a try."

Thought *what* might work? I was too stunned and breathless to ask the question. Still holding on to my wrists, Luke jerked backward again. It felt like he was pulling me into a thick pane of glass, one that refused to break. I tried to free myself from his grip, but I wasn't going anywhere unless he let me go.

I was pressed hard against the barrier, and when he jerked on me, my forehead slammed into it and I saw stars. My knees went wobbly and refused to hold me. I was sure that would convince Luke to let go.

He didn't. Instead, he leaned his body over the border so he could wrap his arms around my waist for a better grip.

"I know I'm hurting you, and I'm sorry," he said, his lips intimately close to my ear. "But I have to try."

I made an incoherent sound of protest and tried to pry his fingers open. The roars and snarls were getting closer, as was the sound of metal hooves and paws pounding like hammers on the pavement. Fifteen or twenty yards away, Leo catapulted out of the darkness.

"Let go!" I screamed at Luke. Bad enough he'd put his hands over the border—he would at least survive if he lost those—but now his whole upper body was on the wrong side.

He lurched backward, and my entire front slammed into the invisible wall. My nose crunched, and pain exploded in my head. I could feel the pounding vibrations of Leo's paws on the pavement, hear the hissing of the snakes in his mane. Luke was going to get himself killed trying to save me when I didn't even want to be saved.

And still the idiot kept pulling, smooshing me against the barrier. I turned my head sideways so my throbbing nose was no longer taking the worst of it. I realized my nose had to be bleeding, though everything hurt too much for me to feel it. The bleeding had been caused by my own friend, someone not affiliated with the night, and I feared that meant the blood might have power. I was seriously considering donating some blood to summon another Night Maker, but if I did it, it would be on my own terms, when I was ready.

It hurt more than I can describe, but I buried my face in the bunched-up shoulder of my coat, hoping all the blood would be absorbed into the fur and not land on the pavement. Leo was so close I was sure his venomed stinger would whip past my ear and into Luke's chest any second now. I was half-smothering myself in my own coat, and my eyes were watering with pain, but I both felt and heard Luke sliding his legs past the barrier, one on each side of me. He planted his booted feet firmly on the pavement, then gave a tremendous heave, pushing with all the strength of his legs.

A thousand knives pierced my body from head to toe. I tried

to scream, but there was no air in my lungs. My vision went black as those thousand knives ripped through my flesh and bones, flaying me alive and then setting me on fire for good measure.

And then the worst of the pain stopped and I collapsed in a groaning, crying, barely breathing heap. In a patch of warm, bright sunshine.

CHAPTER TEN

The moment I realized what Luke had done, that he'd somehow dragged me kicking and screaming back into the light, was the worst moment in my entire life. Every ugly, awful, painful emotion that had felt so comfortably distant when I was Nightstruck came rushing back in, hitting me with the force of a tidal wave, a Mack truck, and a sledgehammer all at once.

Images of my dad's dead body, bloody and torn and limp, being dragged away by Piper's minions filled me, the grief suddenly fresh and sharp as if it had happened yesterday. Then I remembered Piper collapsing to the pavement in the square, her hands clasped around a gunshot wound in her abdomen. It had been night when I shot her, but in my memory the blood that welled from the wound and streaked her hands was a brilliant, accusatory red.

Thanks to being Nightstruck, I hadn't had to live with what I'd done, and now all those wonderful layers of protection were gone.

Close on the heels of those memories were images of the Night Maker entering the square through the gate Aleric made with my blood, of Stuart's body after Leo was done with him—and of his agonized screams while I stood idly by and watched him being brutalized for my amusement. The worst part was knowing Aleric had done it because he believed I'd enjoy it, and I'd let it happen because he'd been right. In some dark corner of my mind I never wanted to peer into again, I had wanted Stuart to suffer for what he'd done to me as a child.

I curled up on the pavement in fetal position, wailing incoherently. There were voices talking to me, and the constructs in the square were all howling and snarling with rage, but I didn't care about any of that. When I felt hands on me, I kicked and flailed until they went away.

I got up on my hands and knees and lurched toward the entrance to the square, too mindless to realize—or care—that merely getting back inside the square wouldn't be enough to make my demons go away. For that, I would have to be Nightstruck again, and the only way to do that was to be outdoors at dawn.

I doubted I could have made it into the square anyway, but the moment I started to move that way, a crushing weight landed on my back, pushing me into the pavement and pinning me so thoroughly I couldn't move. I let out a shriek of fury, struggling like some wild thing, but I couldn't get free.

My litany of horrors wasn't over. While the grief and the guilt still battered at my fragile psyche, I had yet another vivid memory that threatened to make me go mad. I remembered the glittering triumph in Aleric's eyes as he lay on top of me and took the virginity I freely offered him. Bile rose in my throat, and it took every scrap of my willpower to keep my gorge down.

I'm not some medieval maiden whose virginity is her most prized possession, nor did I feel like losing it made me a slut. But for the rest of my life, I would have to deal with the fact that my first time had been with a guy who was evil to his core and wasn't even *human,* no matter what he looked like.

My gorge rose again, and this time I couldn't keep it down. I puked all over myself and the insanely expensive fur coat I had stolen because I'd somehow felt entitled to have it just because I wanted it.

I was making quite the spectacle of myself, and a small crowd had gathered around me. They must have been some brave people to come that close when the creatures of the square were going apeshit. I don't care if you know the creatures can't get out during the day—they are terrifying, and no one in their right mind would want to get anywhere near them. I didn't remember seeing anyone on the street or sidewalk when Luke grabbed me, which probably meant they all thought I was just some random girl having a very public nervous breakdown.

Someone pulled my hair away from my face, though I doubted they'd gotten to it before I'd fouled it. Someone else patted my back comfortingly, and I no longer had the energy to bat that hand away. My vision was blurred with tears, my throat burned, my mouth tasted vile, and my nose was throbbing steadily to the frantic beat of my heart.

A strong pair of arms slid behind my shoulders and under my knees, and suddenly I was off the pavement. I knew it had to be Luke who'd picked me up, and I was vaguely aware of him making soothing cooing noises as if I were some frightened stray he was trying to rescue, but I was far too miserable to care. I closed my eyes tightly and prayed that I would soon wake up from this mother of all nightmares.

I didn't open my eyes when Luke slid into a car with me cradled on his lap, nor did I respond when I heard Luke's mom say my name. I presumed Luke had called her while I was having my fit of hysterics, and she had rushed to come get us.

I thought they were going to take me to the hospital—or at

least to a psych ward somewhere—but somehow I'd forgotten that Luke's mom was an emergency room doctor herself. When we got to Luke's house, she had Luke carry me into the guest bedroom where I had spent many a night. She rattled off a list of supplies she needed, and then when he brought them to her, she shooed him away.

I wasn't exactly calm by now, and if left on my own I probably would have crawled under the bed to hide in the dark, but I was no longer a raving lunatic. When Dr. Gilliam asked me gently to take off my coat, I did so without any help from her. I couldn't bear to make eye contact with her, so I mutely slid the coat off and handed it to her while staring fixedly at the floor.

Dr. Gilliam dipped a washcloth into a basin of water, tipping my chin up and dabbing at the blood and puke that were drying on my face. I still couldn't handle eye contact, so I closed my eyes as the warm, wet cloth cleaned the filth from my skin.

"Are you hurt anywhere else that I can't see?" Dr. Gilliam asked.

My psyche was one gaping, bleeding, festering wound, but I didn't suppose she had anything in her medicine cabinet to fix that. I shook my head. Dr. Gillian probed the area around my nose and promptly pronounced it broken.

"There's not much I can do for it, I'm afraid," she said. "We'll put some ice on it to help with the swelling, and I'll give you some ibuprofen for the pain, but other than that we'll have to wait for it to heal on its own."

Like I gave a shit about a broken nose under the circumstances. I was back to being my old self again, however, so I kept my opinion to myself as Dr. Gilliam fetched me a bag of ice. Touching the ice to my throbbing nose was pure agony, but I firmly believed I deserved it. I might not have personally killed anyone while I was Nightstruck, but I was unquestionably responsible for at least one death, and I had done plenty of other things that were going to be hard to live with. And the worst part of it was that while I could blame my actual actions on the effects of being Nightstruck, the person I had become hadn't been made up out of whole cloth. She had come from inside me, was in actuality a *part* of me. Just knowing I had that inside me somewhere was almost unbearable.

Dr. Gilliam sat on the bed beside me. I liked having her beside me instead of in front, because that made it easier not to look at her without feeling like I was being rude.

"Becket, honey," Dr. Gilliam said, "I know this is going to be an uncomfortable question, but I have to ask for your own good. Is there any chance you might have become pregnant or picked up an STD while you were Nightstruck?"

I flinched, because yup, that was an uncomfortable question all right.

"You have to know I won't judge you," she continued. "You're not responsible for anything you did while you were Nightstruck. I just need to know if there might be something we need to treat you for. We'll do it discreetly, of course. And don't you worry about Luke—anything you say to me is going to be strictly confidential."

I realized she was already convinced I'd had sex, probably with multiple anonymous partners. It was a reasonable conclusion to draw, considering how promiscuous the Nightstruck were. If I tried claiming I was still pure as the driven snow, she'd never believe me.

I cleared my throat before I spoke, but even so my voice came out weak and scratchy. "The only guy I was with was Aleric." I kept staring at the floor, wishing I could disappear into it. "He's not human, so I don't think I could have gotten pregnant or . . . caught something."

"We should probably do some tests just to be sure," Dr. Gilliam said. There was no hint of judgment or disapproval in her voice, and I knew she was suggesting it because she wanted to protect me from any potential consequences. I was almost 100 percent positive it wasn't because she didn't believe me.

I didn't know what kind of tests would be involved, but I knew I wanted no part of them. "I'm sure," I said.

"You said you don't *think* you—"

"I'm sure!" I said more firmly and nerved myself up to meet her eyes. "Aleric isn't human. When I shot him, he didn't bleed. He can't carry blood-borne diseases or make me pregnant if he doesn't have blood."

"But he has magic," she reminded me. "Are you really so sure what he is and what he's capable of?"

Of course I wasn't. "No tests," I said. I hoped she couldn't *force* me to get tested, but since she wasn't even my legal guardian, I doubted she could.

L uke says you tried to get back into the square after he pulled you out," Dr. Gilliam told me after she was finished with her examination and pronounced me basically whole. She said it cautiously, and although I wasn't yet up to making any sustained eye contact, I was very aware of how she was looking at me, with great intensity and scrutiny.

I shuddered at the memory and wished it would all become an indistinct blur. But the visceral physical sensation of being ripped from the darkness was very real and vivid, and I had no trouble remembering my desperate attempt to escape from the realities that had come crashing down on me. Even now, I thought about the emotional distance I'd had as a Nightstruck with a sharp longing that made my chest ache.

I started when I realized why Dr. Gilliam had brought it up and hurried to reassure her. "It was just a shock. Being pulled out and suddenly . . . feeling everything again. I panicked. But I'm not going to go running back to the night the minute you turn your back." I hugged myself and shivered. I hated everything I was being forced to feel right now, but I knew I was back where I belonged. If somehow I went back and became Nightstruck again, I knew I would eventually end up letting more Night Makers into the city and getting more people hurt and killed. Now that I was back in my right mind, I could never allow that.

I shuddered violently as I remembered seeing the darkness growing from my blood. I don't think I'm a particularly naive person, but how had I not seen at the time that I was giving Aleric exactly what he wanted—and that he'd keep pressing me for more? I'd been considering the possibility of summoning another so I could have my house back. I wondered what excuse Aleric would have tried next, but whatever it was, it probably would have worked.

I gasped, dropping my bag of melting ice and jumping to my feet as my mind continued following the trail I'd just set it on. "What time is it?" I cried, forgetting my reluctance to make eye contact as I grabbed Dr. Gilliam's arm.

Her eyes widened, and I could see she was fearing for my sanity. I suppose it did seem like an odd question to ask with such urgency at that moment.

"What's the matter, honey?" Dr. Gilliam asked. She was back to using that frightened-animal-handling voice of hers.

I sucked in a deep breath to calm myself so I could talk without making her think I was a raving lunatic. "He's not just going to let me go. Aleric, I mean. He's going to come looking for me the moment the sun goes down, and this'll be the first place he looks."

Dr. Gilliam's brows drew together with concern. "He hasn't come after Piper. Her parents hired a private security firm to help keep her safe, but so far they haven't had any trouble."

"I'm different," I insisted. "Did Luke tell you about the Night Maker?"

I could tell by her puzzled expression that she had no idea what I was talking about. Luke must have been upset when he found out I was behind what had happened to Rittenhouse Square, and yet he apparently hadn't told his mother about it. Either he just flat-out hadn't wanted to talk about it, or he'd been protecting me in his own way, trying to hide the full extent of what I'd become from someone whose good opinion he knew mattered to me.

But there was no time for that now. My rendezvous with Luke had been at two, and I had no idea how much time had passed since then. I'd been too dazed to pay attention, but I was sure it had been at least an hour, probably more, and sunset would be on its way soon.

I hurriedly explained the Night Makers and my role in creating the gate to Dr. Gilliam.

"So you see," I concluded, "Aleric needs me. And that means he's not going to let me go without a fight. He can come here with an army of Nightstruck and constructs, and they can get in with no trouble. We can't be here."

Being an emergency room doctor, Dr. Gilliam was used to thinking on her feet and not panicking. I could see the worry in her eyes, but her voice came out smooth and level as she glanced at her watch. I saw that as I had feared, it was nearing four o'clock.

"I'll book us a hotel room," she said. "We'll have to come up with something more permanent and secure, but it'll do for now. Pack a bag, and we'll be out of here in fifteen minutes."

CHAPTER ELEVEN

I didn't really have any packing to do. Piper and her Night-struck friends had destroyed just about everything I owned. I had a single change of clothes, a few assorted toiletries—and a gun. I'd had two of them, but I had no idea what had happened to the one I shot Piper with. My dad's backup gun should have been packed in my pathetically empty duffel bag, but it wasn't there. Not surprisingly, considering Luke had shot at me with it on my second visit to his house. Dr. Gilliam probably wouldn't have left me alone in that room if there were a gun handy. If I were her, I wouldn't trust me as far as I could throw me.

I heard a door open down the hall, then heard the heavy thump of paws on the floor. I turned around just in time to see Bob come bursting through the door. He bounded toward me like he was on springs, his tail wagging wildly, his eyes bright with joy. My dad had long ago trained him not to jump on people, but when he came to a halt at my feet, his paws kept dancing, proving how badly he *wanted* to jump on me.

I fell to my knees and put my arms around my dog, hugging him tightly and almost bursting into tears. His fur felt softer than the mink coat, and I didn't even mind the sloppy dog kisses. I looked up to see Dr. Gilliam smiling in the doorway.

"Don't worry," she said, "he's coming with us. I'll find a hotel that will take him."

I worried that might be hard, seeing as even the most pet-friendly hotels usually only take small dogs. But there was no way I was leaving Bob here alone.

I would have loved to have taken a long hot shower and then buried myself under the covers where no one could see me, but that was not among my options. My mind was slowly but surely becoming more my own, my mental processes emerging from the fog of shock. I wished I hadn't told Dr. Gilliam I had slept with Aleric. I should have just lied, even though she wouldn't have believed me. I trusted her not to tell Luke, but I still hated the fact that she knew. Never mind how much I hated the fact that I had actually *done* it.

If I let myself think about it too much, I started feeling like there were worms writhing in my belly, so I tried really really hard not to think about it. Which was easier than it sounds, seeing as I had so many other horrors filling my head.

There were still a good thirty minutes left before sunset when Luke and Bob and I piled into Dr. Gilliam's car. I felt even more shy and tongue-tied around Luke now than I had in the days when I'd been crushing on him from afar. I found the idea of making conversation downright impossible, actually, so I mostly just huddled in the backseat with my head down and my mouth shut. Either Luke was being considerate of my mental state, or he didn't have any more idea what to say than I did, because he didn't try to talk to me during the short drive.

When the city was first put into quarantine, I thought most of the hotels would have to shut down. After all, it wasn't like we had visitors coming in for the night, except for those unlucky people who'd happened to be traveling here when the quarantine hit. I suspect some of the smaller hotels did close, sending any guests to one of the bigger ones that remained open.

Thanks to the depredations of the Nightstruck, the hotels weren't as empty as I would have expected. Property damage was one of the Nightstruck's favorite party games, so every day there were more people needing alternative lodgings for the night. That being said, the hotels weren't so booked up that it was hard to get a room. Dr. Gilliam seemed to have no trouble getting us a two-bedroom suite on about thirty minutes' notice. And, as it turned out, a lot of hotels had also relaxed their pet policies out of compassion, so Bob was actually welcome.

I had naively thought that one room was for the Gilliams and one room was for me, but it turned out Dr. Gilliam and I would be roommates. It sort of made sense for the two women to share a room and let the lone guy have a room to himself, but I knew at once that wasn't the reason. Dr. Gilliam didn't want me to have a room to myself because she was afraid I might sneak out in the night so I could be out at dawn and be Nightstruck again. Just because I told her that wasn't what I wanted didn't mean she believed me.

"Are you working tonight?" I asked her. It used to be she worked practically every night, because the emergency room was always flooded thanks to Nightstruck attacks.

She gave me a knowing smile, telling me without words that she knew exactly why I was asking. If I'd come right out and asked if we were sharing a room specifically because she wanted to keep an eye on me, she'd probably have given me a straight answer. But I wasn't sure I wanted a straight answer.

"We couldn't go on having the same people work every night shift," Dr. Gilliam said. "It was doable for a few weeks, but since the crisis doesn't seem like it's going to end anytime soon, we had to start thinking about long-term solutions. We take turns working the night now, and this week it's not my turn."

I hadn't exactly put a lot of thought into things since I'd been Nightstruck, and I certainly hadn't considered how the city was responding to the way our world had changed. Partially because I hadn't acknowledged, even to myself, just how long I'd been gone. Hell, I didn't *know* how long I'd been gone. It wasn't like I'd kept a diary or jotted appointments in my calendar or anything.

"What's the date?" I asked, fearing I was about to lose what little grasp on reality I'd managed to get. I'd snuck out on my mission to kill Piper shortly after Thanksgiving. I'd been gone a couple of weeks, at least, but that was about as close a guess as I could imagine. Everything that had happened while I was Nightstruck kind of blurred together, some of it feeling like it must have happened just yesterday, some of it feeling like it had to be a month ago.

"It's December twenty-seventh," Dr. Gilliam told me.

I gasped and had to close my eyes to fight off a bout of tears. All the terrible things that had happened, all the terrible things I had done . . . And yet somehow finding out I'd missed Christmas entirely was almost enough to send me into another tailspin of despair.

Not that I'd been looking forward to Christmas this year. The idea of having to spend it without my dad, of knowing I would never again spend a Christmas day with my dad, had filled me with dread. Thanksgiving had been bad enough, even though the Gilliams had been kind enough to include me in their family celebration. So it wasn't missing the actual celebration of Christmas that hit me so hard. It was more the passing of a milestone—and the thought of what my mother and my sister, both of whom lived in Boston and couldn't get through the quarantine, must have suffered. They'd both been in pain from having lost my dad, but they must have felt like they'd lost me, too.

"You should call your mother," Dr. Gilliam said gently. "Give her the best belated Christmas present she's ever gotten."

"You told her . . . what happened to me?"

Dr. Gilliam nodded. "The basics of it, at least." We were both sitting on one of the beds, and she reached over and put her hand on top of mine. "I didn't send her the letter you wrote. I hope you'll forgive me."

I grimaced. When I'd gone out to kill Piper, I'd been pretty convinced I wouldn't be coming back. I didn't want to disappear without a trace, so I'd written good-bye letters to my mom, my sister, Dr. Gilliam, and Luke. Actually physically written them by hand, so that just in case I made it back alive I could destroy them without a trace.

"Why not?" I asked. I hadn't died as I'd expected, but being Nightstruck was the next worst thing. I'd have thought it a good occasion for a good-bye letter.

Dr. Gilliam's hand tightened over mine. "Luke and I are the only ones who know it was you who shot Piper."

I'd had enough shocks throughout the day that I couldn't muster one more gasp, but Dr. Gilliam had no trouble reading my surprise.

"When Piper woke up after surgery, she claimed she was shot by one of the Nightstruck."

"Why would she do that?"

Dr. Gilliam raised an eyebrow. "So that you wouldn't be wanted for attempted murder."

Attempted murder. That was exactly what I'd done, and I'd been fully aware of its moral implications. I had never for a moment considered the *legal* ones. Unless things had changed recently, the law still considered the Nightstruck human beings with rights. I doubted there was much push to prosecute anyone who killed one of the Nightstruck, but it made sense that once Piper came back to herself, the police—and certainly her wealthy parents—would want to prosecute the person who had shot her.

"I think it's very important we keep that a secret," Dr. Gilliam continued. "With neither you nor Piper being Nightstruck anymore, if anyone finds out you shot her . . ."

I totally understood where she was going with that. If there was evidence that I'd shot and almost killed Piper—especially in an obviously premeditated attempt and while I was still of sound mind—I would be arrested and could even go to jail.

It was . . . humbling to realize that Piper had protected me even after I shot and almost killed her. It was also hard to reconcile the Piper who would protect me with the one who'd murdered my father right in front of me. I would always consider my dad's death Piper's responsibility, even though it had been Billy the goat who'd done the actually killing and no doubt it had been Aleric who'd ordered it.

"She's been seeing a therapist ever since she came to in the hospital," Dr. Gilliam said. "I think maybe you should consider talking to someone yourself. I can—"

I held up my hand to stop her. "I don't want to talk to anyone about what happened. I just want to . . . forget all about it."

"We both know that's not going to happen."

I winced, not sure if I was grateful for or resentful of her refusal to sugarcoat things. It was nice not to feel condescended to, but some realities are awfully hard to face. Like the fact that I would never be able to scrub my mind clean of what I'd done while I was Nightstruck. Or the fact that despite all my denials, there was a small part of myself that longed to be Nightstruck again. That wouldn't make the memories go away, but it would make them stop hurting.

"I can't imagine what it must have been like, what you must have gone through," Dr. Gilliam said, "but holding it all in and keeping it to yourself is just going to make things worse. I hope you know there's no shame in seeing a therapist. It doesn't mean—"

"I know," I cut her off. No one would fault me for seeing a therapist after everything I'd gone through. In all probability, it was the smart thing to do, the *healthy* thing to do. "There's just no way I'm going to talk about everything that's happened with some stranger." I shook my head firmly. "Can't do it."

Piper's folks could *force* her to see a shrink, but Dr. Gilliam didn't have that kind of power over me. Besides, a shrink probably wasn't optional for Piper. She'd done far worse than I when she was Nightstruck, plus she'd been shot by her best friend. She had to have some kind of PTSD or something. I was a mess myself, but not *that* much of a mess. At least that's what I told myself.

"I understand," Dr. Gilliam said. "All I'd ask is that you don't close your mind to it entirely. And remember, I'm always here for you if you need to talk but can't face a stranger. I can't help you in the way a therapist could, but I can be a friend. A shoulder to cry on. And I promise, I will never judge you."

"What about Piper?" I asked out of genuine curiosity. "Do you judge Piper?"

She smiled ruefully. "I'm afraid Piper was never my favorite person in the first place, so it's a little harder not to be judgy about her."

I'd always thought of Piper as a person who everyone—except my dad—liked. She'd been outgoing and bubbly, beautiful and friendly—all things I wasn't. Even so, I realized I wasn't entirely surprised to find the mother of the guy she'd been dating wasn't any fonder of her than my dad had been. I wondered if Luke's dad felt the same way. Mr. Gilliam traveled constantly for work, so I didn't know him very well. He'd been on one of those business trips when the quarantine hit, and like my mom, he was unable to get into the city. I assumed the separation was hard on both Dr. Gilliam and Luke, especially as the quarantine dragged on and on.

"Now," Dr. Gilliam said. "Why don't you give your mom a call and let her know you're back. She'll be so relieved. She's been frantic ever since you were taken. She's been working hard to find a way to get permission to come into the city, but so far it's been like banging her head against a brick wall."

I had some serious mixed feelings about the idea of my mom making it through the quarantine. On the one hand, she was the only parent I had left, and though she wasn't the most nurturing mother in the universe, I would love to collapse into her arms and cry my eyes out. I would also love to let someone else be in charge for a while, to not feel like I had to make all the difficult decisions myself—even if I might not agree with a lot of the decisions she'd make.

On the other hand, she would be one more person Aleric could potentially use against me. He already knew that the best way to get me to do what he wanted was to threaten or hurt or kill people I cared about. My mom would have a humongous bull's-eye on her the moment she entered the city. Instead of her protecting me, I would be the one protecting her, or at least trying to, and that was not something I needed right now.

I didn't feel like explaining any of that to Dr. Gilliam at the moment, so I kept all those feelings to myself, shoving them down into my center with everything else that was roiling and squirming there. I reached for the phone, but my hand stalled halfway there.

My mom deserved to know immediately that I was safe and whole and back in my right mind. She'd been suffering for about four weeks, and I could end that for her simply by picking up the phone and giving her a call. If that were all there were to it, I wouldn't have hesitated. But she was going to want to know all about what I'd done and where I'd been during the time I'd been missing. She had a lawyer's knack for asking just the questions you don't want to answer and then persisting until you blurted out everything you were trying to hide. I'd had a hard enough day already, and I just couldn't face the Inquisition that was to come.

"If it's all right with you," I said to Dr. Gilliam, letting my hand fall back to my lap, "I'd rather call her tomorrow." I let my eyes get all teary, not because I felt the desperate need to cry at the moment—I was more tired than sad—but because I wanted to look as pitiful as possible. "I can't . . . handle it right now."

Dr. Gilliam bit her lip indecisively. I was acting like I was still Nightstruck, selfishly putting my own wants and needs before those of others. I knew that, and knew it wasn't like me. I just couldn't find the courage to make that call.

"Maybe you can call her for me," I suggested. "Tell her I'll talk to her tomorrow. Maybe you can tell her you gave me a sedative, and I'm sleeping."

Dr. Gilliam's eyes narrowed. "I'm not lying for you, Becket. And your mother already hates me because she thinks it's my fault you ran off. If I call her and won't let her talk to you, she's probably going to call the police and claim I've kidnapped you."

"It is *so* not your fault!" I cried indignantly. My mom had

always been a champ at assigning blame—she'd done it constantly with my dad—but to think that she was blaming the
woman who'd taken me in when I had nowhere to go, who'd
been unfailingly kind, who was even now risking—

"That doesn't really matter, sweetheart," Dr. Gilliam said. "I
promised her I'd take care of you, and I failed. I'd feel the same
way if our roles were reversed and Luke went missing on her
watch. It may not be entirely rational, but it's human."

I stared at the phone balefully and tried to summon the
strength to make the phone call I needed to make. But in the end,
I just couldn't do it.

"Give me one more day to get my head back together," I
begged. "I promise I'll call her tomorrow."

I caught Dr. Gilliam's disapproving frown out of the corner
of my eye, but I was relieved that she let it go.

I was used to catching what little sleep I could during the day,
so I knew I wasn't going to have a whole lot of luck sleeping
at night even though I was exhausted body and soul. Dr. Gilliam
offered to give me something to help me sleep, but I wasn't really
that eager to fall asleep. I could almost feel the nightmares gathering inside me, elbowing each other aside as they jockeyed for
the chance to get to me first. Dr. Gilliam seemed to understand,
and when she went to bed, she handed me her laptop and a pair
of headphones.

"Won't the light from the laptop keep you awake?" I asked
before accepting.

"I'm used to sleeping in less than ideal environments," she
said with a wry smile.

I took her at her word, and once she turned out the lights,

I sat on my bed with the computer on my lap and tried to catch up with everything that had happened while I'd been Night-struck. Bob decided the bed was big enough for two. I didn't think letting him on the bed was a great precedent, but when he stretched out beside me using my legs as a bolster, I didn't have the heart to make him get down. I used one hand to navigate the laptop while the other idly stroked Bob's fur, enjoying his comforting warmth.

The most disturbing thing I read and that no one had told me about was that Piper's "cure" was public knowledge. She was the only person—before me—ever to have recovered from being Nightstruck, which had apparently made the government really, really interested in her. Unfortunately, the only thing they were able to determine—at least the only thing they reported to the public—was that her recovery was linked to her near-death experience.

At first, there was a widespread fear that people would take to the streets at night and try to almost-kill their loved ones in an effort to bring them back to normal. However, there was an unexpected and interesting side-effect to the city's most selfish and mean-spirited being drawn to the night: the people who were still around in the daytime were all the best citizens. There was no rioting or looting during the day, there were no vigilan-tes screaming for the blood of the Nightstruck and taking it upon themselves to hunt them down. And there were apparently few if any people who thought almost killing the Nightstruck in order to maybe bring them back was a good idea.

Still, I hoped the government wouldn't learn of my own re-turn to normal. I didn't think anyone had seen Luke pull me from the square, and even if they *had* seen, they'd have no reason to believe I was one of the Nightstruck. They probably thought I was some crazy person trying to get into the square, and that Luke had heroically rescued me before I managed it. So it was reasonable to assume no one knew that Piper wasn't the only person ever to have been brought back. I hoped it stayed that way.

But of course the outside world still had all kinds of people in it, and those people had a lot of opinions about what the government should do about the problem of Philadelphia. People who didn't think having the entire city and some of its suburbs under quarantine was enough protection. I kid you not, there were people out there who wanted the military to raze the city to the ground in hopes that it would wipe out the "contamination."

There were also tons of people who wanted to get in past the quarantine. People like my mom, who wanted to do it because she was separated from her loved one, but also people who were dangerously curious or who found the idea of being Nightstruck appealing. Which meant the quarantine was now being steadily reinforced, with both police and National Guard patrolling its limits. Impromptu roadblocks had turned into solid walls, and miles of fences kept people back.

I tried to keep myself from wallowing, but it was damn hard. Everything that had happened was because of me. So many dead, so many hurt, so many who had lost everything or who were separated from their loved ones, unsure if they would ever see them again. Try living with that on your conscience day in and day out and see how you feel.

After a while, I closed the laptop and set it aside. There was only so much I could take.

But there was no way I was going to sleep, either. Dr. Gilliam tried to be subtle about it, but I was aware that every hour or so, she turned over to check on me. I prayed she was just checking to make sure I hadn't left, because I did not want to have another conversation about how I felt.

My prayers were answered, and she let me be.

CHAPTER TWELVE

y luck ran out in the morning, when I tried to put off calling my mom until later in the day. Dr. Gilliam wasn't about to accept any excuses.

"She deserves to know you're okay," she said in a voice that announced there was zero chance she would change her mind. "I'll go into the other room to give you some privacy, but you're making that call. Now."

"Okay, okay," I agreed. I knew a losing battle when I saw one.

Dr. Gilliam handed me her cell phone, and I'm ashamed to say I was sorely tempted to dial a wrong number and have a fake conversation with whoever or whatever answered. The idea of some unknown person checking their voice mail and getting my half of an imaginary conversation with my mom was almost amusing, but I was in no mood for childish pranks. Best to just get this over with.

With a resigned sigh, I placed the call. Dr. Gilliam retreated to Luke's room. I wondered if she and/or Luke would be keeping an eye on the hall outside to make sure I didn't try to slip away, then decided I didn't want to know. I didn't deserve their trust, but it would still hurt to see how little of it I had.

When my mom didn't answer on the first few rings, I thought I'd get away with leaving a message, and my body was flooded with relief. Relief that was premature, because my mom picked up before the call went to her voice mail.

"Yes?" she said in a curt, clipped voice.

I realized she thought it was Dr. Gilliam calling, and it pissed me off that my mom would be rude to someone who had done so much for me. So instead of starting off with a pleasant, heartfelt greeting, I said, "You really should be nicer to Dr. Gilliam. Unless you expected her to put me in shackles, there was no way she could have stopped me from leaving."

My mom gasped. "Becket?"

"Yeah, it's me."

Predictably, she burst into tears. I suppose it was the only response that made sense when she'd thought I was probably lost to her forever, but I was still annoyed with her for how she'd treated Dr. Gilliam.

Actually, in a moment of surprising clarity, I realized I'd been angry with my mother for a long time. Ever since she'd decided to move to Boston, actually. She and my dad had agreed I could choose which parent to live with, but really what kind of choice had they left me? My mom was moving away from the only home I'd ever known, going to a strange new city where I would know no one. I would have had to start a brand new school for my senior year, and because my mom is every bit as much a workaholic as my dad was, I would have been on my own most of the time. My mom had to know that there was only one choice I could reasonably make—and she'd left anyway, just so she could make a little more money and gain a little more prestige at a shiny new job.

"Where are you?" my mom asked when she could form coherent words again. She was still sniffling and hiccuping. "Are you all right?"

"I'm fine. I'm with the Gilliams." She'd probably already figured that out, seeing as I was calling from Dr. Gilliam's phone. "It would be nice if you'd apologize to Dr. Gilliam for being such a bitch to her."

I expected a mom-reflex scolding for my language—even though my mom curses like a sailor when she gets angry—but she let out a shuddering breath instead.

"Are *they* all right?" she asked tentatively. My mom is *never* tentative. I'm sure she has doubts and fears just like the rest of the human race, but she's allergic to showing it.

It took me a moment to understand that sound in her voice, to realize she thought I was still Nightstruck and had hurt the Gilliams. It was a relatively logical assumption, especially for someone who wasn't living in the center of the madness and didn't fully understand what life in this city was like.

"If I were Nightstruck, I wouldn't be calling you at eight in the morning," I pointed out. "The Gilliams are fine. They've taken me in again is all."

"So Dr. Gilliam was wrong and you weren't . . . Nightstruck?" She said it like it was some kind of hard-to-pronounce foreign word. "Then where have you been for the last four weeks?"

"I *was* Nightstruck. I'm not anymore." The last thing I wanted to do was go into some detailed explanation of either how I'd been cured or how I'd become Nightstruck in the first place. I doubted my mom would go running to the authorities to volunteer me as a research subject in the quest to "cure" the Nightstruck, but it wasn't impossible she might say the wrong thing to the wrong person. Like most of the people who lived outside the quarantine, she thought everyone inside it was ill or poisoned or drugged—certainly she didn't believe there was anything magical or otherworldly going on—and who knew what she might do for "my own good."

"I can't explain how it happened," I told her. "I think the night just didn't have a very strong hold on me in the first place. But—"

"We need to get you to a hospital," my mom interrupted. "I want you to have a full physical and a mental health evaluation, just to be safe."

I groaned. "I'm fine, Mom. Dr. Gilliam examined me already and gave me a clean bill of health." Except for the broken nose, but my mom didn't need to know about that.

My mom snorted. "If you think I'm ever again entrusting the life of my daughter to that woman—"

"Don't!" I snapped. "If you say another word about Dr. Gilliam, I'm hanging up. I swear it."

There was a frustrated hiss on the other end of the line. "I still want you to have a thorough physical, and you need to be evaluated by a psychiatrist."

Great. My mom basically wanted to commit me to a mental hospital until I could prove I wasn't batshit crazy. The warm fuzzies were just overwhelming.

"I don't need to see a shrink," I growled through clenched teeth, "and I don't need a physical. I. Am. Fine."

Which of course was a gross exaggeration. I was physically intact, and I wasn't running around tearing my hair and screaming gibberish, but that's not the same as being "fine." Maybe if I kept saying I was, I would magically make it be true.

"I'm sure you *feel* fine," my mother said in a condescending tone that would have grated on my nerves in the best of circumstances, "but people who are sick don't always know they're sick. It would make me feel a whole lot better if you were . . . looked at."

"And this is all about what would make *you* feel better, after all."

If my mom had been in the city when the quarantine started, what were the chances she'd be Nightstruck by now? I'd always thought of her as a good person, but maybe that was instinctual loyalty, not wanting to think ill of my own mother. Certainly she wasn't a *bad* person, but she was in her own way as self-centered as Piper. Nothing and no one could come between her and her goals without suffering the consequences, and that seemed like prime Nightstruck behavior.

My mom was obviously taken aback by my comment, because she was silent for a long moment. I felt no inclination to break that silence or take back the words. Instead, I just stood there stewing in my own resentment.

"I've taken a leave of absence from my job," my mom said quietly. "I wanted to have every minute of every day available for my campaign to force the government to let family members come to Philadelphia to be with their loved ones. I'm working with other families to launch a class-action lawsuit, but I don't give a damn about that. All I want is to find a way to get to you and take care of you. I'm fighting with every breath in my body to be allowed into a quarantine zone, which I may never be allowed to leave, to be with my daughter. I'm doing it even though I know that I'll become sick, too, and have to spend all the hours of every night huddled inside fearing for my life. One thing you can be damn sure of: I'm not doing that for *myself.*"

It seemed like a giant weight was pressing down on my shoulders. I'm not sure my mother's motives were as selflessly altruistic as she made them sound, but it was true that if she got through the quarantine, she'd be giving up everything familiar about her life as well as giving up the career that had always been her be-all, end-all. And if she made it through, not only would she be another potential hostage for Aleric, but she'd also maybe be vulnerable to the night's appeal. Instead of her looking after me, I'd have to look after her, and if the night ever got its hooks into her, if she wandered out and got herself Nightstruck, it would be like Aleric putting a collar and leash on me.

I had to convince her to drop it and stay safely in Boston, but I didn't know how. Especially when I didn't want to tell her that I was at the center of it all. The best-case scenario was that she wouldn't believe me, that she would think it was just a delusion brought on by my "mental illness." But it was hard to predict what she might do if she *did* believe me. If she knew I was "Patient Zero" for all the madness, she might feel like she had to tell someone—both for my own good and for the good of all the other residents of Philly. I don't know what the government would do to me if they found out I'd started this whole thing, but I didn't imagine it would be anything I'd enjoy.

The one thing I knew for sure I couldn't afford to do was encourage her. Ordinarily, after that passionate little speech, I'd have apologized for having implied she cared only about herself. Even if she wasn't as selfless as she'd made herself sound, she hadn't deserved my nasty comment. But hell, who gets what they deserve in life anyway?

"So I guess you aren't getting any press coverage in your efforts to break the quarantine?" I inquired. Of course I already knew she was. When my mom does something, she throws herself into it headfirst, and she was making enough waves to get national attention. "And that isn't the kind of thing that could potentially raise your profile and help you get an even better job? Maybe even run for office?"

I could hear my mom's harsh breathing, so I knew she was still on the line despite her lack of response. I channeled my

Nightstruck self—not hard, when I'd been that person less than twenty-four hours ago—and shoved the blade in deeper.

"The best part about it is you know it's never going to work. The government isn't going to set a precedent by letting someone into the quarantine zone just because she's making a bunch of noise, and you know it. So you get all the fame you want without much risk that you'll actually get what you're asking for and have to suffer the consequences."

Later, I was going to feel bad about the shitty things I was saying to my mom. She's self-centered and ambitious, but I knew she loved me, and I knew she genuinely wanted to protect me. Just like I knew she'd taken the potential impact of her campaign to get into Philly into account before she'd launched it, making a decision guided mainly by love but with other motivations lurking in the wings.

If her motivations had been exactly what she'd said, if she'd been acting only as a desperate mother trying to get through to her child, then my words probably wouldn't have hurt her so much. The fact that she remained speechless when I fell silent told me I'd hit close to home. I was all too familiar with guilty silence.

"I don't need you here," I told her mercilessly, giving her a swift kick when she was already down. "I don't *want* you here. Stay in Boston and be near the daughter you actually like."

I could almost feel the spike of guilt in her heart. My older sister, Beth, is a lot like my mom, driven and completely focused. A chip off the old block, who'd known practically since birth that she wanted to be a lawyer just like our mom, and who'd therefore set her sights on going to Harvard, just like our mom. I had never truly been able to relate to either of them. Or my career-focused dad, either, come to think of it.

My mom still couldn't gather herself enough to reply. I figured it was a good time to quit while I was ahead—and while I was able to stand firm against my desire to apologize. I hung up, wondering if my mom was going to call right back.

She didn't.

CHAPTER THIRTEEN

The next few days were really rough. I still couldn't sleep, so I let Dr. Gilliam give me a sleeping pill one night. It knocked me out like a light—right up until the nightmares started. I woke up screaming three times—that I remember. For all I know, I kept everyone in the entire hotel awake all night. I kept waiting for Dr. Gilliam to suggest a therapist again, but she didn't. I think she knew I still wasn't open to the idea, even though I kind of thought it would be a smart thing to do. But when I thought about telling anyone the details of what I'd seen and done while I was Nightstruck, everything within me recoiled. I couldn't talk about it. To anyone.

I didn't have to convince Dr. Gilliam how much of a threat Aleric could be. She agreed with my assessment that he wouldn't just let me go and that she and Luke would be in danger. I tried to argue that meant I shouldn't stay with them, but of course I didn't have to be staying with them for Aleric to use them against me. Instead, we took the precaution of moving every night, shortly before sunset. Sometimes we just changed rooms within the same hotel, but sometimes we moved clear across the city. I didn't exactly feel safe—there was always a chance that he or his minions could get hold of someone who knew where we were and force them to cough up our location—but I believed we were being as safe as possible.

On the fifth night after my rescue, Dr. Gilliam was scheduled to work a night shift at the hospital. She offered to stay with me instead, but I knew how badly the hospital needed her.

"You're going to be extra careful, right?" I asked her. Even before I'd been Nightstruck, Piper and Aleric had orchestrated an attack against her at the hospital, and it worried me to know she would be somewhere she could so easily be found.

She smiled at me. "Don't worry. The hospital beefed up security since the night I was attacked. I'll be safe there."

I wished I could feel confident of that, but then I didn't feel confident about much of anything.

Apparently Dr. Gilliam felt much the same way. When she'd worked during the day, Luke and I had for the most part ignored each other. He stayed in his room, and I stayed in mine. I had to go shopping a couple of times to buy some new clothes, but though Luke came with me to keep an eye on me, we didn't talk a whole lot. I didn't know what to say to him, and he didn't seem to have much clue what to say to me, either. But just before Dr. Gilliam left for her evening shift, Luke came into our room and announced he felt like watching a movie. He didn't ask me if I wanted to watch one with him, instead picking up the remote and flipping to the hotel's movie selections. I didn't miss the brief but definite eye contact between him and his mom before she slipped out the door.

"What are you in the mood for?" he asked with forced cheer. "Comedy? Drama? Action?"

"So you and your mom think I need a babysitter," I said. "Are you planning to spend the whole night in here watching me?"

He hit the mute button on the TV, tossing the remote onto one of the beds and sitting down. "I'm supposed to play it by ear.

If I'm feeling worried about you, I'll 'accidentally' fall asleep while watching a movie, and you'll be too polite to wake me up and kick me out."

I'd expected a denial, not an honest answer, so I momentarily wasn't sure what to say. To cover my confusion, I beckoned to Bob, inviting him up onto the bed with me. When we lived at home with my dad, Bob had been officially banned from all furniture—a rule that I had been known to bend on more than one occasion—but that was a change he had no trouble adapting to. Ears perked and tail wagging, he jumped easily onto the bed and flopped down beside me, putting his head on my lap in case I was in the mood for a good ear-scratching. He made a contented moaning sound when I obliged.

"My mom is worried about you," Luke continued, "but I don't see any reason why you'd want to go running out into the night again."

I appreciated his vote of confidence, though I doubted he could grasp just how badly a part of me wanted to go back to that carefree oblivion. I kept telling myself nothing I'd done while I was Nightstruck counted. Therefore I wasn't responsible for bringing the Night Maker into the city, or sleeping with Aleric, or tacitly condoning a horrific murder. It would have been much easier to convince myself if I didn't suspect . . . no, *know* . . . that I'd been acting on my own deeply buried desires.

"Why would I want to go back to that," I asked with a bitter edge in my voice, "when I can spend all day every day wallowing in guilt and grief and disgust? While fearing for my life and the lives of the people I care about and having nightmares every time I sleep?" I was being weird about it, but I would almost have preferred it if he weren't so . . . accepting. If he'd looked at me like I was some kind of freak, if he'd been angry, if he'd been mean to me . . . Those things I could have fought. I might even have made myself feel stronger as I built a fortress of defenses around me. But his kindness and his lack of judgment made me feel vulnerable and exposed.

"Piper would go back in a heartbeat," Luke said. "She says she feels terrible about everything she did, and she says she hates what she became. But her folks have to lock her in her room every night to keep her from leaving."

I winced. I'd never been all that impressed with Piper's parents. They were total snobs, and I think if they had paid more attention to her, she might not have been so fond of getting herself into trouble. I understood the necessity of keeping her home and safe, but surely there was some better way than to lock her up as if she were a prisoner. Not that I had any idea what that way might have been.

"You were never as far gone as she was," Luke said. "I can't see you voluntarily going back."

I tried to latch onto something that would let me be angry and strong. "I kept telling you I hadn't changed that much, and you kept telling me I'd changed more than I thought. You can't have it both ways."

Instead of rising to the bait, Luke shrugged. "You know exactly how much you changed, now that your head is clear. You have to have an easier path back than Piper does."

There he was, being all reasonable again. Back when I was Nightstruck, I'd thought he'd written me off entirely. He'd seemed pretty pissed off at me, and it wasn't unreasonable for him to blame me for what had happened. It had been my decision to run off and confront Piper, after all. But then if he'd written me off entirely, he wouldn't have met me at the square when I'd asked him to. I wondered if he'd have shown up if he'd known I was sleeping with Aleric and had basically murdered my old classmate.

I was suddenly flooded with hot shame as I realized that not once had I even *thought* to thank him for saving me. He had pulled me out of the square at great personal risk. If it had taken even a fraction of a second longer for the night to lose its hold on me, Leo would have bitten, clawed, or stung him and he'd have died.

Not only had I not thanked him for it, I'd fought him like a wild thing. I could barely remember the blur of time right after it happened, but I was pretty sure I'd called him some terrible names and told him I hated him. And it had never entered my mind to take any of that back.

Maybe some of the night was still inside me, slowly poisoning me.

That was not a comfortable thought. Most of the time, I thought I was completely back to normal, but what did that really tell me? I'd thought I was pretty close to normal while I was Nightstruck, and I could clearly see now that I hadn't been. So if I was warped and twisted in more subtle ways now, would I even know it?

I shivered and hugged myself, fearing I was about ten seconds away from having a complete meltdown. So much for the quaint illusion that I'd been getting a little better every day.

"I'm sorry about some of the things I said to you when you were Nightstruck," Luke said.

The injustice of *him* feeling like he had to apologize to *me* almost made me laugh out loud. "You don't have anything to apologize for," I hurried to reassure him. "You didn't say anything that wasn't true."

"That doesn't mean I had to say it. I know better than to just blurt out the first thing that comes into my head. And I had no right to be angry at you. Nothing that happened was your fault."

I bit back my urge to remind him that *everything* was my

fault. Wallowing in self-pity is not an attractive habit, and I was determined not to do it. Well, not much, at least.

"Thank you for getting me out of there," I said, before I could forget those important words again.

Luke grinned at me in a way that never failed to make my heart flutter. I remembered simultaneously how wonderful his lips had felt on mine when he kissed me, and that my last act before being Nightstruck was to text him a declaration of love. It had been almost reflexive, something I'd done without thinking and certainly without worrying about the consequences. Thank God he hadn't said anything to me about it, but it was still insanely embarrassing, and the memory made me blush.

"You sure didn't seem very happy about it at the time," he said. That grin of his said he was teasing, but something in his eyes told me there was more to it than that. He was hiding some secret pain behind that teasing. I was sort of glad I didn't remember just what kinds of awful things I'd said to him.

I grimaced and looked away. "I wasn't," I admitted. "Being Nightstruck was kind of like being anesthetized, and it wasn't easy to go back to having to feel . . . everything." I scraped up a little scrap of courage from somewhere deep within and met his eyes once more. "But you did the right thing. I'm really glad to be back."

I looked away again, because I wasn't sure if I was telling the truth or not. I'd never had so many mixed feelings in all my life. I *wanted* to be glad I was back. I *should* be glad I was back. And there were times when I was, times when I thought about how much it must have hurt Luke and Dr. Gilliam—and even my mom—to think they'd lost me forever. If only there weren't always a sense of impending doom hanging over my head. If only I didn't keep hearing my father scream when Billy the goat savaged him. If only I didn't remember tumbling naked into bed with Aleric in our tent in Rittenhouse Square, or standing by and watching Stuart be killed when I could have saved him. What I wouldn't have done for a nice case of amnesia . . .

"If you're feeling very generous," Luke said, "maybe you and I can go see Piper tomorrow and you can thank her, too. She was the one who suggested I might be able to pull you out of the square."

Thanking Piper—for anything—was not a high priority on my to-do list. Maybe she'd had a hand in helping Luke pull me back from the night, but if it weren't for her, I wouldn't have been Nightstruck in the first place. Hell, if it weren't for her, my dad would still be alive!

I didn't say anything, but obviously Luke had no trouble reading my ungracious thoughts on my too-open face.

"She's in a lot of pain, Becks," he said.

His use of my nickname felt almost accusatory, but that was probably just my own guilt talking. Piper had been my best friend for a long time, and if I hadn't been tricked into letting the magic into the city, she would have gone right on being that wonderful—if occasionally infuriating—best friend for who knew how long. It was because of me and my actions that she'd changed, and yet I couldn't stop blaming her for what she'd done.

"That's why she's seeing a shrink, isn't it?" I asked. I tried for an almost callous tone but found my voice coming out tight. I then noticed that my hands had both clenched into fists. Bob noticed, too, sticking a cold wet dog-nose into one of those fists to remind me of my duty to pet him at all times. I gave him a quick, irritated glance. "You're not the boss of me."

Luke and Bob made almost identical snorting sounds, startling me into a quick, half-choked laugh.

"You two have been spending *waaay* too much time together," I muttered.

We had a good laugh about that. Then we both laughed even harder when I reflexively started petting Bob again, proving that he was, in fact, the boss of me. For a few heartbeats, things felt almost . . . normal between us.

But of course that couldn't last. The awkwardness came back as soon as I noticed its brief absence. Maybe the best thing would be to try to talk it out, but I wasn't up to that. Not in my fragile mental state.

"How about a comedy?" I said in response to his long-ago, almost forgotten question about what type of movie to watch. "I think we could both use a few good laughs."

My suggestion made the awkwardness spike again. We both knew I was looking for an excuse for the two of us not to talk anymore. I tensed up, just in case Luke wasn't going to let me change the subject so easily, but after one long, uncomfortable stare, he shrugged and picked up the remote once again.

"Comedy it is."

CHAPTER FOURTEEN

I was sick and tired of feeling guilty. Guilty about letting the magic into our city, guilty about what had happened to my dad, guilty about putting Luke and his mom in danger, guilty about . . . Well, about just about everything. And thanks to that conversation with Luke, I was now feeling guilty about my attitude toward Piper.

She had done awful things to me when she was Nightstruck. But then when I'd shot her, instead of being angry with me, she'd desperately tried to save me. She'd practically shoved me away, screaming at me to run for safety and leave her there in the square to bleed to death. And then after she'd miraculously recovered from my attempt to kill her, she'd helped Luke come up with a plan to drag me from Aleric's clutches. Clearly, she had forgiven me for trying to murder her in cold blood. It seemed the least I could do was try to forgive her.

It was embarrassingly hard to do—hence, the guilt-fest. However, I decided my best chance at achieving something approximating forgiveness was to pay her a visit. If nothing else, she was probably the only person on the planet who could come close to understanding what I was feeling. Maybe we were beyond having any touchy-feely moments, and maybe there was no hope of ever healing my bruised and battered psyche, but at least I could say I tried.

Luke drove me to Piper's house out on the Main Line while Dr. Gilliam caught what little sleep she could before she'd have to arrange for a new hotel room for the night. Things were still uncomfortable between Luke and me, but I was glad for his presence anyway. I was so nervous my stomach was tied up in knots, and I wanted to scream. I didn't know how I would react to seeing Piper, and I was terrified of finding out.

"You didn't bring a gun, did you?" Luke asked in a poor attempt at a joke when we pulled up in front of Piper's stately home.

I gave him a glare that probably didn't have any heat behind it because I was too freaked out to manage a good one.

He grinned unrepentantly. "Too soon?"

I appreciated his attempt to lighten the mood, but even his good cheer couldn't lift the dread that was weighing me down. I considered telling him I'd wait in the car while he visited with Piper, but I refused to be that much of a coward.

Piper's mom let us in. Even with the city in chaos and her daughter recovering from a gunshot wound after turning into a psychotic bitch from hell, Mrs. Grant was clearly convinced that a lady was never to be seen in anything but designer clothes and full makeup. She had the same pressed and starched look she'd always had, and based on how straight her back was and how high she held her chin, I swear she spent half her childhood walking around with a book on her head to create perfect posture.

I imagined she didn't think much of my jeans-and-hoodie outfit, or of the fact that I'd made no attempt to hide the bruising and swelling around my nose with makeup. It looked a little better each day and no longer throbbed relentlessly, but it wasn't exactly pretty.

She greeted me stiffly, and Luke a little more warmly. I wondered if she knew her daughter had killed my dad, but I wasn't about to ask.

"You can go on back," Mrs. Grant said to me. "Luke, why don't you come to the kitchen and I'll make you some tea."

I felt a stab of something between panic and confusion. Luke wasn't coming with me?

"You're not coming to see Piper?" I asked in a squeak. It was all I could do not to reach out and grab him like a security blanket.

"Piper said she wanted a chance to talk to you alone first," Mrs. Grant said. "She says you had a fight and she needs to clear the air."

Well, that was one way of putting it.

"I'll come with you if you want," Luke said quietly. "Piper doesn't get to call all the shots."

God, it was hard to turn him down. So often in the past, I'd used Piper as a shield to help me deal with how nervous Luke made me. Maybe someday I would laugh at how things had changed. You know, when the pigs are gracefully soaring over the glacial landscape of Hell.

I reminded myself that I was not a coward. I'd dredged up the courage to go marching out into the night and try to kill Piper, knowing I was more likely to get myself killed than succeed. Surely going to talk to her one-on-one now was no big deal compared to that.

My mental pep talk didn't make me feel any better, but I resisted the urge to accept Luke's offer. This was something I had to do on my own.

"Thanks," I said to him, "but it'll be okay."

Mrs. Grant was looking at me oddly. I'm sure she was wondering what kind of fight could justify my level of reluctance when Piper and I had once been so close. Knowing Piper, she'd probably passed it off as some minor disagreement.

141

I hadn't spent tons of time at Piper's house, but I knew how to get to her bedroom without a native guide. You'd never have guessed it from how long it took me to get there, though. My palms were sweating as I reached up and gingerly knocked on the closed door.

"Come in," Piper said.

I took a deep breath and pushed the door open, trying to brace myself for the shock of emotions I was sure to feel when I laid eyes on her.

No amount of bracing could prepare me for the sight that met my eyes when I stepped into that room and got my first look at the post-Nightstruck Piper. I barely recognized her, and all the anger I'd been afraid would come bursting out of me took cover in the deepest recesses of my mind.

I'd always been just a little jealous of my former best friend, because as well as being insanely popular, she was also drop-dead gorgeous. Exactly the kind of girl you'd expect a guy like Luke to be with. She'd made herself less gorgeous even before she was Nightstruck by chopping off her beautiful red-gold hair and dyeing it a stark, unappealing white. Seeing her like that for the first time had been a shock, but nothing like the shock of seeing her now.

She'd lost so much weight her clothes were hanging on her like a sack. Her skin was sickly pale, which made the bruise-like blotches around her eyes look even deeper and darker. She'd dyed her hair back to some approximation of its natural color and it had grown out some, but it was brittle-looking and had no luster to it.

But the most shocking change, the one that immediately hit me the hardest, was something less tangible than that. Something to do with the slump of her shoulders, the curve of her back, the hollowness in her eyes. This Piper was a shadow of her former self, with none of the confidence, vivacity, and cheer I'd come to expect from her.

She was sitting on her bed, her back against the wall, and she didn't get up when I came in. Maybe that seemed like too much of an effort. I saw her notice my nose and frown. Then she managed a tired-looking smile that didn't come close to reaching her eyes.

"Wow," she said. Even her voice sounded different, less firm. "I must look even worse than I thought."

I swallowed hard, stepping tentatively closer as if I were approaching a potentially dangerous stranger. The polite thing would be to reassure her that she really didn't look so bad after all, but I couldn't seem to make myself do it. Hell, I couldn't seem to make myself say anything at all.

Piper looked down at her hands, which she held clasped in her lap. "My folks keep threatening to force-feed me, but I have trouble keeping much of anything down, so I don't think it would help."

Luke had told me she wasn't doing well, but somehow I had never envisioned her doing as badly as she obviously was. She looked like she belonged right back in the hospital, and I was actually a little surprised they'd let her out in her condition.

"I would totally have understood if you decided not to come," Piper said, still staring at her hands.

"I almost didn't."

Her flinch made me regret the harsh words almost immediately. Don't get me wrong: I was still enormously angry with Piper. But only the most heartless bitch wouldn't feel sorry for her in the state she was in. I took a deep breath and let it out slowly.

"Like I said, I would have understood." Piper met my eyes briefly and tried a tentative smile. "But I'm glad you came."

I wasn't. I wanted out of that room so bad I could taste it. Part of what had made me like Piper so much in the past was that she was so easy to talk to. That certainly wasn't the case anymore, and I was at a loss for what to say.

Piper hugged her knees to her chest, and I noticed how bony and frail her wrists looked. "I hope you know that if I could go back in time and undo everything, I would."

I did know that, although it didn't make me feel a whole lot better. Every time I found myself thinking I should maybe let Piper off the hook and say she wasn't responsible for everything she'd done while she was Nightstruck, I got stuck on the fact that no one had forced her to go running out into the night.

"Why did you leave?" I demanded. Piper had become Nightstruck on the night my next-door neighbor was killed by some unknown beastie. I'd gone out to see if Mrs. Pinter was all right after having heard her scream, and when I came back into my house, Piper was nowhere to be found.

Piper shuddered and hugged her knees more tightly. "I don't have a good answer," she said, so softly I had to move closer to hear her. "Ever since the city started changing, I've felt . . . uncomfortable in my own skin. Like I don't quite belong anywhere, or like I'm playing a role, pretending to be someone I'm not." She laughed nervously. "It's really hard to explain." She let go of her knees and planted her hand in the center of her chest. "There's this constant, restless ache coming from deep inside here, and that night . . ." She shuddered again, her shoulders hunching defensively. "That night, I just couldn't take it anymore. I was so scared, Becks . . ."

I shook my head. She'd been scared because some unseen construct had been trying to break in to the house. The power had been out, the two of us had been alone, Bob had been in a mindless frenzy of barking and snarling, and we didn't yet know that constructs couldn't actually come inside. "So your logic was, 'something's trying to get inside and rip us to shreds, maybe I'll feel safer if I just go outside'?"

"I know how stupid it sounds," Piper said. "It wasn't like I was really thinking that. It was just . . . a feeling. And then Aleric came to the door and promised that everything would be all right." She held up a hand to stave off the protest I'd opened my mouth to make. "I know, I know. I barely knew him, and I had absolutely no logical reason to believe a word he said. But at the time, I felt like . . . like I was drowning. And Aleric had just thrown me a life preserver. Grabbing onto it seemed like the only sensible thing to do."

Unfortunately, I had a pretty good idea what she was talking about. When the dawn had swept over me on the morning I became Nightstruck, my rational mind had been 100 percent certain I didn't want it to happen. I'd tried desperately to get indoors. But I'd been a total emotional wreck, and when the first light of dawn came upon me, I knew I had a choice as to whether to let the night sweep me away or not. I could have refused to budge and stayed myself, but in my wrecked state of mind, the temptation to escape all the turmoil had been too great to resist.

Maybe being angry with Piper was completely hypocritical, no matter what she'd done. But anger just isn't that easy to let go of.

"If you'd known what would happen, would you still have gone with him?" I asked.

Piper shook her head, but not in denial. "I don't know, Becks. I think the night already had its hooks deep into me, and I was just too damn weak to resist it."

There was a wealth of self-loathing in her voice, and her eyes looked even more haunted now than they had when I'd first walked in. I finally forced myself to close the remaining distance between us, to sit down on the bed beside her like I would have back when we were friends. I couldn't quite manage a hug, but I gave her a light pat on the shoulder. It was a pretty feeble olive branch, and my heart wasn't entirely in it, but at least it was something.

Piper let out a shuddering breath, and some of the tension eased out of her shoulders. "I feel a bit like Dr. Jekyll and Mr. Hyde, only instead of being just one at a time, I'm both all the time." Tears shimmered in her eyes. "I want Mr. Hyde to go away, but he won't, and he's stronger than Dr. Jekyll." She blinked away the tears, but not the misery.

"It's Jekyll I'm talking to right now," I said, but Piper shook her head.

"Hyde's here, too. And Hyde hates your guts because you're the reason I'm not Nightstruck anymore."

For the briefest moment, I had a very clear glimpse of that hatred lurking in her eyes, but then she blinked and shook her head violently.

"I don't want to feel that way," she said between clenched teeth. "I want to be back to how I was before the city started changing, before the magic came."

Before I let the magic in, she was thinking, but Dr. Jekyll stopped her from saying it. Apparently we each had plenty of reasons to be angry at the other.

"We're never going to be friends again, are we?" I said. It was something I'd known since the moment I'd encountered the Nightstruck version of Piper, but somehow it was just sinking in now.

"Not like we were," Piper agreed. "But we can try like hell not to be enemies, at least."

I nodded, though I wasn't sure that effort would succeed. I

146

was never going to be able to look at her again without remembering the night of my dad's death—and I was never going to forget that brief glimpse of the hatred she carried within her.

"It's never going to be the same between me and Luke, either," Piper continued. "I know the two of you are into each other, and I want you to know that that's okay."

That was one conversation I definitely did not want to have. My first instinct was to deny that there was anything going on between me and Luke—after all, there wasn't, at least not right now—but I didn't think Piper would believe the lie. "That won't be an issue," I said, perhaps a little too fast.

Piper managed a lopsided grin that was almost convincing. "Like hell it won't. I saw the way you two looked at each other while I was Nightstruck."

"That was then," I said with what I hoped was a dismissive shrug. "We were spending a lot of time together because our parents didn't want us alone at night and—"

"It was more than that," Piper interrupted. "And it's still more than that. I don't want to stand in the way."

For the entire time Piper and Luke had been dating, I had assumed Piper had no idea I was interested in Luke. Surely she wouldn't have come on to him at my birthday party as she had if she'd known I was interested. She could sometimes be careless, but she was a better friend than that, at least back in the day. Now I wondered if maybe some part of her had had a clue all along. However, if that was the case, I didn't want to know. Sometimes ignorance really is bliss.

"Don't worry, you won't," I said. There were plenty of things standing in the way, but Piper was no longer one of them, at least not for me.

Piper gave me a knowing look. "Is that because there are bigger issues?"

My skin went all crawly as I thought about Aleric's hands—and other things—on me, and I suspect my face went a too-revealing shade of pale. Piper knew exactly how seductive Aleric could be, and she knew exactly how many defenses I would have had against him while I was Nightstruck.

"The absolute last thing I want to talk about is my relationship with Luke," I said.

For the second time that afternoon, I caught a glimpse of something ugly hiding behind my former best friend's eyes. She knew exactly why I didn't want to talk about it, and at least some part of her was maliciously glad I would have to live with that shame for the rest of my life. And glad that it might get in the way of me ever having a real relationship with Luke.

The malice vanished as fast as it appeared, but I knew it was still there, still lurking. The Piper I'd once known—or thought I'd known—was long gone, even if she was occasionally capable of playing the part still.

"You should tell him the truth about Aleric," Piper advised me. "It'll probably bother him even if he says it doesn't, but it's the kind of thing he'll get over. He won't get over it if you lie to him about it."

"What part of I don't want to talk about it didn't you understand?"

Piper laughed. "You don't have to talk. I'm just giving you advice as someone who knows Luke better than you do."

I realized at that moment that I would never be able to take anything Piper said at face value again. Was she giving me genuine advice based on her understanding of what made Luke tick? Or was Mr. Hyde chortling and rubbing his hands together in glee as he did his best to sabotage whatever was left of my relationship with Luke? I had no way of knowing.

Not that it mattered, I told myself. Everything had been awkward and strained between Luke and me since he'd dragged me from that square, so it wasn't like we needed the issue of Aleric to keep us apart. There was already a gaping chasm between us, one I couldn't see any way to cross.

CHAPTER FIFTEEN

I spent a lot of time feeling like total crap, not without good reason. But even when you're living this totally bizarre life, spending every night huddled in a different hotel room jumping at every shadow, you start to develop a kind of routine and it becomes your current definition of normal. Many of the city's schools had reopened, although on limited hours, but Dr. Gilliam didn't seem inclined to push either Luke or me into going back to school. It might have added a degree of semi-normalcy to our lives, but it might have added predictability, too, and that was something we couldn't afford. Aleric and his people might not be able to get to us during the day, but they were perfectly capable of forcing ordinary people to do their dirty work for them. The routine became, then, to have as little routine as possible.

I was always worried about Dr. Gilliam, because she had to go to work at the hospital, and the bad guys could easily know that. The only consolation was that she wasn't an idiot, and she was serious about taking precautions. I still let out a breath of relief every time she made it back from a shift safely.

I didn't hear from my mom, but I knew from checking on the Internet that she had not abandoned her quest to get in past the quarantine. She was pissed at me and hurt by the things I had said, but she hadn't changed her mind about coming to get me. I talked to my sister Beth a couple of times, but it seemed Mom had quoted our entire argument to her verbatim, and she was pretty pissed at me as well. She and Mom had always been more alike than not.

I wasn't under the impression that Aleric had given up on me, but I have to admit I had relaxed my guard just a little bit when New Year's came and went without any sign that he was homing in on us. The idea that I would live the rest of my life in hiding, constantly on the move, was hardly appealing, but considering all the other unpalatable changes that had happened in my life, it was something I could live with.

Everything seemed to be going about as well as could be expected, which was why it came as quite a shock when in the second week of January, there was a knock on our hotel room door at just after noon. Dr. Gilliam was at work, and Luke had headed down to the hotel's gym to get a workout in, so I was the one who had to answer the door.

I assumed it was housekeeping at first, but then realized that housekeeping would usually announce itself. Bob wasn't quite as territorial now that his territory changed every night, but he could still muster a seriously intimidating bark. However, he wasn't in full Hellhound mode, and I noticed as I went to the door that his ears were perked up and his tail was wagging, which suggested he recognized the scent of whoever was out there.

I wasn't about to take Bob's word for it, so I checked out the peephole. I wasn't sure how I felt about seeing the familiar face of Detective Sam Bellows, one of my dad's protégés, standing in the hallway. Sam had always seemed like a nice guy, and he had come to dinner on any number of occasions, but I hadn't seen him since my dad had died, and his presence on the doorstep of my hotel room seemed ominous. Or maybe that was my paranoia speaking.

He knocked a second time while I stood there indecisively wondering what he could want and how he had found me. I decided there was only one way to find out, but since I was feeling paranoid, I left the safety latch on the door as I opened it a crack and looked out warily.

Bob did not have my mixed feelings, shoving his way past my leg so he could stick his nose through the crack in the door. Neither I nor my dad had ever caught Sam feeding Bob scraps when he came to dinner, but we were both sure he had to have done it. Bob isn't usually much of a people person, but he'd always loved Sam, and food was the surest way to Bob's heart.

"Hi, buddy!" Sam said, sounding as delighted to see Bob as Bob was to see him. He squatted so he could be on eye level with Bob, reaching out to scratch behind his ears, much to Bob's delight. Sam grinned up at me as he continued to scratch. "Oh, yeah, hi to you, too, kiddo."

I snorted, but couldn't help smiling. It's a good bet someone's a true dog person when he greets the dog before the human. I like dog people. But I kept the latch on, my inner alarms continuing to blare a red alert.

"Hi, Sam," I said cautiously. "What a nice surprise."

You didn't have to be a detective to notice I was acting a little squirrelly. Sam stood up straight and looked me in the eye. The bruising and swelling from my broken nose were almost completely gone, but I caught the quick frown when he noticed the remnants. I hoped he wouldn't ask me what had happened.

"Sorry to drop in on you out of the blue," he said. "And I'm sorrier than I can say about your dad." The slight rasp in his voice told me his sorrow was sincere, but if he were just dropping by to offer his condolences, he'd have done it ages ago.

There was some other reason he was here, some reason I was sure I wouldn't like.

"How did you find me?"

"I'm a detective. It's what we do." He gave me a jaunty smile that failed to put me even remotely at ease. He glanced at the latch on the door. "May I come in?"

If Aleric was going to threaten and bully someone into snatching me during the day, I seriously doubted it would be someone like Sam. How would he even know my connection to Sam? No, if Aleric sent someone after me, it would be some hapless stranger like the poor man who had long ago tried to deliver Dr. Gilliam to the Nightstruck. But even so I was reluctant to trust anyone these days.

"What is this about?" I asked, not taking the latch off.

Sam sighed. I'm sure he would have preferred if I acted all friendly and trusting, but I didn't have it in me. "I need to ask you a few questions about the night Piper Grant was shot."

The blood drained from my face so fast I had to clutch the door to keep myself upright. I will never be a professional poker player. I could almost feel Sam's interest piquing. *It's perfectly natural to be freaked out,* I told myself. Even if I didn't have a guilty conscience, I would know his showing up to question me meant he thought I was somehow involved, and that would be shocking.

"Please let me in," he said softly. "For now, I'm here as your friend, not a detective. I'll keep anything you say in strictest confidence."

I believed he meant what he said about coming as a friend, but I did not believe he was going to keep anything I said to himself. Detectives lie about that kind of stuff all the time in an effort to lull suspects into saying something incriminating.

"I'm a minor," I reminded him. "You're not allowed to talk to me without a parent's permission. I can give you my mom's phone number if you'd like." And my mom would tell him exactly where he could stuff his questions.

Sam held his hands up and gave me innocent eyes. "I'm just here as a friend," he reminded me. "I'm sure you had nothing to do with it, but I'd like to be able to prove it."

I snorted and shook my head. "I'm the daughter of a cop and a lawyer. Do you honestly think I'm going to fall for the 'if you've got nothing to hide there's no reason not to talk to me' ploy?"

My heart was pounding, and I had a panicky vision of Sam hauling me off in cuffs and locking me up in some juvenile detention center. Maybe I'd be safe from Aleric there, but I'd face plenty of other dangers. I didn't think the daughter of the late police commissioner would be better liked in juvie than a cop would be in prison.

Had Piper decided to tell the truth and admit I was the one who shot her? I remembered those brief glimpses I'd seen of the malice and hatred she was trying so hard to fight off. Had Mr. Hyde won?

But if Sam were planning to arrest me, he wouldn't have come all by himself, and he'd be taking a very different tone with me.

He gave me a wounded look. "I'm not trying any kind of ploy. I wouldn't be where I am today without your dad, and it seems like looking after his daughter is the least I can do to repay that debt. I shouldn't be telling you this, but I will, just to prove that I really am looking out for you. We received an anonymous tip from someone who said they witnessed the shooting and named you as the shooter. No one actually believes the tip, but it would be easier to fully dismiss it if you had an alibi."

One thing I was sure of: there had been no witnesses to the shooting other than Aleric. No non-Nightstruck witnesses, at least. Sane people stayed inside at night, and we'd been too deep in the darkened square for anyone to see it from a window. One way or another, Aleric was the source of this anonymous tip. Which was better than it coming from Piper, but not by much.

"Friend or not," I said implacably, "you're a detective, and I'm going to do exactly what both my mom and my dad would advise me to do under the circumstances. Sorry, Sam."

I was worrying him. He'd expected me to talk to him and give him an easy alibi so he could just dismiss the tip as the bullshit it was. My refusal to talk made it seem like I was hiding something, and he didn't like that one bit. However, he was obviously not in the position to force me to talk to him. Not yet, at least.

"If you change your mind, give me a call," he said, handing me his card. "Anytime, day or night. I really want to help."

I took the card and nodded. "I know you do, and thanks. I'm sorry I can't be more helpful."

He hesitated a moment before turning away, probably hoping I would have an instantaneous change of heart. I didn't.

I was completely freaked out when Sam left. I probably wasn't going to be arrested based on nothing but an anonymous phone call, but that didn't make me feel any less panicked. My life was complicated enough without becoming a fugitive from justice on top of everything.

When the hotel phone rang, I was so wired I jumped and almost screamed. The sound seemed shockingly loud—and ominous.

Who would be calling on the hotel phone? Surely anyone who wanted to reach me would call me on my new cell phone, though less than a handful of people had that number. And anyone I hadn't given that number to would not know I was staying at this hotel.

I bit my lip and stared at the offending phone as it rang again. Maybe it was just the front desk. Or housekeeping. Some innocuous hotel business that I'd laugh about later. Yeah. That had to be it.

I continued staring at the phone until it stopped ringing, then blew out a sigh of relief. Relief that was premature, because after about a ten-second pause, it started ringing again.

"There is zero reason to answer that," I told myself, and I knew I was right. In all likelihood, it wasn't for me. And if it was for me, it was someone I didn't want to talk to. I should just unplug the phone so I didn't have to listen to it ringing and go right back to panicking over Sam's visit.

I crept indecisively closer to the phone as its shrill ringing grated on my nerves. I wanted to follow my own advice and yank the cord out of the wall, but I wasn't sure that would make me feel much better. If I didn't answer, my mind would start churning away thinking about all the possibilities. Which would be pretty amazingly useless—and downright stupid if the call was a wrong number or something trivial I hadn't thought of.

Maybe it was some telemarketer who'd somehow got hold of the wrong number.

I didn't believe my own reasoning. I knew who would be on the other end of that line if I picked up, knew it with a gut-clenching certainty no amount of logic could counteract.

I picked up anyway, holding my breath and not bothering to say hello, praying for that telltale silence then click that meant it was a telemarketer. No such luck.

"Surprise!" Aleric said with exaggerated cheer.

My knees went weak and I sank down onto the bed. For a moment, I actually thought I was in danger of throwing up. I glanced out the window just to assure myself that the sun hadn't somehow set while I wasn't looking. But no, it was still daytime, the sun bright and high in the sky. I supposed he was calling from the square.

"What's the matter?" Aleric asked with a laugh. "Cat got your tongue?"

At that moment Bob, no doubt sensing my distress, rested his chin on my lap and whined softly. I grabbed hold of his fur with my free hand, and it took a concerted effort to keep the grip light enough not to hurt him.

How had Aleric found me?

I reminded myself that it was still daytime, that he was stuck in the square and couldn't get to me. Finding me would do him no good when we were going to move to a new hotel as soon as Dr. Gilliam got back from her shift.

None of that kept me from breaking out into a cold sweat. *Hang up the phone,* a very reasonable voice inside my head urged me.

"I'm getting the feeling you're not very happy to hear from me," Aleric said. "I find that . . . disappointing."

I managed a snort at that, digging up my voice and my courage. "I'll bet. I can't think of any good reason why I shouldn't hang up on you right now."

"Don't you want to know how I found you? After all, you do seem to be doing your best to dodge me. Not that your best is good enough, obviously."

"You're calling just to tell me how you found me? I know you like to brag about how brilliant you are, but . . ."

"It isn't just the Nightstruck you have to be wary of if you want to avoid me, Becket. I'm very good at finding ways to convince people to cooperate with me. For instance, a little birdie told me you had a chance to catch up with your old friend Sam Bellows not too long ago."

Bob whined again, and I realized I'd been squeezing too hard after all. I let go and settled for resting my hand on his warm, soft body, taking comfort from him as if I were a five-year-old and he my teddy bear. I wanted to jump to my feet and run screaming from the room, but reminded myself one more time that just because Aleric knew where I was—and who'd been here to see me—didn't mean he could get his hands on me.

"Would you be shocked to hear that I phoned in an anonymous tip to the police about you?" Aleric asked.

No, of course I wasn't surprised. "I figured it was you. I'm not an idiot."

"I could argue, but I suppose I should let you cling to at least one of your illusions."

"I could argue," I countered, "but you're really not worth the trouble."

He laughed. "Do you miss me?" He didn't wait for an answer. "Don't worry, we'll be together again real soon."

"In your dreams," I said with as much bravado as I could scrape up.

"It can happen one of two ways. You can do it the easy way and just come back to me. I'm sure you're not under the same level of lockdown as Piper. You can get away if you want to.

"Or you can continue to be difficult about it, and things will get unpleasant for you. Again. I'd rather not put you through that if I don't have to."

"Then don't!" I snapped, once again urging myself to hang up. However, as much as I didn't want to talk to Aleric, I didn't think refusing to listen to him would improve my situation. I needed to get the clearest picture possible of what I was up against, and since Aleric did love to hear himself talk, it was possible he'd reveal something I needed to know.

"Come back to me," he said. "It'll be easiest for everyone that way. I promise I'll do a better job of making you happy the second time around."

I closed my eyes and fought a wave of longing I wished I didn't feel. We both knew that I'd been plenty happy to be Nightstruck, that Luke had dragged me away from that life kicking and screaming. And it certainly would be easier for me if I could duck away from all the grief and guilt and sense of responsibility.

"It's not going to happen," I said, my voice uncomfortably hoarse.

"Look, you're being very clever with all this moving around you've been doing, and so far I haven't been able to find you fast enough to get to you. But if you don't come to me of your own free will, I'll make sure you get arrested for shooting Piper. They'll lock you up nice and tight, and you won't be a moving target anymore. Do you really think you'll be safe from me behind bars? That I can't get to you if I want?"

Between his army of Nightstruck and his terrifying constructs, I had no doubt Aleric could get to me anywhere as long as he knew where to look. Maybe I really was making things unnecessarily difficult for myself by fighting him like this.

"How hard do you think it'll be for me to convince Piper to accuse you?" Aleric continued. "I bet she'd be more than willing."

"They wouldn't believe her," I argued weakly. "She's already told them it was some Nightstruck guy."

"I bet they'd understand how she'd be reluctant to admit it was her very best friend in all the world who shot her. And even if they didn't, it might be enough to get you arrested when there's that anonymous tip on record, too. And if it isn't, I'm sure I can come up with more evidence to incriminate you. After all, you *are* the one who shot her."

True enough, but not something I was about to admit on the phone. I seriously doubted Aleric was recording me, but there was no reason to be stupid about it.

"It doesn't have to be this way," Aleric said, his voice taking on a cajoling tone. "Just come back to the square, and your life will go back to being easy and carefree and fun. I really do miss you, and I bet somewhere deep down inside you miss me, too."

I shuddered. Just thinking about him touching me made me want to hop into a hot shower and scrub off a layer or two of skin in a futile attempt to get clean. There was no part of me that even remotely missed him. At least, I was pretty sure there wasn't.

"Well it's been lovely catching up," I forced myself to say, "but I've got some packing to do, so I'm gonna have to say good-bye."

"Before you go, let me tell you about the carrot. I think you understand the stick part of this equation pretty well."

"I don't want anything to do with your carrot!" I snapped. I was glad we weren't having this conversation face-to-face, because I probably turned beet red when I thought about what I'd just said. I braced myself for Aleric to make fun of the double entendre, but he either missed it or was just too focused on the job at hand to bother with it.

"Your father isn't dead," he said.

Tears instantly sprang to my eyes, and my throat squeezed completely shut. I could barely breathe, much less find my voice to shout out my opinion of Aleric's blatant lie.

"My Nightstruck brought him to me after his encounter with Billy, and I've been keeping him in the basement of one of the abandoned houses I like to visit."

"Bullshit," I finally managed to croak out.

"Hey, you thought Piper was dead, and it turned out she wasn't. Why shouldn't you believe me when I tell you your dad's alive?"

Well, for one thing, I'd seen my dad die right in front of my eyes. I'd assumed Piper was going to die, but she hadn't been dead when I'd left her. The same had not been true of my dad when the Nightstruck dragged his body away.

"If you had my dad locked up in a basement somewhere, you'd have told me before now."

I could almost hear his nonchalant shrug. "Would you have cared if I told you while you were Nightstruck?"

"Yes!" I bit out. "I still loved my dad!"

"Tell yourself that if it makes you feel better. But he would have been useless to me as leverage against you while you were Nightstruck."

"Then why did you keep him alive?"

I knew my dad was not alive. I knew it. But I wanted it to be true so, so badly. I had never wanted to be convinced of something so much in my life.

"Just in case he might turn out to be useful someday."

Even wanting to be convinced, that wasn't a remotely convincing answer. If he thought my dad might be useful to him someday, but wouldn't be useful to him while I was Nightstruck, then logic said Aleric had suspected I'd escape somehow. Aleric was not the kind of guy who made contingency plans or expected to fail at anything.

There was no way my dad was alive, and realizing that brought on a fresh wave of crushing grief. I didn't know how to absorb the reality that I would never see my dad again.

"I know it's a lot to take in," Aleric said, trying to sound gentle—something he sucked at. "I'll give you a day or two to think about it, then I'll get back to you. I'm sure I can find you again. And who knows—maybe next time, I'll get a fix on your location before dawn. Then we can be reunited without your having to spend any time in jail first."

He hung up before I had a chance to demand proof that my dad was alive. Which was just as well, because I knew there was no such proof forthcoming.

I thought I'd been panicked after Sam's visit, but that was nothing compared to how I felt after talking to Aleric.

The fact that he'd somehow located me was disturbing enough, but paired with his threats, it was downright terrifying. It was all too easy to imagine the police showing up one day with a warrant for my arrest based on updated testimony from Piper. And because Aleric was a vindictive bastard, he'd probably try to get Luke and Dr. Gilliam arrested for harboring me.

I winced as I realized that once again, Luke and his mom were in danger because of me.

My next realization, which made me go cold all over, was that they both seemed to have relaxed their guard around me. It used to be Luke was always by my side when Dr. Gilliam was at work, but today he'd felt confident enough in me to go down to the gym for a workout. If I wanted to save the Gilliams both from Aleric and the police, the best thing I could do was to slip out now, while I had a chance.

The thought started gathering momentum in my brain as I hurried to pack a bag with my meager belongings. I had no idea how I could protect myself out on the streets, but I could worry about that later. Surely I could find *somewhere* to hole up for the night incognito.

I slapped myself in the forehead as I came to the obvious conclusion that instead of sitting around feeling sorry for myself day after day, I should have been working on a plan to get myself out of Philadelphia. If I was outside the quarantine, where the city didn't change at night, then Aleric really couldn't get to me, and there was no threat that I'd become Nightstruck again.

My mind was racing so fast, flitting from one unfinished thought to another, that I became completely oblivious to my surroundings. So much so that I somehow managed to miss Luke getting back from his workout and coming through the door from the adjoining room. When I turned to get the last of my clothes out of the dresser, I finally noticed him and let out a choked scream.

He was leaning against the door frame between our rooms, his arms crossed over his chest. Damp with sweat, his hair curled enticingly at the base of his neck. His similarly damp T-shirt clung to the lines of his chest, and somehow he managed to make even saggy gym shorts look sexy. I shouldn't have been noticing how hot he looked, not when he was glaring at me like that, but I couldn't help it.

I glanced over my shoulder at my duffel bag, which sat on the edge of the bed and had a pair of jeans hanging out of it—I hadn't exactly been packing neatly. My face burned with a blush that declared my guilt, but I tried to deflect it with a logical explanation.

"I'm just getting a head start on packing for tonight," I said.

Which made perfect sense, seeing as we changed hotels or rooms every night. But he'd obviously been standing there long enough to see how quickly and furtively I was moving, so I probably couldn't have sold him on the explanation even if my face hadn't turned into a giant neon sign shouting: I'M GUILTY!

Luke just stood there staring at me. It was clear he was pissed as hell, but I also saw a hint of hurt in his eyes. I hadn't given a moment's thought to how he and his mom would feel when they discovered I was gone, though to be fair I'd only hatched this barely half-formed plan of mine a couple of minutes ago, and there were a lot of thoughts I hadn't gotten around to yet.

"Were you going to leave us notes this time, or were you just going to disappear without a word?" Luke asked. The look he was giving me was so cold I half expected frost to start coating the room.

I bit back a defensive answer. He had every right to be pissed, especially if he thought I was running because I wanted to go back to being Nightstruck. I took a calming breath and, facing him as boldly as I could, told him about Sam's visit and Aleric's call.

I'd thought maybe he would understand once I told him everything, but his face remained closed off, his voice not much warmer.

"You were going to run away because you were afraid my mom and I would get *arrested*?" he asked incredulously. "Here's getting arrested," he said, holding his right hand out palm up, "here's getting caught by Aleric and his crew." He held up the other hand at the same level, then dropped it dramatically lower as his right hand flew upward.

When he put it that way, well, of course the scales didn't balance. My instinct to run away hadn't been based on logic, just on knee-jerk panic. So really I didn't have a leg to stand on defending myself, but that didn't stop me from trying.

"If I can get out of the quarantine zone, then there'd be no way Aleric can ever get to me and force me to open another gate," I said, well aware that that had been an afterthought. But probably a pretty good afterthought, and one that should have occurred to me earlier.

"Uh-huh," Luke said, stalking into the room and giving the connecting door a gentle slam. The sound made me jump, though if he'd wanted to Luke could have slammed it hard enough to make the entire room shake. "And you thought this was such a good idea you had to run off half-cocked without talking it over with anyone. It's just a coincidence that you came up with this idea while my mom and I were both out of the room, right?"

Damn it, he had me again.

I shoved my duffel bag out of the way with more force than necessary and plopped down on the edge of the bed. Predictably, Bob immediately started nosing my hand, asking for a pet. With a frustrated huff, I complied.

"I panicked," I admitted, finally able to let go of the fight. "I'm afraid Aleric can convince Piper to tell the police I was the one who shot her. If that happens, they'll probably arrest me, and that'll make me a sitting duck."

Luke was still frowning at me, but less fiercely, and his shoulders had lowered. "I don't see how running away with no money and nowhere to go—especially at night—would have helped the situation."

"It wouldn't. Like I said, I panicked. I figured I'd work out the details later. I admit, I was being stupid."

Luke came all the way into the room finally and sat on the edge of the other bed. The anger seemed to have drained out of him, leaving behind sadness and worry.

"Was that it?" he asked quietly. "Or did some part of you want to go back to being Nightstruck again?"

I flinched at the question, because it wasn't one I wanted to think about. "I'm about ninety-nine percent sure that had nothing to do with it," I told him.

"Then what it really comes down to is that you don't trust my mom and me."

I gave him an incredulous look, having not seen that one coming at all. "Of course I do!"

"Then why would you try to run away a second time? Why

didn't you consider, I don't know, talking it over with us or something instead of acting like we were some kind of obstacle you had to get around?"

"I told you I wasn't thinking straight!"

"And were you thinking straight the night you snuck out to kill Piper?"

I groaned and lowered my face into my hands. I'd thought both Luke and his mom had somehow understood why I'd done what I'd done. Up until now, neither one of them had even mentioned that terrible decision of mine, much less questioned it. I guess they were just being nice in deference to my fragile state of mind.

My first instinct was to clam up and refuse to talk because it was too uncomfortable. But I owed Luke an explanation even though he'd never asked me for one. Before now, at least.

I raised my head and rubbed at my eyes, feeling suddenly exhausted. It's amazing how tiring it is to ride an emotional roller coaster that plunges to such deep lows.

"You and your mom are both good people," I said. "The *best* people. I knew if I told you what I was planning, you would have stopped me. You wouldn't have wanted me to take that kind of risk."

"And we would have been right. Maybe if you'd talked to us instead of taking off like you were the Lone Ranger, you would have realized that and spared us all four weeks of misery."

I shook my head. "Maybe you and your mom would have felt better about it, but *I* wouldn't. You have no idea what it's like carrying all of this around with me, knowing that none of this would have happened if it hadn't been for me. All the people who've been hurt, all the people who've died . . ." I let my voice trail off and shuddered. My back and shoulders bent under the weight of it.

Luke stood up, and at first I thought he was about to walk out, that he was sick of my whining and complaining. I knew he understood, at least to some extent, but that didn't make it any easier to be around me. But Luke really is one of the best people on the planet. Instead of leaving me to mope in solitude, he sat on the bed beside me and wrapped his arms around me. I didn't feel like I deserved a hug after what I'd just tried to do, but I didn't have the willpower to resist it. I sagged into his arms, heedless of the dampness of his shirt.

"You don't have to carry it all alone, Becks," he said into my hair, his arms warm and firm and perfect around me. "I'm willing to help you if you'll just let me."

I put my own arms around him, squeezing tight as my heart swelled with emotion. "I'm not great at accepting help," I said into his shoulder. "You may have noticed that about me."

He laughed briefly. "I may have."

I expected him to let go of me any moment now, but his arms remained around me as one of his hands stroked slowly up and down my back. I wasn't about to let go until I had to.

"Did you mean what you said in that text?" he asked.

My chest constricted. I knew, of course, exactly which text he was referring to, and I was completely unprepared to answer him. I'd never thought he'd bring it up, thought he'd treat it like the embarrassing secret it was and let me off the hook. It would have been so much easier that way, if we'd just pretended it never happened.

What could I say? Surely I couldn't say yes, couldn't say I loved a guy I'd made out with, like, twice. And who had technically still been my best friend's boyfriend at the time. I didn't want him to think that I was some psycho stalker girl who saw true love at the slightest provocation. And yet saying no seemed even worse. Cruel, somehow. Not to mention probably a lie. I think

I'd loved Luke for a long time and just never allowed myself to admit my feelings were anything more than a juvenile crush.

Luke was still patiently waiting for an answer. I hoped the awkward silence would convince him to change the subject, but no such luck. He was holding me close to his chest, and I could hear the thumping of his heart against my ear, the sound strangely comforting. I just wanted to cuddle there without thinking or talking, but that wasn't among my options.

"I don't know," I finally murmured, since I couldn't convince myself to say either yes or no. The hand that had been stroking my back stopped moving, and I realized that was probably the worst possible answer. I was brave enough—or maybe just stupid enough—to run out into the night and try to kill Piper, but I wasn't brave enough to own up to my own feelings. How pathetic is that?

My cheeks were flaming hot as I wriggled out of Luke's embrace, and there was no way I could bear to meet his eyes. Luke had risked his life to drag me out of the square and save me from the night, and I didn't even have the guts to admit how I felt? God, I loathed myself in that moment.

"It's all right, Becks," Luke said. "I shouldn't have pushed it. Sorry."

Oh, man. Now he was apologizing because I was being a wimp? He was most definitely too good for me.

"I meant it," I blurted out unexpectedly. I couldn't believe those words had escaped my mouth, and I immediately wanted to sink through the floor and disappear. The heat in my face was epic, and my fingers were digging into the mattress as if somehow holding on tight enough would make this all better.

"I thought I would never see you again," I said, forcing my voice out through a tight throat. Then I shook my head. "No, that's not right. What I was really afraid of was that I'd see you again and I'd be like Piper. That I'd say cruel things and hurt you just for the fun of it. I couldn't bear to let that happen without telling you how I really felt first. I know that was, like, super melodramatic, and—"

I didn't get to finish the sentence because Luke's lips were suddenly on mine.

CHAPTER SIXTEEN

Luke had kissed me a couple of times before, and it had been fantastic. I had wanted him for so long, and had never felt any hope that I might get him. Kissing him was like finding the Holy Grail.

At least it had been before.

Remembered glories flooded me as I savored the warmth and softness of those lips, but hard on the heels of those memories came other, much less pleasant ones. Memories of Aleric kissing me, of my body responding to him in all the ways it had to Luke. Memories of Aleric helping me out of my clothes, pressing his naked body against mine.

I shuddered and pushed Luke away, though part of me screamed to forget all about Aleric and take what Luke was offering. That part of me couldn't outshout the other, which cringed with revulsion at the memory of what I'd done. Of what I'd let Aleric do. And most of all, of what Aleric was.

I'd always harbored the suspicion that I wasn't worthy of a guy like Luke, that he was totally out of my league. Now I felt dirty and damaged on top of it. How could I relax into his kiss, how could I give him what he deserved, when I had *that* floating around in my memory banks?

"I'm sorry," Luke said the moment I pulled away. "I didn't—I wasn't—"

He sounded alarmed, like he was afraid he'd hurt me, or like he thought his kiss had been completely unwelcome. I felt warmth flooding my face and once again was tempted to crawl under the bed and hide. I didn't want to give him the "it's not you, it's me" speech, but that was the only thing I could think of to say.

"Don't be sorry," I said. My throat tightened up, my voice getting thick. Luke was not naive, and he knew what the Nightstruck were like. He probably already had a good idea that I wasn't a virgin anymore. Hell, he probably already guessed I'd slept with Aleric. Maybe he'd have been perfectly content if that knowledge could remain nothing but uncorroborated speculation, but I didn't think there was any way I could avoid hurting him. If I didn't give him a good explanation for why I pulled away, he couldn't help but take it personally. I know I would have in his shoes.

"I had sex with Aleric," I forced myself to say, nausea roiling in my belly. The fact that I'd actually *enjoyed* it at the time made the memory worse, not better. I almost thought I would feel less dirty if he'd raped me. "Until I can find a way to . . . to scrub that from my memory, I don't think I can . . ."

Of course I didn't have the guts to look at Luke when I made the admission, so I couldn't see his first reaction. I had to believe he'd made a face of disgust. I was probably lucky he hadn't leapt to his feet and run to the bathroom to wash his mouth out.

There was a painfully long moment of silence before Luke spoke again, and when he did, it wasn't to say any of the awful things I was expecting. Not that Luke would ever say anything awful, not really. He's too nice a guy for that. But still, I was braced for something unpleasant.

"Am I supposed to be shocked?" he asked instead. He was still sitting intimately close to me, and he reached over to take my hand, twining his fingers with mine. "It certainly seems like the kind of thing Aleric would do."

"But I *let* him," I rasped, the shame weighing on me so heavily my shoulders bowed. No, I hadn't just *let* him—I'd encouraged him.

"You were Nightstruck."

"That's no excuse!"

I tried to pull my hand away from his, strangely angry that he didn't seem in the least bit surprised or disappointed in me. He squeezed my hand tighter, not allowing me the easy escape I craved.

"So if some guy slips a roofie into a girl's drink, it's her fault if he assaults her while she's out of it?" Luke asked.

"That's not the same thing."

"It's *exactly* the same thing," he argued.

He certainly sounded like he meant it, not like he was just saying the words he thought I wanted to hear. I glanced at his face and saw nothing in his eyes but sincerity and concern. It seemed too good to be true.

But, I reminded myself, he'd figured out what had happened long before today, and he'd had plenty of time to digest it and get past his first reaction. Maybe he'd even talked it over with Piper, or with his mom, and that was why he was able to be so reasonable and sweet. Obviously I didn't have a whole lot of experience with guys, but I didn't think books and TV shows and movies were just making up the whole testosterone-fueled jealousy and possessiveness that the male of the species was capable of. Even Aleric had been jealous, and he wasn't even human. Besides, Luke didn't know what *else* I'd done while I was Nightstruck. Would he still be this understanding if he knew about Stuart's death and the part I played in it?

Luke's hand tightened convulsively on mine, making me wince. He loosened his grip immediately but leaned forward so he could look me in the eyes with extra intensity.

"Don't let that asshole screw with your life any more than he already has. You didn't do anything wrong, and I'm not the kind of guy who thinks any girl who's not a virgin is a slut. I mean seriously, Becks, how many boyfriends had Piper been through by the time she got around to me?"

Even in my misery, I managed an almost amused snort at that. Before Luke, Piper had flitted from boyfriend to boyfriend so fast it was hard to keep track of them all. I don't think she slept with all of them, but certainly some of them.

Unbidden, another memory assailed me, that of Nightstruck Piper mocking Luke, suggesting she had been his first.

"At least her boyfriends were all human," I said.

Luke sighed heavily and finally let go of my hand. "If you're determined to make everything be all your fault, then maybe I can't change that. But it gets old, you know. So you made some mistakes! Everyone does. Maybe running off half-cocked acting like you're the only one in the world who can fix things isn't the best way of handling it. Maybe you should just deal with it already."

"I'm trying!" I protested miserably.

"Well try harder."

I half-expected Luke to park himself in my room and play watchdog until his mom got home, but either he trusted me to stay put or he was just sick of me and my attitude. He went into his own room and shut the adjoining door. Soon, I heard his shower turn on.

I looked at my half-packed duffel bag, then at the door. If I wanted to get away and face my troubles on my own, now was the time to do it, but running away didn't seem like such a hot idea anymore. My best chance of staying out of Aleric's clutches was to get past the quarantine and escape Philadelphia. For that, I would need help. I didn't know if Luke and his mom were exactly the kind of help I needed—would they really know any better than me how to sneak past a military blockade?—but at least I'd have someone to bounce ideas off.

I finished packing for our evening room change, but I stayed put. When I heard the shower go off in Luke's room, I made sure I was making noise in my own so that he'd know I hadn't left. I can't imagine how he would have felt if I'd disappeared on his watch, and I really hoped his decision to leave me alone was a sign of trust and not just disgust.

Dr. Gilliam had already made a new reservation for us, so we moved the minute she got off her shift at the hospital. It was always a close shave to get moved before the Transition hit and the city turned into its nightmare self, so by mutual—if silent—agreement, neither Luke nor I brought up the afternoon's events until we were settled in our new room. Then, he fixed me with a significant look, one that said if I didn't start talking, he would.

So I told Dr. Gilliam about Sam's "unofficial" visit, and about the anonymous source who'd named me as the shooter, and about Aleric's ominous threats. I conveniently left out the part about how I'd tried to run away and Luke had stopped me. If he wanted to rat me out, that was fine, but I saw no reason to bring it up myself.

Dr. Gilliam looked appropriately concerned after I'd finished, her brows furrowed. "We need to get you a lawyer," she said.

It seemed like such a . . . mundane thing to do. Something

you would do when life around you was otherwise normal. The thought hadn't even entered my mind until Dr. Gilliam mentioned it, and when she did I felt like an idiot. Hiring a lawyer was the obvious thing to do when you were worried you might soon be arrested. However, there was a big, big problem with the idea.

"I can't afford a lawyer," I said. "Not unless I use my mom's credit card to pay for it, and I don't want her to find out about this."

Dr. Gilliam's eyebrows shot up. "Why on earth not? She'd probably have some suggestions for who you should call."

I shook my head. I had no doubt my mom would have suggestions. Although she was a corporate lawyer herself, I knew she had plenty of friends who were criminal attorneys. I had the dark thought that there were probably a lot of attorneys who'd been Nightstruck, but that was probably my dad and his low opinion of criminal attorneys talking. Back when he and my mom were married, they used to get into big arguments whenever he made some snarky comment about how much harder lawyers made his job.

"If she finds out I'm in legal trouble, she'll try even harder to get into Philadelphia. And a judge somewhere might think me being arrested for murder and having no family member to look after me was a good reason to let her come."

"Maybe that wouldn't be such a bad thing."

I'm sure Dr. Gilliam would have been overjoyed if my mom showed up to take me off her hands. Her life was already stressful enough without me. Working in the emergency room at a time like this would be enough to drive most people to a padded cell, and she also had to deal with the strain of being forcibly separated from her husband. Even if my mom came for me, Dr. Gilliam and Luke would have to live in hiding, because

Aleric knew I cared about them. But at least if I was gone, she wouldn't have to worry about me doing anything stupid—like, say, running away—or about my mom blaming her for anything that might happen to me.

"My mom doesn't understand the threat," I reminded her. "She thinks we're all sick and hallucinating, so she's not going to want to listen to me about taking precautions. Maybe after her first night here, she'll be convinced, but maybe not. Maybe she'll just think she's sick, too. And even if she doesn't . . . You know my mom. Don't you think she might be vulnerable? I mean, she's not a *bad* person, but then neither was Piper."

Dr. Gilliam thought about it a moment, then conceded my point with a little shrug. "I see where you're coming from, I really do. But she's your mother. She has a right to know that you're in this kind of trouble."

"If I *do* get arrested, then yeah, she has a right to know. But right now all that's happened is Aleric placed an anonymous tip that made Sam ask me some unofficial questions. I'm not in any real trouble yet."

"Which is a good reason to get a lawyer now. Waiting till you're in real trouble will complicate things."

I shook my head. "If I get into the kind of trouble Aleric's threatening, being prosecuted will be the least of my worries."

Not the most comforting thought, and Dr. Gilliam didn't look convinced.

"If I can talk to a lawyer without my mom finding out, then I'll do it," I conceded, but that was as much of a compromise as I was willing to make.

I decided now would be an excellent time to change the subject. "I've been thinking about it a lot, and I think we need to get me out of the city."

Dr. Gilliam looked like she was halfway toward a big laugh before she realized I was serious. I decided to hurry on before she had a chance to tell me exactly how impossible my idea was.

"As long as I'm within Aleric's reach, there's a chance he's going to get to me eventually. That would suck for me and for everyone who cares about me, but what's even worse is that I know he'll convince me to open more gates. He won't be happy until the Night Makers have taken the entire city. I can't let him catch me, and the best way to avoid that is to get me out of the city where he can't follow."

Dr. Gilliam was looking at me as if she were mentally measuring me for a straitjacket. I guess I couldn't blame her. Breaking out of the quarantine zone when it was being guarded by the military sounded like the longest of long shots. Not to mention that it would be both dangerous and highly illegal. After all I'd already put Luke and his mom through, I was now asking them to break the law for me. Again.

"That sounds good in theory," she said, which was a more positive response than I'd expected. "But even if we could manage it, I'm not sure it would work."

"Why not?"

"The magic obviously has a strong affinity for your blood, right?"

"Um, yeah," I admitted uncomfortably.

"So I'm not sure that it wouldn't follow you if you left the city."

I felt as if someone had just used a vacuum cleaner to suck all the breath out of my lungs. I'd always assumed the magic was attached—for lack of a better word—to the city itself. That after having accidentally contributed to its arrival with a single drop of my blood, my role in what had happened to the city was over—as long as I didn't open more gates for the Night Makers, at least. But if it was *me* the magic was attached to . . .

"May I use your laptop?" I asked Dr. Gilliam, then dove for the computer without waiting for permission. Dr. Gilliam said something that I couldn't hear over the rushing of the blood in my ears. I quickly got on the Internet and searched for a map of the quarantine zone, having never before put any thought into where its borders lay, how far the nightmare stretched.

All of Center City was within the quarantine, but there was a fingerlike extension to the northwest, covering parts of Montgomery County.

Montgomery County. Where my school was located.

I'd first met Aleric just outside the gates of my school, after the night magic had turned a pile of spilled trash into a man-shaped monster that had chased me.

Could it possibly be a coincidence that the magic was tied to my blood and it extended beyond the city limits only in the one direction I routinely traveled?

"I had noticed that before," Dr. Gilliam said quietly, standing behind my chair as I stared at the map. "Maybe it's past the point of spreading now that it's taken root so solidly and the changes are . . . stable. But it's also possible that your mom's almost right about this being an illness, and that you're Patient Zero."

"Possible isn't certain," I said. I really wanted to cling to the hope that there was a way out of this.

"No, but do we really want to test the theory? Think of how terrible the consequences would be if the magic spread."

No, thank you. That was not something I wanted to think about.

"So then what do we do?" I asked in a small voice. In only a few hours, I had built escaping the city into this grand plan, this shining hope that there was a way to end at least some of the hell we were going through. I did not want to slide back into the darkness, but I could feel my grip on that hope slipping.

Dr. Gilliam put her hands on my shoulders and squeezed. "I don't know, Becket. For now, we just keep on keeping on."

I closed my eyes, not at all sure I could pull it off.

CHAPTER SEVENTEEN

D r. Gilliam found a lawyer for me. A friend of a friend who was willing to talk things over with me and come to my aid should the worst happen. I put his number into my phone, but he told me to carry his card around with me at all times because I might not have access to that phone if I got arrested. He seemed to think that was unlikely based on the evidence the police had, but I hadn't told him just how likely it was that other evidence would surface. One thing he told me unequivocally: unless I had an ironclad alibi that would exonerate me completely, I was to say *nothing* to the police without him present.

For the next couple of days, our lives went on in what I was thinking of as the new normal. I'd always hated the term in the past, but I didn't know what else to call it when "normal" meant being on the run and staying in a different hotel room every night.

So far, at least, our constant hotel-hopping seemed to have kept Aleric off our tail. He'd said he'd give me time to "think things over," but if he were able to track me down every day, I was sure he'd have called to let me know. He'd just gotten lucky when he found me on the day Sam came by to ask questions.

But as Aleric pointed out, he didn't need to find my hotel room to make trouble, as we found out the hard way when a couple of detectives I didn't know showed up on our doorstep.

Luckily for me, Dr. Gilliam wasn't at work yet because she was working the night shift, and she was the one who answered the door while I held on to Bob's collar to help remind him that *stay* meant *stay*. His training had slipped a bit since my dad's death, but he didn't struggle against my hold. I saw the detectives glance at him nervously anyway as he greeted them with flattened ears, bared teeth, and a deep, rumbling growl.

"I'm Detective Franklin," the older of the two cops said, "And this is Detective Woods. We'd like to talk to Becket Walker for a little bit. Mind if we come in?"

Dr. Gilliam remained firmly parked in the doorway.

"I'm sure Becket would like to consult her attorney before answering any questions," she said smoothly. I was really glad she did, because my tongue appeared to be attached to the roof of my mouth with Krazy Glue.

Detective Franklin gave Dr. Gilliam a shifty-eyed look. "We just want to ask her a few questions. Nothing official."

Dr. Gilliam pulled her cell phone out of her pocket. "That's fine. I'll just give the attorney I hired for her a call. And of course I'll have to call her mother. I know a lot has changed in the last couple of months, but I doubt you're allowed to question a minor without a parent or legal guardian present."

Both detectives scowled, though they couldn't have been surprised. They might not know me personally, but they certainly knew who I was, and I doubted they expected the late police commissioner's daughter to be completely ignorant of her rights. They were there to intimidate me—and it worked.

They grumbled at Dr. Gilliam a bit and gave me looks that said I was digging the hole deeper by not cooperating. Which might have bothered me, if it weren't for the fact that cooperating would turn the hole into a bottomless pit. They might have a hard time getting a conviction because Piper was Nightstruck at the time I shot her, but being convicted was the least of my worries. I hoped their claim that they were here unofficially meant that Aleric hadn't persuaded Piper to talk. Or manufactured any new evidence.

"All right," Detective Franklin said with a big sigh that told us we were being a major pain in his ass. "If it's not possible for us to speak with Miss Walker, then you'll do." He glanced at his watch. "We promise to have you back well before sundown. We'll keep you for an hour or two, tops."

"Me?" Dr. Gilliam asked, clearly startled.

Internally, I groaned. Of course the police were going to want to question Dr. Gilliam and Luke, considering I'd been staying at their house on the night of the shooting.

"If you can provide an alibi for Miss Walker, then we can put this whole business to rest," Detective Franklin said with false cheer. Obviously he knew Dr. Gilliam couldn't alibi me. If she could, one or both of us would have mentioned it by now, and I probably would have told Sam that in the first place.

As usual, Dr. Gilliam stayed calm under pressure, and she recovered from her initial surprise quickly. "I don't see why I'd have to go to the police station to do that," she said. "I'll tell you now that as far as I know, Becket was in her room all night on the night Miss Grant was shot."

I learned in that moment that Dr. Gilliam is a pretty good liar. She sounded natural and unrehearsed, giving away nothing in her voice or face. I, on the other hand, probably gave away everything, because no matter how hard I tried to hide my reaction, my cheeks heated in a guilty blush. I was caught between a feeling of intense gratitude that Dr. Gilliam would lie to the police for me, and a crushing guilt that she would have to. I was not her daughter, not her family, and she shouldn't have to put so much on the line for me.

"That's great," Detective Franklin said, again with the false cheer. "Now if you'll just come down to the station and sign a quick affidavit to that effect . . ."

"I'd be happy to," Dr. Gilliam answered, "but it will have to wait until tomorrow. We'll be changing hotel rooms tonight, and I still have to pack and make the reservations."

"Just why are you staying in a hotel, anyway?" the detective asked. "We haven't seen any reports of damage to your house. You wouldn't be trying to avoid the police, now, would you?"

Dr. Gilliam rolled her eyes. "Yes, I'm trying to avoid the police by staying in hotels under my own name. And going in to work my shifts at the hospital, where of course there are no police around at all."

Franklin's face flushed, and I gathered he didn't much appreciate the disrespect. However, it was hard to argue Dr. Gilliam's logic—though it was probably equally hard from his point of view to come up with another explanation for our odd behavior.

"We'll see you bright and early tomorrow morning then, shall we?" Detective Franklin asked.

"Yes, of course," Dr. Gilliam said, conveniently not mentioning that she was working the night shift tonight and would be sound asleep bright and early tomorrow morning.

Grudgingly, Detective Franklin accepted her promise and left, but I doubted we'd seen the last of him.

"You shouldn't have lied for me," I told Dr. Gilliam when I was certain the detectives were out of earshot.

Dr. Gilliam shrugged. "It's not against the law to lie to the police."

"I know, but it tends to piss them off. And if you sign an affidavit . . ."

"We'll cross that bridge if and when we have to. For now, I just wanted to get rid of them. I think we both need to have another

183

talk with your attorney. And you and I have to revisit the idea of telling your mother the truth, because it's only a matter of time before the police contact her. If they haven't already."

Unfortunately, Dr. Gilliam was right about that. I might have hoped the police department would cut me some slack because I was the late police commissioner's daughter and because life in the city had become so crazy. In fact, the more I thought about it, the more unlikely it seemed that they would try to question me based only on Aleric's anonymous call. If Piper had named me as the shooter, I probably wouldn't have been able to get out of this interview so easily, but I felt certain Aleric had done something to make the police look more closely at me as the possible shooter.

Reluctantly, I dug out Sam's card and gave him a call. I felt bad calling him for help after I'd treated him like the enemy, but he and my dad really had been close. Maybe if I acted pathetic enough, Sam's compassion would get the best of him and he'd let me know if the police had any further evidence.

It made me feel somewhat dirty—and question once again whether being Nightstruck had left any lingering effects—to manipulate someone the way I was planning to manipulate Sam if I could, but I needed to know how close I was to being arrested.

Sam, of course, was still full of questions, none of which I could answer, but I came up with something plausible and vague to try to satisfy his curiosity.

"One of the Nightstruck has it in for me," I told him. "That's why the Gilliams and I keep changing hotel rooms. We want to make it hard for him to find me. I think he's the one who called in the so-called anonymous tip, and I think if he can find a way to implicate me, he'll do it."

Sam thought that over for a moment. "Why didn't you say so from the start?"

"Because the police have enough trouble dealing with the Nightstruck already. You can't afford to go chasing after this guy when there are packs of them roaming the streets at night breaking into houses and killing people. But detectives came by the hotel today and wanted to take me to the station for questioning and then wanted to take Dr. Gilliam in. I'm worried that this guy might have planted some other kind of 'evidence.'"

Sam's hesitation could have meant he was trying to decide which question to ask next, but I suspected it was more about trying to decide what to tell me. He'd known me—albeit not super well—since I was a little girl, and surely he didn't believe I'd actually shot somebody.

"I think I may be in real trouble, Sam," I said, and it wasn't hard to sound pathetic and scared. "I don't know what the Nightstruck are capable of, but I don't think it's hard to imagine them being able to use magic to manufacture something that makes me look guilty."

"I don't know, Becket. That sounds a little subtle for them. They're more into murder and mayhem than frame jobs."

I shivered involuntarily. "Not the guy who's after me. Trust me, he's plenty subtle."

Sam made a noncommittal noise. "How'd you get on this guy's radar, anyway?"

"I'm not sure." I lied convincingly, or at least I hoped so. "It has something to do with Piper. She was obsessed with me when she was Nightstruck, and I guess she got this guy interested in me. Please, Sam. Can you tell me if some other evidence has conveniently sprung up out of nowhere to convince the police I shot Piper?"

"You know I can't share information like that with you."

Which was almost as good as a yes, because he probably would have said so if the answer were no. "I know you're not supposed to. But you know me. You know I didn't shoot anyone. And with my dad . . . gone . . . I'm all alone here. My mom's still in Boston. Dr. Gilliam's been great, but she's not family." I put a hitch in my voice that wasn't entirely phony. I was playing shamelessly on Sam's loyalty to my dad, but I was willing to do whatever it took to keep from being blindsided. "You said you would be my friend," I finished in a small, forlorn voice.

There was a long silence as Sam thought it over. I found myself holding my breath and forced myself to breathe. The silence felt weighty and oppressive, and I was almost scared for Sam to break it, scared of what he was going to say.

"My advice to you as a friend," he finally said, "is to come in and give us a statement about what happened that night. Even if you were to admit to being the shooter, it wouldn't have to be the end of the world. Your friend was Nightstruck, so no one's going to have trouble believing you did it in self-defense."

Shit. I'd been banking on him not believing I was the shooter, but he sounded like he was already convinced of my guilt.

"You see, Becket," he continued, "if you admit you shot her in self-defense, it's not hard to believe the charges would be dropped. But if you keep denying it and, hypothetically speaking, another anonymous tip would happen to lead us to a gun and its ballistics should happen to match those of the gun that shot Miss Grant and that gun should happen to be registered to your father . . . Well, it might look bad."

My stomach turned over. I'd known the gun was a possible vulnerability, and now that fear had been justified.

"If hypothetically speaking that gun had been found, then why would I not hypothetically be under arrest already?"

"Because anonymous witnesses can't testify in court, the evidence is circumstantial, and most importantly the victim has already positively identified a shooter who isn't you. The state isn't convinced they have enough to win a conviction against the late police commissioner's daughter on what they have, so they're not willing to arrest you."

The "yet" was silent, but we both knew it was there.

"You can talk to me if you're not comfortable with Detective Franklin," Sam offered, still hoping that I'd see the writing on the wall and let the police have their interview.

"Thanks, Sam. I'll think about it."

We both knew what that meant, and I could almost hear Sam's disappointment over the phone.

CHAPTER EIGHTEEN

With great reluctance, I accepted the reality that there would be no keeping my mom out of this. I hadn't talked to her since our big blowup, though she had called several times. She hadn't left any voice mails, which was either because she knew you couldn't make up for a fight in a voice mail or because she just didn't know what to say to me. But since the police were clearly going to contact her—if they hadn't already—it was time to end the radio silence. Much though I dreaded the conversation.

I called in the evening, when Dr. Gilliam was at work. Luke retreated into the adjoining room to give me privacy. For about fifteen minutes I stared at the cell phone Dr. Gilliam had given me before I finally scraped up the willpower to make the call.

I knew the police had been in touch with her already when the first thing she said after a perfunctory greeting was that I should call her back on the landline. My mind immediately jumped to the conclusion that she thought my cell phone might be monitored, and I cursed myself for not having thought of it. Who knows what I might have naively blurted out if the police hadn't already alerted my mom?

Dutifully, I called my mom back on the old-fashioned corded phone by the bed. I thought we might have to go through some awkward and painful attempt at reconciliation first, but my mom got straight to business.

"Tell me everything," she demanded. "I promise you I won't judge you, but I have to know all the facts so that I can come up with the best plan to keep you out of jail."

I sat heavily on the bed, wishing I could have used the cell phone so I could pace while I talked. I had already decided it was time to tell her the whole story, even though I didn't expect her to believe me. But it was really hard getting started, so I stalled a bit. "Dr. Gilliam hired a lawyer for me, so—"

"I don't care," my mom interrupted. "She wouldn't know a brilliant criminal attorney from an ambulance-chaser, and you're *my* daughter. I am going to take care of you, whether you want me to or not. Now tell me what happened."

I bristled all over again at the way my mom dismissed Dr. Gilliam, but now was not the time to start another argument. So I started at the beginning, telling my mom about the night I found the not-a-baby in that dark alley and inadvertently opened a door to another world. I also told her about Aleric, the creature that was formed by the combination of my blood and the night magic. I told her about opening a gate for the Night Maker in Rittenhouse Square, and I told her about Aleric's desire to have me open more. I also explained why I was so desperate for her not to come to Philadelphia, though I only mentioned her potential as a hostage, not my worry that the night might tempt her.

And finally, I told her about the night I shot Piper. I found that my courage and honesty had its limits, however, because I couldn't bring myself to give my mom all the details about that night. For instance, I didn't tell her that I'd intended to kill Piper all along, nor did I tell her that Piper was just standing there harmlessly when I pulled the trigger. I made it sound as if I had legitimate reason to believe I was in mortal danger, when in fact I'd done it because Aleric had goaded me beyond my endurance.

My mom listened to the story in silence. I wished I could see her face so I could have some clue what she was thinking. I had to admit, it had to sound pretty crazy from where she was sitting, especially if she was buying into the government's claims that we were all suffering from some kind of mass hallucination. And the fact that I was claiming to be the center of it all, the person who had triggered the nightmare and whose blood could be used to make the nightmare infinitely worse must have made me sound like I was some troubled teen desperately seeking attention.

When I finally finished with my story, she neatly sidestepped all the most important issues and homed in on the one that was most familiar, that she could wrap her brain around.

"So it was self-defense then," she said with satisfaction.

"Um, yeah." I'm not sure what I was hoping to accomplish by lying to her, but I just couldn't force myself to tell her that I'd tried to commit cold-blooded murder—while I wasn't even Nightstruck yet. "Look, Mom, I'm not so much worried about being prosecuted as being arrested in the first place. It's Aleric who's feeding the police the evidence they need, and he was very certain he'd be able to get me out of jail."

"If we find you the right lawyer, we can make sure it never comes to that," she answered without a hint of doubt in her voice. She's not stupid, so she had to know this wasn't something we could control no matter how good my lawyer was. I suspected she was merely trying to comfort me.

"Somehow I don't think it's going to be that easy," I muttered, and wasn't surprised when my mom ignored the comment completely.

"I think your legal troubles are going to give me the extra

push I need to get into the quarantine zone," she said, making me groan out loud. She ignored that, too. "You should not be deprived of your legal guardian when you're facing potential criminal charges, and I think once I've signed several libraries' worth of waivers they're eventually going to let me come to you and take care of things."

Exactly what I was afraid of. "You can't come to the city, Mom. You'll have a giant target printed on your back." I let my voice quaver instead of keeping a stiff upper lip. "I couldn't bear it if you ended up like Dad."

"I'm not going to let that happen, honey," she assured me.

I wished I could believe her. "You don't have to come here to hire a good lawyer for me," I tried, knowing full well her mind was already made up.

"I am your mother, and I'm not letting the police question my little girl without me present. In person. So I'm coming for you, whether you want me to or not."

"You're going to get yourself killed! You don't understand what it's like here, what we're facing."

"I'll figure it out when I get there. I've already arranged for a cleaning service to take care of the damage to our house, and when I get there, you and I can replace anything that needs replacing. You'll have your home back again and be able to sleep in your own room. You'd like that, wouldn't you?"

"Have you been listening to anything I've said? I'm in *hiding*, Mom. People in hiding don't get to go home and sleep in their own bedrooms. Not unless they're terminally stupid." I had stopped by my house only once since Luke had pulled me from the square. I hadn't been surprised to find that Aleric had sent his buddies in to trash it once again. It was a remarkably petty gesture, but then that was Aleric for you.

"Becket, honey, you're making yourself hysterical over

nothing. You're sick, and it's making you see threats where none exist. I can't imagine all the stress you've been under is helping the situation. What you need is to get back to your home and get some rest and let me handle things for a while."

"I'm not sick!" I said, but what chance did I have of convincing her? The press and the government had laid down this narrative about sickness, reinforcing it with the draconian quarantine, and no one who wasn't experiencing the madness firsthand could possibly understand. And as long as no camera could capture the way the city changed at night, the outside world was going to cling to the illusion that we were all hallucinating because it was the only thing that came close to making sense to them.

"The city really does change at night, and I really am the center of it all. Dr. Gilliam says I'm like Patient Zero in some big outbreak, only in this case it's an outbreak of magic instead of disease."

As soon as the words left my mouth, I realized I'd made a big mistake. My mom was still blaming Dr. Gilliam for me having been Nightstruck for almost a month, and she was supremely uninterested in anything Dr. Gilliam had to say.

"We'll talk about this more when I get there," my mom said. "It should only be a couple of days now, and I've made it very clear to the Philadelphia police department that I will slap them with a lawsuit if they try to question you before I get there."

Her mind was completely closed, and I didn't have a battering ram big enough to break down her barriers. If she really meant to take me back to our house and install me in my own bedroom, then I might as well walk out into the street and hand myself over to Aleric right now. At least if I were in a prison or some juvenile detention facility, Aleric would have to work to break me out. The Nightstruck had broken into my house before without any difficulty, and they could easily do so again.

The walls were closing in on me, and I had a hard time seeing any hope of escape.

Things had been weird between Luke and me since I'd told him about what happened with Aleric. It was hard to say for sure whether the weirdness was coming from me or from him, but it was definitely there. But after getting off the phone with my mom, I needed someone to talk to. Someone who would believe me when I said my mom coming to the city would be a disaster. Dr. Gilliam was at work, I had no desire to call Piper for a friendly chat, and that left Luke. Little by little, my world kept shrinking.

The hotel that we were staying in that night had a kitchenette, and after I recounted my conversation, Luke used the microwave to make us each a cup of soothing hot cocoa while he thought it all over. Chocolate can solve a lot of problems, but this one was far out of its league. I set my mug on the coffee table and took a seat on the hard-as-a-rock sofa. I have yet to stay in a hotel that has a comfortable one. I meant for Luke to sit next to me, but Bob got to the middle seat faster. A furry chaperone.

Luke smiled as Bob laid his head on my lap and gave me imploring eyes. That dog knows exactly which buttons to push. Instead of picking up my cocoa again, I started scratching behind Bob's ear. He signed contentedly and closed his eyes, not bothering to open them when Luke moved his tail out of the way so he could sit down.

"Maybe when your mom gets here and gets a firsthand look at what's going on . . ." Luke suggested, but his voice trailed off. He knew that was wishful thinking.

"She'll just believe she's sick, too. And there's nothing short of Aleric showing up to drag me away that's going to convince her I'm not suffering from some kind of paranoid delusion when I say I'm in danger. She's going to take me home the first chance she gets, and that'll be the end of it."

Aleric would drag me out of my house, and he'd probably bring my mom, too, to use as leverage against me. Letting another Night Maker into the city was about the last thing I wanted to do, but how could I possibly resist him if he started hurting my mom in front of me? My hand tightened in Bob's fur as I remembered the sick, unbearable feeling in my gut when I'd seen Billy ram my dad, when I'd heard my dad's screams of pain. There was no way I could withstand that, even knowing that Aleric would have no reason to keep my mom alive after I'd given him what he wanted. He'd probably kill her just to punish me for having run away from him.

"Well then you obviously can't let her take you home," Luke said, reasonably.

"How can I stop her? She's never going to listen to reason. Not until it's too late, at least."

Luke grinned at me, a hint of genuine humor in his eyes. "You are the most stubborn, pigheaded person I know. I think I still have bruises from dragging you out of that square. Do you honestly think your mom can force you to go anywhere you don't want to go?"

I smiled involuntarily, and I suspected I blushed just a little bit as well. A lot of guys would find stubbornness unappealing in a girl, but it didn't sound like Luke was one of them. The smile faded quickly.

"My mom's the one who taught me to be stubborn, and let me tell you, I learned from a true master," I said. "If I dig in my heels and refuse to go, she'll probably get the police to drag me there in handcuffs or something. She's sure she's right and this is all in my head."

Luke thought that over for a moment and nodded. He didn't know my mom as well as he'd known my dad, but he knew her well enough.

"So what are you planning to do? Just give up and go quietly?"

I spared him a sour look, but I knew he was poking at me with a purpose. He was right, too. Thinking about all the ways I was screwed wasn't going to help the situation. Unfortunately, I wasn't brimming with clever solutions.

"I'm not going to give up," I assured Luke, "but my mom is pretty good at being an unstoppable force, which kind of leaves me at a loss."

"Your mom isn't the real problem here. Aleric is."

"Well yeah, but . . ." My voice trailed off as I realized Luke had just cut directly to the heart of the matter.

Ever since Luke had pulled me from the square, we'd been playing defense, running and hiding, our situation never improving. How long could we possibly keep it up? Even without the threat of arrest hanging over me or my mom making herself a potential victim, the chances that Aleric and his people would eventually get to me or Luke or Dr. Gilliam were frighteningly high. To the point that it seemed nearly inevitable.

"The only way any of us will ever be free is if we can stop Aleric," I said, then let out a bitter snort of laughter. "Which was exactly what I was thinking when I snuck out to kill Piper, and look how well that turned out."

"But you weren't wrong. You just didn't take the idea far enough."

"I took it as far as I could," I retorted. "Piper's just a human being. Aleric is something altogether different. And in case you've forgotten, I tried shooting him point-blank and it didn't bother him a bit."

"There has to be some way to kill him," Luke said. "Or at least send him back to wherever he came from. And I'd bet anything you're the one who can do it."

I was still unconvinced. Aleric was an unnatural being who by all rights shouldn't exist. Why should I believe there had to be some way to kill him? Hell, I wasn't even sure he was exactly alive by any definition we would use.

"There's a reason he's so obsessed with you," Luke said when I was silent for too long. He took my hand and squeezed it. Bob didn't appreciate this interference with his petting machine and shoved his nose upward into our joined hands, making us both smile briefly.

I used my free hand to resume petting, because having Luke hold my hand felt way too good to let go.

"He's obsessed because he wants me to open more gates so he can bring more Night Makers through."

"But maybe it's more than that. He sure seemed awfully possessive of you when you were Nightstruck. Why did he feel the need to seduce you? And why did he start pounding his chest whenever I showed up?"

"Because he's a guy."

"That's just it: he's *not* a guy. You spent a lot of time with him when you were Nightstruck. Did he show a lot of normal human emotions?"

"Well, no," I had to concede. "He got grumpy with me sometimes when I didn't immediately do what he wanted me to, but then I was the only person around him who didn't bow and scrape to him." I thought about it a little harder, furrowing my eyebrows as I tried to bring to mind a time when Aleric had seemed to be emotional over anything other than me. And I couldn't do it. He barely interacted with the Nightstruck at all, except to issue orders now and again. There were no ups or downs to his moods, at least not that he showed.

"Don't you think it's a little strange then that he acted so jealous?"

"To be fair, you did pull me out of the square. Maybe he knew all along that was a possibility and that was why he didn't want me around you."

Luke didn't look convinced. "That makes it sound like something completely pragmatic and rational. You getting away wasn't just some inconvenience for him. It really mattered. Enough for him to feel threatened by me."

"Well it's not because of his deep and abiding love for me," I said, but Luke's argument was starting to make a little more sense. His jealousy of Luke was the only genuine, lasting human emotion I'd ever seen in Aleric, and there had to be a reason for it. "Maybe it's just really important to him that I be Nightstruck so he can convince me to open more gates."

"If he was that eager to bring more Night Makers through, why did you only open one gate in the whole month you were with him?"

"I wasn't jumping for joy at the thought of slicing myself open for him. Maybe he was just trying to slowly coax me down the slippery slope."

"Or maybe he was afraid of what you might do if you weren't under his thumb anymore."

Luke had theorized before that I might somehow be the key to getting the night magic out of the city for good, that because it was tied to my blood, I had some kind of power over it. But I'd seen no evidence that would help sell me on the idea. As far as I could tell, the only thing I could do was make things worse.

I was about ready to pull my hair out with frustration. "If I have some magical way to make Aleric go poof, then I'm too stupid to figure it out." I leaned my head against the back of the sofa and closed my eyes to avoid the look of reproach Luke was giving me.

"The good news is that you don't have to figure it out all on your own. We have at least a couple of days before your mom gets here. Maybe if we put our heads together, we can come up with something."

I was clearly in a glass-half-empty frame of mind, but if I was going to keep out of Aleric's clutches, I was going to have to fill up that glass real fast.

CHAPTER NINETEEN

I wouldn't have thought it was possible, but Piper looked even worse than she had the last time I'd visited. The hollows under her cheekbones were deeper, the bruise-like shadows around her eyes darker. Her nails were bitten to the quick, with little bloody spots around the edges that said she'd been chewing her cuticles as well. Clearly whatever shrink her parents had hired wasn't making any progress.

Disturbingly, there was now an ornamental grille stretching all the way across her window. I didn't think it had been put there to keep anyone *out*.

Piper saw me staring at it and grinned wryly, a shadow of her former self flickering briefly. "Isn't it sweet how my folks are protecting me from any Nightstruck who might come calling?"

"Are they just being cautious, or did they put it there for a reason?"

Piper shrugged, but didn't answer. In the past, her room had always been in a state of organized chaos. Relatively neat because her parents had a maid service come in every day, but always overflowing with evidence of a full life. Now it seemed barren, almost sterile, and the air felt close and stale. Or maybe that last part was just my imagination.

"I'm probably lucky it's just a grille and not bricks," Piper said, kicking listlessly at the rolling chair that sat in front of her computer desk. A desk that in the past had always been piled high with dog-eared books and doodle-covered papers, but was now empty except for her sleeping computer.

I still harbored a lot of anger toward Piper, but even so I felt a pang of sympathy. This was no way to live, and jailing her in her room didn't seem like the best way to help her get back to normal. Not that normal was possible for her anymore, but surely she could be better than this. If Aleric and the night magic were out of the picture, would she finally recover? It might well be her only chance, but I wasn't so sure she'd see it that way.

"If you had a choice," I asked, though I already knew the answer, "would you join the Nightstruck again?"

Piper pulled the rolling chair toward her, straddling it and sitting on it backward with her arms draped over the back. The only other place to sit was on the bed. In the old days, I'd have flopped there carelessly without a second thought. Now, I sat stiffly on the edge and felt restless and out of place. There wasn't a whole lot of life in Piper's eyes—certainly not like there used to be—but something flared for a moment before it almost instantly died back down. The expression was gone before I could interpret it, but I couldn't help wondering if she felt I was invading her space by sitting on her bed without an explicit invitation.

"I want to say no," Piper said, not meeting my gaze. "It's the only decent thing to say, right? I mean, I know what I turned into, and no one in their right mind or with a hint of conscience would want to be like that." Her shoulders slumped, and she let out a hissing sigh. "I swear to God I still have a conscience. I don't *want* to want to go back. But sometimes it's so hard . . ." Her voice trailed off, and she blinked rapidly to stave off tears.

I knew exactly how she felt, because that was how *I'd* felt for a little while after Luke had pulled me out of the square. The difference between her and me was that I'd gotten over it within a few hours. I won't lie: there were definitely times when I felt a little tug of longing, when I missed how carefree I'd felt when I didn't give a crap about anyone but myself. But despite Luke's and Dr. Gilliam's worries, I had more than enough willpower to fight that yearning off. Piper was a different story.

"So, yeah," Piper concluded, her voice stronger. "I want to go back. And I think maybe *you* should want me to go back, too."

I raised my eyebrows at her, bewildered by the statement. "Oh?"

"I've heard through the grapevine that the police have recovered your dad's gun. The one you shot me with." She looked away as she said it, but not before I caught the flash of anger and malice in her eyes. I might sympathize with her and might occasionally forget that she wasn't my friend anymore, but Mr. Hyde would *not* forget.

"How did you hear that? The police don't run around sharing the results of their investigations." I'd been lucky when I'd persuaded Sam to tell me anything, and there would be no way I could have managed it if he hadn't been such a good friend of my dad's. No one would tell Piper or her parents anything.

"It's amazing what rich parents and influence will do," Piper said, but something about her tone was off, and I knew at once that her parents had nothing to do with it.

"You've been talking to Aleric, haven't you?"

One corner of her mouth lifted then dropped in an aborted smile. "Maybe I have. Hell, I have to talk to *someone* other than my shrink and my parents. I don't exactly get a lot of visitors you know."

Before the city had started changing, Piper had been one of the most popular girls at our school, her social calendar always chock-full. I had often suspected a lot of those friendships weren't much more than skin-deep, and it seemed I was right. If they'd been real friends, then as long as Piper hadn't done anything heinous to them while she was Nightstruck, they'd have stuck with her. Or at least popped in for a visit now and then. Hell, if *I* could come visit her after what she'd done to me, you'd think some of her other friends could have, too.

I almost laughed at myself, because let's get real, I wasn't visiting for Piper's benefit or out of the goodness of my heart.

I glanced over at the metal grille over Piper's windows. I didn't know what it turned into at night, but I was sure Aleric could find a way to get his Nightstruck in here regardless. Piper followed my gaze—and my line of thought.

"I asked him if he could break me out," she said. "He said he could, but he wouldn't. Not until I've told the police that you're the one who shot me."

I fought off the wave of panic that threatened to flood me. How long could Piper resist an enticement like that? I was probably lucky not to be in handcuffs already.

I caught another glimpse of malice on Piper's face before she managed to hide the expression. She'd intended to scare me, and she'd succeeded. I hated feeling like I was somehow following her script. Or worse, Aleric's.

I crossed my arms and gave her my blankest stare. "So why haven't you done it?"

"Gee, I don't know. Maybe it's because I'm not the coldest bitch in the universe and don't want you to go to prison for something I goaded you into doing."

"That's not it," I said promptly. "You hate my guts. I can see it in your eyes."

"I do not!" she protested. "*You're* the one who hates *me*."

She was looking at me with wide, innocent eyes, the picture of sincerity. Maybe there was even a part of her that meant it, that knew she was to blame for her current situation.

"So your Mr. Hyde has gone away?" I asked.

Piper groaned and closed her eyes. She was silent so long I thought maybe she was finished with our conversation. "He's still here," she finally admitted, eyes still closed. "And yeah, you're right. He hates you." She opened her eyes and met my gaze. She looked a little more like her old self in that moment, but I knew it was a lie. "I told Al no, that I wouldn't do it. I have no *intention* of doing it. But I can't swear I *won't*. When I hit the lowest of the lows . . ." She finished the sentence with a helpless shrug.

Great. Even if my mom didn't get permission to cross into the quarantine zone, there was no question in my mind that Aleric could wear Piper down until she turned me in. I *had* to find a way to fight him.

"I don't want you to get hurt, Becks," Piper said. "Really I don't." She reached out and put a hand on my arm. Things had changed between us so much I had to fight the instinct to flinch. "Help me get out of here," she begged, her hand clenching convulsively on my arm.

"What?"

"I want to be Nightstruck again. I want to stop caring. I want it so bad that I know eventually I'm going to do what Aleric wants just so he'll get me out. But if *you* get me out first . . ." Her eyes gleamed with a sudden, manic energy. "All I have to do is be outside at dawn. I'm so broken inside I *know* I'll get swept away. And if I'm Nightstruck, then the police won't be able to make me come in and make a statement or anything. They would have to drop the case."

She was so eager for me to say yes she was panting with it, like an addict hoping she was about to get a fix. And it made a certain kind of twisted sense, what she was asking. There was no way the police would arrest me if Piper was Nightstruck.

"It might destroy your parents if you were taken again," I reminded her.

Piper scoffed. "Like hell. I'm the family embarrassment in the state I'm in. They used to love to show me off to their friends and brag about me—though Lord knows I was never that much to brag about. Now they lock me in my bedroom and barely bother to look in on me. They've probably told their friends I'm dead just so they don't have to admit their daughter is one step short of being institutionalized."

I'd never had a high opinion of the Grants, and there may have been a kernel of truth in what Piper was saying. They weren't the warmest and most affectionate parents I'd ever met, and they'd shown a fair amount of indifference to Piper's well-being even before she'd been Nightstruck. But I did believe they loved her—the shadows around her mother's eyes weren't as deep as Piper's, but they were there nonetheless—and I knew they would be devastated if she disappeared again. Not that I expected Piper to take my word for it.

"I think if they were that eager to be rid of you, they wouldn't have put bars on your windows," I pointed out. Not to mention that if they'd been as uncaring as she thought, they would probably both have been Nightstruck by now. "And even so—how do you think Aleric is going to feel if you turn up Nightstruck and haven't helped deliver me into his hands?"

Piper snorted. "You think I give a crap how he feels?"

"I think you'll give a crap if he's pissed off enough to kill you. Which I wouldn't put past him."

She dismissed the threat with a wave of her hand. "He's not

going to kill me. And even if he does . . . I'd rather be dead than locked up in here for the rest of my life."

I couldn't tell if she meant that, or if she was just trying to manipulate me. For all the anger I felt toward her, I didn't want her to die. There was no question that she was desperately unhappy, but I couldn't take anything she said at face value.

Piper heaved an enormous sigh. "I was always jealous of you, you know."

I blinked uncomprehendingly. Piper being jealous of me made about as much sense as Donald Trump being jealous of some starving orphan in Africa.

"Your dad could be a pain in the ass sometimes," she continued, "but it was always so obvious he loved you. I wished my folks could be more like him."

"Your parents love you," I protested. "And seeing as you killed my dad, you should maybe just shut up now."

Piper was undeterred. "They don't love me the way your parents love you. I've seen articles about your mom and her crusade to get into the quarantine zone. Neither of my parents would ever dream of doing something like that for me."

I snorted derisively. "Yeah, like it would be so great to have her show up here and get herself killed just like my dad. I'm doing everything I can to *keep* her from coming, and Aleric's little games are making it almost impossible."

"My point is that she cares enough to fight for you, and my parents . . . don't. I know my shrink has told them I should be hospitalized, but they'd rather keep me in prison here than suffer the embarrassment of having a daughter in a mental institution."

"Or maybe they think your shrink is wrong and you're better off at home. Maybe they can't stand the idea of trusting a bunch of strangers to keep you safe."

205

"That's what they say, but I don't believe them. I *have* to get out of here. Please help me. For both our sakes."

"I've got a better idea," I said. *Idea* being a very loose term for what I had. "How about if instead of giving up, we try to win this fight?"

Piper arched an eyebrow at me. "Sounds great. If I can find a way out of this that doesn't involve me ratting you out to the police or becoming a monster again, I'm all for it. What do you have in mind?"

I gave her a sheepish smile, feeling like I'd just pulled a bait and switch. "Um, well, that's the tricky part."

Piper snorted and shook her head at me. "In other words, you don't have an idea, you just wish you did."

"Luke's convinced there has to be some way I can kill Aleric. I figured since you've spent almost as much time with Aleric as I have, you might have some ideas. If Aleric's gone, it's possible the night magic might go with him and the city might go back to normal. And without the night magic nibbling at you, you might start to feel better."

"Do you realize you said 'might' four times?"

I huffed in irritation. "When we're looking for an alternative to you being Nightstruck again and/or me being captured by Aleric and making Philadelphia into Night Maker Central, I think we can live with a few mights."

"What makes you think I know anything more about how to kill Aleric than you do anyway?"

"You were always more attuned to the night magic than I was. You told Luke his idea to drag me out of the square might work. I never would have thought of that myself. At least it never would have occurred to me that it would work."

Piper looked down at her hands and started picking at her

ragged cuticles. "That was just . . . instinct. It's not like I actually knew anything."

"If I wait until I find something I know will work, I'm doomed and so is the city. Is there anything Aleric did or said while you were with him that made you think he had a vulnerability?"

Piper glanced up at me briefly with a hooded expression then quickly looked away again. I suspected her jittery behavior and lack of eye contact meant she had ideas she wasn't sure she was willing to share with me.

"Anything at all," I pressed. "You want a chance to go back to normal, don't you?"

When she met my eyes this time, there was no question it was Mr. Hyde who stared out. "What I want is for you to help me get out of this goddamn prison. It's your fault I'm here in the first place!"

Practically before the last word was out, she clapped her hand over her mouth and her eyes widened and filled with remorse. "I'm so sorry," she said from behind her hand. "Can we just pretend I didn't say that?"

My blood thundered in my ears, and my hands clenched into fists so tight my fingers dug into my palms. I ground my teeth and kept my mouth shut to keep a torrent of angry words from spilling out of me. Maybe if I hadn't felt so guilty about letting the night magic into the city in the first place, her words wouldn't have had so much power to wound.

"I don't know if or how he can be killed," Piper said, "but Aleric definitely has a vulnerability: you."

It was an olive branch, and the only reasonable and productive thing to do was to take it. If only I didn't feel so . . . raw. But with everything that was happening in my life, with all the weight I carried on my shoulders, Piper's condemnation was just too much to bear, and I was shaking with the effort to keep from screaming at her.

"He was completely obsessed with you, Becks," Piper continued, undaunted by my furious silence. "I thought when he lured me out of your house that it was because he saw something in me, because he wanted me, but it was always all about you. I wanted you to come out and join me, but I wouldn't have worked at it so hard if Al hadn't insisted."

I finally found my voice, though it came out sounding tight and angry. "Because he needs me to bring in more Night Makers."

Piper shook her head. "It's more than that. It has to be. I mean, I'm sure it's nice for him to have that little patch of night in the city, but what is he really getting out of it that's such a big deal?"

It was a question I'd never put a moment's thought into. I knew why I had wanted that patch of night, but as far as I could tell, Aleric had little to nothing to gain from it. He usually disappeared in the day even when he didn't have to.

"Maybe it's some kind of territorial thing," I mused, but the idea didn't feel right. "He wants more Night Makers in the city because he wants to conquer the world, and that helps him. Somehow."

"Don't get me wrong: I'm sure he wants to bring more Night Makers into the city, and I'm sure expanding his territory is part of his plan. But he doesn't want it enough to explain how badly he wanted you to be Nightstruck. I think Luke's right and you might be dangerous to him somehow."

"If I'm dangerous to him, why doesn't he just kill me?"

"Maybe he can't. You were the key that let him into our world. Maybe if you died—"

Piper's voice cut off abruptly, and she swallowed hard. I

didn't know why at first, but then I really thought about what she'd just said: Aleric couldn't kill me because I was the key that let him into this world. In other words, she was suggesting that if I was dead, Aleric and the night magic would vanish back to wherever it was they came from.

"So your suggestion is I should kill myself?" I asked coldly. "That's what you've been leading up to?"

I should have known better than to think Mr. Hyde had crawled back into his hiding place, but I'd allowed myself to be lulled out of my anger. What an idiot. I jumped from the bed like there was a spring in my butt, my eyes stinging with tears of rage and hurt. I knew I shouldn't allow her words to hurt me, that she was not the Piper I knew anymore. She was practically a stranger to me, and why should a stranger have the power to hurt me? But knowing it wasn't the same as feeling it.

"I didn't mean it that way," Piper said miserably, but I didn't wait around to hear what else she had to say.

The thought that haunted me as Luke drove us back to that night's hotel was that Piper might be right. Maybe if I were dead, the magic would all go away and no one else would have to die. But as miserable as I had been ever since the night I'd unwittingly opened the first gate, I wasn't suicidal. Maybe if I'd been *sure* my death would banish the magic, I'd have had to put a little more thought into the idea, but even if I bought into Piper's logic, there was no proof of any of it.

I told Luke that nothing useful had come out of our conversation, and as far as I was concerned, that was the truth. I wasn't going to kill myself for the greater good, and I hadn't learned anything important from the conversation. After all, I already knew Aleric was obsessed with me. I was no closer to figuring out what to do about Aleric than I had been before I'd talked to Piper.

I figured I still had at least a couple of days to try to come up with a plan, but it turned out my mom had been working overtime. She called about a half hour after I got back from talking to Piper and dropped a bombshell.

"I've been granted permission to enter the quarantine zone," she told me. Her tone told me she was riding high from the victory—like all lawyers, she really loves winning, especially when the odds are heavily against her. Even if we didn't have the looming threat of Aleric, I wondered how she'd feel about her victory in a few days, when she'd had a chance to experience the nightmare and it finally sank in what she'd done.

I know I've made some pretty scathing remarks about my mom. I always felt like her career was more important to her than her family, and I'd always felt that she loved Beth—the chip off the old block—way more than she loved me. There were about a million reasons I didn't want her to come to Philadelphia, but I had to admit I was both touched and humbled that she'd do it.

For all we knew, Philadelphia was going to be under quarantine forever, which meant that not only was my mom giving up her career to be with me, but she was giving up her ability to see Beth, her golden girl. I'd told myself in the past that her campaign to break through the quarantine to get to me was an act of vanity, that it was all for show. But if that were the case, she wouldn't actually *do* it. And none of that takes into account that Philadelphia was not a pleasant or safe place to live these days. Mom thought she was going to be breathing toxins or viruses or something that was going to make her hallucinate—and she was still coming for me.

"I can't fly into the city," my mom continued, "but I'm going to fly into Newark and rent a car. I should be there at about three."

I think my heart stopped beating for a couple of seconds. "Wait. At three? You can't possibly mean *today*."

Surely not! Surely I'd misunderstood her. I hadn't had nearly enough time to plan for her arrival.

"Yes, today. I don't see any reason to draw this out. Not when you need me."

"But what about Beth? You know you may never see her again if you come here."

Mom's voice got tight, but she didn't sound any less determined. "I'm sure it won't come to that. They can't keep Philadelphia under quarantine forever."

"They're not going to let you bring a rental car into the city," I said in a desperate search for something to make her hesitate, at least take a little time to think it over. (And give me a little more time to figure out how I was going to keep her from becoming my Achilles' heel.) "Rental car places generally want to get their cars back."

I regretted the sarcasm the moment the words were out of my mouth, but my mom didn't seem to mind. "I realize that, honey," she said gently. "I'll leave the car when I get to the quarantine zone, and I've arranged for someone to return it for me. When I'm through, I'll call a taxi. I've rented a room at the Rittenhouse, but I'm hoping that by tomorrow, we can get the house cleaned up enough for us to move back in."

I almost laughed, more out of hysteria than humor. Mom clearly had no concept of what she would be facing when she entered the city, and by the time she got a look at the view from the Rittenhouse Hotel—which overlooks Rittenhouse Square with its now permanent night—it was going to be too late to turn back. Also, if she thought we were going to be able to live in our old house by tomorrow, she had no clue the extent of the damage Aleric's Nightstruck had done. That might mean I'd have a couple of days before I had to face the fight that was coming when I refused to go home. Maybe in a couple of days, I'd come up with an idea for how to make the night magic go away.

"At least wait until tomorrow to come into the quarantine zone," I begged. "If you get here at three, you'll only have a couple of hours before Transition, and if you get delayed . . ."

"I'm going to get there in plenty of time," she assured me in the soothing croon you might use with a frightened child—or a crazy person. "Don't you worry. I'll meet you in the lobby of the Rittenhouse at three o'clock sharp. That's a promise."

"Please, Mom. Don't—"

"I'm coming, and that's final. Now I have to get moving or I'm going to miss my flight."

"At least choose a different hotel! Trust me, you don't want to have to look at Rittenhouse Square all day."

The Rittenhouse was the closest hotel to our house, and therefore the one we were most familiar with. It wasn't at all a surprising choice for my mom to make. It was just the worst possible one. Thanks to the perpetual night in the square, Aleric or one of his minions was bound to see me go in, and then they'd go on the attack as soon as night fell.

"The arrangements are already made," my mom said. She was like a bulldozer, and no puny human being was going to stand in her way. "If the square will give me a preview of what it'll be like at night, then all the better to prepare myself."

"You can 'prepare yourself' when Transition hits."

"I have to go, honey. The taxi just honked. I love you, and I'll see you soon."

She didn't wait for my reply. No doubt she already knew

I would keep arguing if she gave me the chance. Which is why she didn't answer the phone when I tried to call right back. I was tempted to hurl the phone against the wall in frustration, but settled for hurling it onto the bed instead. The impressive bounce off the mattress wasn't anywhere near as satisfying as the spray of plastic shards and spilled innards would have been.

CHAPTER TWENTY

I wish I could be there with you just in case," Dr. Gilliam said as we all packed our bags. She and Luke were going to move to a new hotel, but I hoped the pressure would be off them when I was with my mom. No way it would be safe for them to go home, but with Aleric focused on me, he probably wouldn't go hunting for them, and they could probably afford to stay in the same hotel at least for a few days at a time.

"Don't worry," I said. "I'll be fine, and the hospital needs you more." Not to mention how bad an idea it was to have Dr. Gilliam and my mom in the same room together.

Bob probably sensed the tension in the room. He was practically glued to my side, and I had to be careful not to trip over him as I moved to give the dresser drawers one last inspection. We didn't really unpack when we moved into new hotels, but our stuff did tend to find its way into drawers and odd corners anyway.

"Thanks again for taking Bob," I said as I bumped into him for the thirtieth time. There was no way I was taking Bob anywhere near the square and its endless night. He's eighty pounds of pure muscle, and if he wanted to have it out with some nasty construct in the square, I doubted I would have the strength to hold him back. Even if I did, he would draw way too much un-wanted attention.

Dr. Gilliam had helped Luke and me put together disguises that might fool casual observers, but I doubted they would fool anyone in the square. Most of the Nightstruck in there would be asleep, but the constructs made a habit of patrolling the borders, and I suspected they would recognize me—and report back to Aleric—no matter how thick my disguise.

"If your mom doesn't make it to the hotel by four o'clock," Dr. Gilliam reminded me, "I want you and Luke to get out of there."

I swallowed against an urge to argue. Luke was going to drive me to the hotel, and having his car there meant we could make a speedy getaway if necessary. Sunset wasn't until about a quarter to five, so running away by four seemed a little extreme. We could *walk* to their new hotel and get there before sunset. Still, it was hard to accuse Dr. Gilliam of being overprotective considering the circumstances. If I were her, I probably wouldn't have even allowed Luke to drive me to the square.

"Sure thing," I said, hoping my mom wouldn't make me put that promise to the test. I fully expected her to be late. Even if she got through the quarantine as fast as she thought she would, the city was vastly changed from what she knew. The Nightstruck caused new damage every night, and there weren't enough hours in the day to fix it all. Mom wasn't going to recognize the city she had once called home, and though there were many fewer cars on the road than there used to be, there were also a lot more streets closed due to damage. You couldn't drive straight from point A to point B, so everything would take longer than she expected.

Dr. Gilliam closed her suitcase, and I zipped up my duffel bag.

All that was left to do was get me and Luke into our disguises, and then it would be time to go.

I hugged Dr. Gilliam hard when Luke dropped her off in front of their new hotel, and it took an effort of will to let go. I owed her more than I could possibly repay, and no quantity of thank-yous would ever be enough.

"Take care of yourself, Becket," she said as she picked up her suitcase.

"Sure thing," I promised, but I didn't think parading myself in front of the square—even in disguise—was a great start to keeping that promise.

I gave Bob a good scratch behind the ears. "You guard Dr. Gilliam and Luke with your life," I ordered him. He responded by giving my cheek a lick. I figured I'd better get moving if I didn't want to dissolve into a puddle of tears, so I jumped into the car and tried not to look back.

I felt like there were eyes on me the moment Luke turned the car onto Walnut Street and the square came into view. It was the first time I'd seen the square since Luke had pulled me out of it, and to say it was spooky was an understatement.

It was a bright, sunny day, but the sunlight came to an abrupt end all around the square. Inside, it was so dark you could barely see anything except a few shadows. Especially with the bright sunlight making it impossible for your eyes to adjust. The imposing form of the nighttime iron fence loomed ominously in the darkness, and if you squinted enough, you could just see the shadows of fang-covered benches waiting for unwary prey to take a seat. There was no prey unwary enough to try to sit on one, but sometimes the Nightstruck thought it was fun to throw the benches a treat.

I shivered and crossed my arms over my chest, trying to re-

216

member what it had been like to live inside that darkness, to see people thrown screaming into those fangs and shrug it off.

"I did that," I whispered under my breath.

"Huh?" Luke said.

"Nothing."

But it wasn't nothing. I had brought that permanent darkness to the square, and if Aleric had his way, I would do it again to some other part of the city. I patted the pocket of my jacket, where I'd stashed my dad's backup gun once I'd gotten it back from Luke. My mom would probably freak out if she realized I had it on me, but there was no way I was going near the square without it.

Luke parked his car on the street, just short of the hotel's driveway. In the good old days, he'd never have found a spot on the street unless he got incredibly lucky. Now, his was the only parked car in sight. Hell, the only car in sight *period*. No one who didn't have to would so much as drive by the square, and *this* was where my mother thought we should stay?

I reminded myself for the millionth time that my mom thought we were all hallucinating and that the square was perfectly normal. I wondered if she would still believe that when she saw it in person or if she would just accept it as reality that she was hallucinating as well.

I got out of the car and peered at the darkness across the street. I could see nothing but shadowed shapes, but I felt sure there were eyes watching me. The air seemed to crackle with excitement and anticipation, the evil inside the square licking its chops at the sight of me. I wished I believed my disguise—an itchy wig, dark glasses, and a hoodie—would fool anyone watching. Luke's disguise was even thinner, just a hat pulled low over his ears and a pair of mirrored sunglasses.

"Let's go, Becks," Luke said, placing a gentle hand on my arm and giving it a tug.

I hadn't even noticed that I'd stopped in my tracks and was staring like one entranced. Luke's touch snapped me out of it, but I couldn't help frequently looking over my shoulder as we hurried toward the hotel's front entrance. My lizard brain was sure that if I turned my back, something would leap out of that darkness and run me down.

I expected the hotel to be a total ghost town and was surprised it was even open. However, I'd forgotten just how *nice* a hotel it was, and I'd forgotten about all the out-of-town visitors who'd been trapped in the city when the quarantine hit. If they'd been staying in this lovely hotel before the square went dark, it probably would have become their home away from home, and some of them would have been reluctant to leave.

The lobby was quiet, but not entirely deserted, and the hotel staff hadn't let a little thing like the nightmare outside their doors stop them from putting out stunning floral arrangements that were works of art. There were several people sitting in the comfortable lobby chairs, all of them tapping away at laptops, and all of them positioned so they couldn't see out the front windows toward the square. It was surprisingly easy to do, because the hotel's front was on an angle instead of facing the square head-on.

Not surprisingly, my mom had not yet arrived. She'd already called me once today to let me know that her plane had been delayed, but only for fifteen minutes, and she didn't expect it to make her late. She hadn't called back since then, so I assumed that meant there hadn't been any further delays.

Luke and I sat down in an otherwise empty seating area, facing the front doors. Partially because I wouldn't have been comfortable with the square at my back, but also because it made no sense not to face them when I was waiting for someone. I unzipped my coat, but didn't dare take it off for fear the gun might spill out at some inopportune moment. It wasn't like I had a permit for it or anything, and it probably wouldn't do an attempted murder suspect much good to be caught with an illegal weapon on her person. I was overly hot, but the gun was a comforting weight at my side and made it easier to cope with the creeping sense that there were eyes watching me from the darkness across the street.

"You know they can't see in here during the daytime," Luke said, reading my thoughts. "All they can see is reflections on the glass." He took off his shades and the hat, stuffing them both carelessly into a coat pocket.

"That makes me feel much better," I grumped, but I followed it with a weak smile to let him know I was kidding. I'd have loved to take the stupid wig off, but it wouldn't be as easy to put back on as Luke's hat. I hoped we wouldn't have any need to make a quick getaway, but I'd be more comfortable knowing I could bolt at a moment's notice without blowing my disguise.

I realized with a renewed sinking feeling that I might never see Luke again after today. We were never going to go back to living across from each other, not while Aleric was after me and knew Luke and his mom were important to me. His mom and my mom obviously were not getting along, so it wasn't like we'd be hanging out together. My throat tightened up, and I swallowed hard past a painful lump. Now was not the time to start crying over everything that I'd lost. I *should* be spending this time putting together a strategy to make my mother believe that we were genuinely in danger, not sinking into a pathetic funk.

"I'm going to miss you," Luke said in a whisper so soft I could barely catch the words.

His mind and mine were obviously traveling down the same

rails. If I said something serious and heartfelt, I was sure I would burst into tears, so I fell back on comfortable sarcasm and gave him a sardonic grin. "You mean because I've been such a pleasure to live with?"

Luke's lips thinned, and he shook his head and looked away. Sometimes, humor just isn't the way to go. I wanted to kick myself for the smart-ass remark.

"Sorry," I said on a sigh. "I was afraid I'd start crying if I tried to say it back." Right on cue, my eyes started stinging, and my vision went blurry. I blinked and swallowed and just barely managed to keep the tears at bay.

Luke nodded, still not looking at me. I'd hurt him with my show of indifference. Considering how many times I'd done the same thing since he'd rescued me from the square, it would take more than a quick, glib apology to undo the damage. I was just going to have to risk losing my dignity and having an ugly crying jag in front of him. It wasn't like he hadn't seen worse from me in the past.

I took a deep, shuddering breath. "You're the best person I know," I said, talking fast as if that would help me get the words out before I dissolved. "You didn't give up on me when all logic said you should, and you put your life in danger to save me. I've basically treated you like shit because I was too absorbed with feeling sorry for myself to think about how other people felt, and through it all you've been way nicer to me than I had any right to expect." Tears were leaking from my eyes, spilling down my cheeks, and it was getting harder to form words.

There was more I needed to say. I was sure of it. But Luke put his arms around me, and that was when I lost it completely, sobbing against his shoulder. Funny how much harder it is to keep your emotions contained when you fear you may never see someone again.

"It's okay, Becks," he said quietly as he stroked my hair. "You've been through hell, and I *haven't* been as nice about it as all that. It wasn't fair of me to expect you to just get over it."

His arms squeezed tighter around me, and I felt no urge to complain. He felt solid and warm and real against me, the one constant in my turbulent and chaotic life. I inhaled the scent of him and tried to commit it to memory. There was no reason we couldn't keep seeing each other if we both wanted to, but I couldn't shake the feeling that this was good-bye.

I wanted to assure him that he'd been as nice as humanly possible and that all the responsibility for the tension that had come between us sat squarely on my shoulders, but I couldn't seem to suck in enough air to form words, much less sentences.

Eventually, the tears ran their course, and I started to regain control of my breathing. I could have spoken then, but words seemed an inadequate vehicle to express what I was feeling.

"Cheer up," Luke said. "Maybe your mom won't be able to make it here today and we can do this all again tomorrow."

We both laughed at the joke that clearly wasn't funny. I drew away and wiped my eyes. I pretended I didn't feel the curious stares I was receiving from the few other people in the lobby. A quick glance at my watch told me it was three-thirty. I checked my phone to make sure I hadn't received any messages while I was too busy bawling to notice, but there was nothing.

"If she doesn't get here by four," Luke reminded me, "we're outta here."

I nodded. I sent my mom a quick text, asking her if she had an updated ETA. She texted back that she was running late and would meet me at four-thirty at the latest. I groaned and showed the text to Luke, who shook his head.

"She does know sunset's at quarter till, right?"

"She knows," I said. I texted that I was leaving at four, and we then went through an odd, disjointed negotiation that ended with me agreeing to wait until four-fifteen.

"Will your mom be okay with that?" I asked Luke. After all, it was mostly for *his* safety that she'd insisted we not wait past four.

"It'll be fine," Luke said. "Our hotel's only five minutes away. I'll have no trouble getting in before dark."

I hated that I was compromising Luke's safety yet again, but we both knew my mom was never going to change her mind and come in the morning like a sensible person. If we had to leave before she arrived, I was just going to have to hope the creatures in the square had no idea what my mom looked like and wouldn't realize they had a potential hostage making herself so temptingly available.

CHAPTER TWENTY-ONE

At about a quarter to four, I texted my mom to see if she was still on track to get to the hotel by four-fifteen. There was no response, but I wasn't immediately alarmed. She could be in the middle of something, or maybe she didn't hear the phone. It was no big deal. Or so I tried to tell myself.

I tried again at four o'clock, but still no response. My heart rate sped up, and I couldn't sit still, so I stood up and started pacing in front of the sofa, trying to calm my pulse with some slow, deep breaths. Luke stood up and blocked my path, putting his hands on my shoulders.

"I'm sure there's some innocent explanation," he said, but his eyes said he was worried, too. "Try calling."

I did, but the call went to voice mail. I immediately tried again. And a third time.

"Aleric's got her," I moaned, but Luke shook his head.

"It's daytime," he reminded me. "Aleric can't do anything to her in the daytime."

I wished I could believe that, but I feared the length of Aleric's reach. "He doesn't need to get to her himself," I said. "He just has to force some innocent day person to do what he wants. How hard would it be for him to get a hostage?"

"He'd have to know your mom was coming."

"Piper could have told him."

"Piper didn't know she was coming *today*. No one except you, me, and my mom knew that. So let's not jump to conclusions. Maybe the battery on her phone died."

It was a perfectly logical explanation, but every instinct was screaming at me that something was dreadfully wrong. I glanced at my own phone and saw that it was already ten after four. "She's too careful to let her phone die at a time like this. Something's wrong."

The reckless—and frustrated—part of me wanted to rush out the doors into the square to find Aleric and demand answers. I was 100 percent certain he was behind this, that he had my mom. But as panicked as I felt, I wasn't stupid enough to deliver myself directly into the enemy's arms.

"We have to get out of here," I said, already moving toward the door. "If Aleric has my mom, she'll tell him we're here at the hotel." If he didn't know that already. It was possible the creatures of the square would have recognized me even if I showed up covered head to foot in a gorilla suit.

Luke followed without protest, hastily tugging on his hat and glasses—and grabbing my duffel bag, which I'd completely forgotten about. He was probably still hoping there was an innocent explanation for the sudden radio silence, but he surely wasn't anxious to hang around the hotel any longer than necessary. If he was right and my mom showed up after we left, we could always meet up tomorrow, and I could hope she acted sensible and stayed inside as any sane person would do after dark.

My mind was whirling futilely, trying to come up with a resolution when I didn't even know what the problem was yet. Luke and I hurried to his car, both ready to get the hell out of there.

But Luke cursed when he went around the front of his car to

get to the driver's side. "I have a flat," he told me, staring at his front tire.

I shivered in a chill as I glared across at the square. What were the chances that Luke would just happen to have a flat at a moment like this? I wondered if we'd find a bullet hole if we looked at the tire closely—the Nightstruck didn't use guns as a general rule, but that was mainly because they preferred to perform their mayhem with their bare hands. There were certainly Nightstruck who had guns, and they'd use them in a pinch.

But it was no big deal to have the flat. We could get to Luke's new hotel on foot with time to spare.

Luke gave his tire a swift kick, then came back to the sidewalk. As he approached, we both looked up when a pair of police cars rounded the corner from Walnut Street onto W. Rittenhouse, coming toward us. No lights or sirens, and there was no reason to think those cars had anything to do with us, but a new set of alarm bells started clanging in my head anyway as I thought of another reason my mom might have failed to answer my texts.

I reached over and grabbed Luke's free hand, hoping those cruisers would go ahead and cruise right by, but they pulled in to the driveway in front of the hotel, and moments later the doors opened and revealed several cops—and my mom.

My heart sank like a stone, and I felt like I was going to be sick. My mom hadn't stopped answering my texts because Aleric had her. She'd done it because she was planning to hand me over to the police.

I had no doubt that she thought she was doing it for my own good. If they finally had enough evidence to arrest me—if, say, Piper had fingered me—then she probably thought surrendering was my best option. In her mind, she wasn't so much betraying me as forcing me to make the "right" decision.

225

But damn, it felt like one hell of a betrayal anyway.

It was always possible the police had taken the decision out of her hands, had used threats or intimidation to get her to tell them where I was—and taken her phone away from her to keep her from warning me. But I knew my mother, knew how she thought. She was not one to be intimidated. By anyone. If she was here with the police, it was because she chose to be.

I tugged on Luke's hand, urging him toward Locust Street, which was less than half a block away. Neither the cops nor my mom had noticed us yet—or if they'd noticed us, they hadn't recognized me in my disguise—and the sooner we got out of sight, the better. But before we took a single step, my mom looked over her shoulder at the square. I froze like a rabbit, hoping that if I stood still, she wouldn't notice me.

She was looking at the square, not at me, but I was in her peripheral vision, and I saw her take a quick glance at me. She looked away again, momentarily fooled by the disguise, but then she started, and I knew it was all over.

Luke gave my shoulder a sudden, urgent push. "Run!" he said. "I'll try to slow them down if I can."

I wasn't sure what good running from the police would do, especially when it was so close to Transition and I had nowhere to go. However, if they arrested me, then it was all over, so I took Luke's advice and ran.

I heard my mom calling to me, then the police shouting at me to stop, but I just put my head down and ran harder. I turned right on Locust Street to get out of the cops' sight as fast as possible, and I looked frantically around, hoping to see a likely escape route or hiding place.

There was nothing obvious, and I didn't dare slow down to look more closely. I kept running toward Twentieth Street, figuring my best bet was to turn yet another corner and hope to lose them that way. It was a flimsy hope at best, but at that moment flimsy was better than nothing.

I heard the pounding of shoes on pavement behind me, and once again someone shouted at me to stop. I wondered if that ever worked once a suspect had taken flight. I also heard the screech of tires and cursed. I'd expected them to pursue me on foot only, seeing as Locust was a one-way street and went the wrong way. There wasn't any traffic this close to Transition, but the cops couldn't be sure they wouldn't barrel into an oncoming car the moment they turned that corner.

I ran harder, my legs burning with the strain of my all-out sprint. I probably didn't have a chance of outrunning the guys on foot, much less the car, but I had to keep trying.

The gun in my coat pocket thumped against my hip with every step, and I realized there was one way I could ensure they couldn't take me to jail, where Aleric could get to me. The cops would be reluctant to shoot a seventeen-year-old girl—especially when she was the daughter of the late police commissioner—but if I pulled out that gun, everything would change.

I could draw the gun, turn to face my pursuers, and fire a shot into the pavement, making myself an active shooter. There would be only one action they could take. I remembered Piper's sly suggestion that if I died, Aleric—and the gateway that let the night magic in—would die with me. That might have been complete bullshit, just her Mr. Hyde planting the idea in my head as revenge, but it was also possible she was right. Maybe the one truly heroic thing I could do right now was turn and shoot, commit suicide by cop. If it didn't work, if the night magic retained its iron grip on the city, then at least people wouldn't be any worse off. And there would no longer be any chance Aleric could get to me and convince me to open more gates.

It's the right thing to do, the only *thing to do,* a voice whispered in my head, and I believed it.

I plunged my hand into my coat pocket and wrapped my fingers around the butt of the gun, but I couldn't seem to make myself pull it out. Damn it, I didn't want to die!

The car that was chasing me finally came into my peripheral vision, and I realized I was almost out of time. *Pull the gun, pull the gun, pull the gun,* I ordered myself, but my hand stayed in my pocket as the car drove halfway onto the sidewalk in front of me, barely missing a fire hydrant. and shrieked to a stop.

My first thought was that it wasn't a police car. Police don't drive fire-engine-red BMWs. My next was that I recognized that car.

The passenger-side door sprang open, and I saw Piper leaning over the seat.

"Get in!" she shouted at me.

I didn't have time to think about what I was doing, didn't have time to wonder what the hell Piper was doing here, how she'd gotten out of her house, why she just happened to be driving by the hotel at the exact moment I was running for my life.

I dove into the passenger's seat, and Piper took off without waiting for the door to close. The tires shrieked and squealed in protest, and the scent of burnt rubber filled the air. I clawed for the door, almost falling out of the car when Piper flew over a pothole. I finally got hold of it and yanked it closed just before it hit a post that would probably have torn it off entirely.

Piper was driving like a maniac, foot to the floor, still going the wrong way on Locust. I was bouncing around so much I couldn't even get my seat belt on, but I wasn't about to tell her to slow down.

She blew through the red light at Twentieth, punching her horn as she nearly T-boned another car that had the right of way. If some unsuspecting driver turned onto Locust, we were all going to die, because Piper was going too fast to stop, and the street was narrow and tree-lined so there was no room to swerve.

We reached Twenty-First without a head-on collision. Piper spun the steering wheel and stomped the gas pedal again, making the car fishtail and nearly taking out a fire hydrant. I reached for the grab bar, holding on for dear life as Piper righted the car and started tearing down Twenty-First. Thankfully, we were at least going the right way now.

I glanced over my shoulder and saw no sign of the cops, though I heard sirens in the distance. The cops were probably just now back in their cars after the foot chase and were taking off in pursuit. We weren't out of the woods yet, though I was half convinced Piper was going to get us both killed the way she was driving.

It wasn't exactly a smooth ride, and we were bouncing over potholes and manhole covers so hard my teeth kept clacking together, but at least we were going straight for a moment, and I was able to wrestle my seat belt into position. Piper skidded around another corner, going left despite a red light. I clung to the grab bar and stared at her, finally out of fight-or-flight mode enough to allow rational thought some room.

She looked every bit as bad as she had the last couple of times I'd seen her. Maybe even worse, with those sunken eyes and those bony fingers gripping the wheel. Her hair looked like it hadn't been washed or combed for at least a couple of days, and her clothes were covered with spots and stains.

My heart seized in my chest when the dying light shone through the windshield and I saw the color of those spots and stains. I wanted to reach for my gun, but I couldn't convince my fingers to release their death grip on the grab bar. That was when I noticed the hint of white bandage that peeked out from beneath both of her sleeves.

"Did you try to kill yourself?" I blurted. There were probably a lot more important questions for me to ask at the moment, but I couldn't seem to drag my eyes away from those bandages. I'd known that Piper was in bad shape, but somehow it had never occurred to me that she was *that* bad.

She flicked a quick glance my way as she turned yet another corner. Her speed was dropping as we went, and she was no longer drawing the attention of every pedestrian we passed. We were still going well above the speed limit, but considering how close it was to Transition, that was hardly remarkable. I wondered where we were going. I also wondered if I should be trying like hell to get out of that car. After all, if she'd had time to have her wrists neatly bandaged, then she'd had time to change clothes, too. Instinct told me the blood on those clothes wasn't her own.

"I'm not really sure what I was trying to do," Piper said. "It was somewhere between a genuine attempt and what my shrink would call a 'cry for help.'"

I couldn't figure out what to say to that. The person sitting next to me in this car might as well have been a total stranger. A potentially dangerous one at that.

"I never used to have trouble making up my mind," Piper continued. She glanced over at me, and I nodded in agreement. I felt wary enough of her that I probably would have nodded in just the same way if she'd told me she'd been abducted by aliens. Her mouth lifted in a half grin that told me I was wearing my feelings clearly on my face.

"Don't worry, Becks. I know how crazy I look and sound, so you don't have to worry about offending me."

I looked up at the sky nervously. We were getting way too close to Transition. "Where are we going?"

"There's an empty house I used to like to hang out in when I was Nightstruck. It's as good a place as any to hide for the night. We're almost there."

"If any of Aleric's watchers in the square realize I got in your car, they might guess where we are if it's somewhere you used to hang out."

She raised an eyebrow at me. "You got a better idea? We're kinda short on time here."

I still had 1,001 questions—and about 1,002 reasons not to trust Piper—but I had no idea where else I could go in the short time we had left before Transition. She pulled the car to a rough stop in front of an unremarkable row of houses. I had the brief thought that her red BMW would be way too easy for the police to spot parked openly out in the street, but of course after Transition, the police would be way too busy protecting people from the Nightstruck to look for little ol' me.

I followed Piper up a short flight of stairs and watched the sky anxiously as she unlocked the door. The key was on a rabbit's foot key chain. The rabbit's foot had blood on it, and it looked pretty fresh. I fingered the gun in my pocket.

The door swung open, and Piper stepped inside, beckoning me to follow. I hesitated on the threshold. The sky took on telltale hues of orange and red. I could tell I was facing directly west, because it looked like I could walk down the street straight into that blazing fireball. As the sun disappeared, the Transition began, the forms of the buildings and the familiar features of the city's streets blurring and waving as shadows of people who hadn't been there moments ago began to appear.

There was no time, and there were no other options. I crossed the threshold and pulled the door closed behind me.

CHAPTER TWENTY-TWO

The abandoned house Piper led me into was the polar opposite of the elegant one in which she and her parents lived. I suspected that was the point. It was cozy and homey, all the furniture functional rather than decorative. Whereas Piper's house was pristine, with all things kept in their designated places unless in use, this house was cheerfully chaotic. There was a bicycle in the foyer, a half-finished jigsaw puzzle on the coffee table in the living room, and books with ragged covers and dog-eared pages arrayed on every flat surface. A guitar was propped against one arm of the sofa, and an ornately carved ship's wheel—what on earth was that doing in someone's living room?—against a fluffy armchair.

Piper made herself at home, plunking down on one end of the sofa and lighting a battery-operated Coleman lantern that sat on the nearby end table. "Power and water were shut off by the time I got here," she explained. "Hope you don't need to use the bathroom, because they're pretty gross by now."

I could only imagine. Actually, I had no inclination to imagine.

"So what's the story?" I asked, far too agitated and pumped up on adrenaline to sit down.

"The story?" Piper asked with a pseudo-innocent raise of her brows. It's hard to look even pseudo-innocent when you've got blood splattered on your clothing.

I just stared at her, wondering if I wouldn't be better off taking my chances outside. The only thing I knew and understood about Piper right now was that she wanted to be Nightstruck again, no matter what the cost. That didn't seem like the kind of person who'd be eager to come to my rescue. Not out of the goodness of her heart, at least.

"How come you showed up at the hotel at the exact moment I had to make a speedy getaway?" I tried again. "How come you showed up at all?"

"Remember how I said earlier that I never used to have trouble making up my mind?" She waited for my nod of confirmation. "Well, obviously I mentioned that because these days I *do* have trouble. I can't make a decision without second-guessing it two seconds later."

"What does that have to do with anything?"

Piper leaned back on the couch and crossed her arms over her chest. It looked like a defensive posture, only the way she then propped her feet on the coffee table—heedless of the puzzle pieces she knocked to the floor—looked pretty relaxed.

"I figured you weren't going to help me escape," she said. "Not that I blame you, really, but still. The only way I could see to get out of that room and live again was to give Aleric what he wanted. So I called the police and told them you shot me."

I had pretty much figured that out on my own. There was no other reason they would have suddenly decided to arrest me now, and I'd always known it was a risk.

"But then you changed your mind and decided to become my getaway driver?" That still didn't make any sense. She might have known I was about to be arrested, but that didn't explain how she'd been at the hotel. She couldn't possibly have known where I was. And yet obviously, she had.

"There were a few more steps in between," she said, her nose wrinkling. "I felt really bad about it almost as soon as I hung up the phone, but I figured it was too late. That's when I did this." She held up her arms to display the bandages. "I changed my mind again while I was cutting, so that's why I'm not, like, dead or anything."

"I'm glad you did," I said, surprised to discover I actually meant it. No matter how many mixed feelings I had about Piper, I didn't want her dead.

She cocked her head at me. "Are you?"

I sighed and finally sat down on the couch, though I kept a respectful distance between us and made sure my coat draped in such a way that I could get to the gun if I had to. "Yeah, I am. Though that may change when you finish your story. I don't know how you found me, and I can't think of an innocent explanation." I glanced at the blood on her clothes. "And I don't know how you got out of the house and why you've got blood on you."

"I already explained about the blood," she said, not making any particular effort to mask the fact that she was lying, that the blood was not hers. "As for being at the hotel, well, no, I don't suppose there's an innocent explanation. I'm sure you know Aleric was planning to break you out of jail, but when I called and told him I was free, he came up with an easier plan."

I groaned. "You mean the plan where I stupidly get in the car with you and you take me straight to him?"

"Yeah, well, that was his idea." She grimaced. "Okay, it was my idea, too. But like I said, I change my mind every two-point-five seconds. Once you got in the car . . ." She shrugged and hunched her bony shoulders. "I don't want you to get hurt, and I don't want Aleric to get you. At least I don't most of the time."

I touched the comforting weight of the gun in my pocket. I'd seen no sign that Piper was armed, but I didn't know what she was capable of, what dangerous and unpleasant skills she had picked up when she was Nightstruck. And again, there was the issue of that blood on her clothes. Just the fact that she wouldn't talk about it told me she'd done something terrible.

"So what's to stop you from changing your mind again and handing me over to Aleric?" I asked. I would have pressed her some more about the blood, but I was pretty sure I didn't want to know the answer.

Piper swallowed hard and finally met my gaze with those hollow eyes of hers. "Is that a gun in your pocket, or are you just happy to see me?"

I didn't get it at first. I patted the pocket with the gun. "Yeah, I have a gun, but—"

I cut myself off as I realized she wasn't just talking about me being armed and therefore hard to kidnap.

I guess it shouldn't have shocked me. She'd already admitted to having slit her wrists, after all. But shock me it did, and all I could do was stare at her with my mouth hanging stupidly open. She raised her chin and continued to meet my gaze, her eyes showing fear and despair and anger and hope all at once.

"I didn't mean to imply you should commit suicide the last time we talked," she said. "I *swear* I didn't. But after I said it, I started thinking maybe it was advice for me instead of you."

I tried to remember the Piper of before, that laughing, vivacious girl who always found a way to make a bad situation seem better. I remembered tearful phone calls from the dreadful months when my parents' marriage was imploding before my eyes, calls that invariably ended with me laughing, my heart lighter. I remembered the beauty of which I'd always been just a tad bit jealous, and I remembered her carefree spirit and her love of life.

Today, she looked almost like an extra in some zombie movie, with her dull, listless hair, her corpse-white skin that clung too closely to the contours of her bones, and the bleak expression in her hollowed eyes.

I felt a pang of yearning so strong it brought tears to my eyes. God, how I wanted my best friend back! How I missed the easy camaraderie and the feeling that there was always someone who had my back. I'd known from the moment my dad died that I could never have any of that back again, but when I found out she'd survived the gunshot wound, I'd had hopes that she could become herself again. Even if we couldn't be friends, I would have been comforted by the knowledge that she was out there, that the friend I had once been so close to still existed.

I wanted to believe that she could still come back, that some-how lots of time away from Aleric and the night—and lots of meds and hours with the shrink—could still restore her. But as I looked at her now, that hope was impossible to find.

"The way I see it," she said, "there are two choices. Either you let me live and I eventually change my mind and betray you to Aleric, or you shoot me and put an end to things. I should have died the first time anyway. It would have been easier for every-one involved."

"Easier isn't always better," I countered.

"But this time it is." She sat up a little straighter, her stare be-coming more intense and focused, like she was *willing* me to do what she wanted. "Most of the time, I hate your guts, Becks. Take advantage of this little window where I don't. Put me out of everyone's misery, including my own."

Suddenly, I could see exactly how this was all going to play out. If I didn't do it, if I didn't shoot her, Piper was going to force my hand. She was either going to try to put in a call to Aleric, or she might even attack me, force me to defend myself. If she did either of those, I'd be forced to shoot her.

I'd shot Piper once in a blaze of mindless fury, and it was the act I regretted more than anything else I'd ever done. Even more than I regretted watching Stuart get brutalized and killed before my eyes, since that was something I never would have done if I'd been in my right mind. But shooting Piper had been an act of hatred, and it had put the huge dent in my soul that had finally made me vulnerable to being Nightstruck.

I refused to shoot her again, even in an act of pity. But if I said that out loud, she was going to take the choice away from me. So I lied, slipping my hand into my coat pocket and pulling out the gun.

"Okay. I'll do it."

I pointed the gun at Piper, and she recoiled, her whole body going tense as her eyes went wide. I thought she was going to climb over the arm of the couch to get away from me, but she stopped herself, panting, her hands digging into the cushions like claws. There was a wild mixture of terror and hope on her face.

"Do it," she whispered, then squeezed her eyes shut.

I hadn't yet figured out how I was going to get out of this, so I stalled for time.

"Not here," I said. "I may want to . . . to sleep on this couch."

Piper opened her eyes and looked around. I thought for sure she'd see through me in a heartbeat. Did she really think I was the type of person who'd be putting thought into the potential inconvenience her dead body might cause me? But then she wasn't exactly thinking like a normal human being right then.

"How about the laundry room?" she suggested. Her voice

shook, and her hands hadn't released their death grip on the couch. She watched the barrel of my gun like a rabbit might watch a circling hawk. "Y-you can j-just close the door a-and forget I'm even there."

Oh yeah, *that* was likely to happen. But maybe once I got her into the laundry room, I could figure out some way to lock her in so I wouldn't have to worry about what she'd do if I turned my back.

"All right," I agreed. "Show me where. And move slowly. I'm not a hundred percent convinced this isn't still all some part of an elaborate setup."

Even in her terror, Piper managed to roll her eyes at me. "How can me asking you to kill me possibly be a setup?"

I shrugged one shoulder while making sure to hold the gun perfectly steady. "I don't know, but I've already been set up at least twice today. If it happens again, I'll have to consider that I may be the stupidest person on the planet. So cue the paranoia, and don't make any sudden moves."

"Fine, fine." Annoyance seemed to have dulled some of the fear. I hoped that annoyance wasn't severe enough to make her change her mind and do something drastic.

She rose slowly from the sofa, her hands up. I followed at a cautious distance as she moved toward the hallway.

"Grab the lantern," I ordered. I'd have felt safer if both her hands were empty—the lantern was probably heavy enough to be a dangerous weapon—but we would need the light, and I preferred to keep my two-handed shooting grip.

Piper did as she was told, turning her back on me and leading me down a hallway and into a basement laundry room. I carefully checked out the door as I walked through, hoping there would be a nice, sturdy lock, but of course there wasn't.

The laundry room itself was as chaotic as the rooms above,

with overflowing hampers against one wall and a clothesline draped with sheets and towels crossing from one side to another. Why the former residents dried their sheets on an indoor clothesline when they had a dryer was beyond me.

Piper came to a stop just short of the line of sheets. Still moving slowly, she put the lantern down then stood up and raised her hands again. She kept her back to me, though the rigid tension in her shoulders said it cost her.

"Maybe it'll be easier like this," she said. "If you don't have to look me in the eye. If you don't have to remember what I once was."

I realized with a rush of relief that she had just given me the opening I needed. I sucked in a deep, dramatic breath and moved in closer to her, until the barrel of my gun just brushed the back of her head. She gasped and jerked, but didn't try to get away or tell me she'd changed her mind.

I'd never in my life actually hit anyone—at least not since I was old enough to remember. Certainly I'd never conked anyone on the back of the head with the butt of a gun. I had no idea how hard I had to do it to knock her out—nor did I know how hard I'd have to hit to kill her.

Figuring I was much more likely to hit too soft than too hard, I pulled back my hand and brought it down as hard as I could make myself on the back of Piper's head. The sound of the impact—and Piper's pained groan—made me wince, but she collapsed to the floor in a heap.

Because I was fresh out of trust and innocence, I held the gun at the ready while I bent down to check on her. She appeared to be out cold, but she was breathing. Still operating on suspicion overload, I kept a careful eye on her while I dumped the sheets and towels off the clothesline, then unhooked it and used it to tie Piper's hands behind her back, trying to find the perfect balance between tying them tight enough to hold her and loose enough not to cut off circulation to her hands. I then patted her down and confiscated her phone so that she couldn't call Aleric even if she somehow got her hands free.

She was starting to come to by then. I feared when she reached full consciousness, she was going to be furious with me and that maybe having her hands tied wasn't going to be enough to protect me from her wrath. While she moaned and stirred, I quickly untied her boots and pulled the laces out, using them to secure her ankles. The bindings weren't exactly foolproof, but I hoped they'd be enough to hold her.

CHAPTER TWENTY-THREE

Piper was beyond furious when she woke up, to the point that there was no reasoning with her. She thrashed around so hard I worried she would reopen the wounds on her wrists. She screamed at me incoherently, alternately begging me to kill her and threatening to kill me. I couldn't even begin to calm her, so I did the only thing that made sense: I left her alone in the basement, closed the door, and returned to the living room to try to figure out what to do next.

I wasn't exactly bursting with ideas. With the police after me during the day and Aleric after me during the night, I didn't know where to go. Nor did I know what to do with Piper. I tried calling her house, thinking I could at least let her parents know she was safe—and maybe work out how to get her back to them—but all I got was an answering machine. The sound of that beep made me shiver and wonder again how she'd managed to get out. No one went out at night these days except police and emergency maintenance workers. I'd have expected the Grants to be hovering over their phone.

If they were alive, that is.

I shoved that thought aside. They *had* to be alive. Piper was pretty messed up right now, but she wasn't Nightstruck, so surely she wouldn't have killed her own parents. They were probably out looking for her or staying with family or friends for comfort and support.

Wherever they were, they wouldn't be helping me solve the problem of Piper anytime soon. More than anything, I wanted to get away from her, to put some distance between myself and the threat her mercurial moods posed. And I wanted to get out of the house Aleric probably knew she'd liked to hang out in—if only I could think of somewhere safe to go and some safe way to get there.

I risked peeking out the front window to see if it looked like I could get out of the house without being seen. Unfortunately, the street was lined with parking meters, or at least things that were parking meters during the day. At night they were heads on sticks. The heads looked dead, but I knew from my days of being Nightstruck that they were capable of opening their eyes—and of reporting what they saw to Aleric. I bit my lip and hoped like hell they weren't reporting the presence of Piper's car even now.

I sat back down on the couch—in the dark, because I'd left the lantern downstairs with Piper—and did battle with my own despair. I had never felt so utterly alone in my life, and if I allowed myself to think about what my mom had done, how she'd brought the police with her instead of warning me or protecting me, I'd probably succumb to an epic crying jag. I'm sure in her own mind, she was doing what was best for me, but that did nothing to lessen my sense of betrayal.

Thinking of my mom reminded me that there had likely been interested observers in the square when she and the police had arrived. Aleric and his minions might not have known my mom on sight, but thanks to Piper, they probably knew she was coming. We look enough alike that under the circumstances I had to assume someone in the square would guess her identity. And

242

that meant they knew exactly where she was. The hotel was well-guarded at night, but Aleric could probably muster a freaking platoon of Nightstruck to storm the place. And there was nothing I could do to help her, especially when she refused to believe I was at the center of everything.

I was angry and hurt at what she'd done, but she was the only parent I had left, and I couldn't bear to lose her. I pulled out my phone to warn her even though she wouldn't listen and I doubted she could protect herself anyway. I'd taken the battery out earlier as a precaution, but I seriously doubted I'd have to worry about the cops tracking my signal at this hour. My finger hovered over her name, but my hand seemed to have a will of its own. I didn't want anything bad to happen to her, but the idea of hearing her voice right now, of hearing her justify herself and tell me she'd brought the police for my own good, made my stomach churn.

I decided to call Luke instead. I told myself it was because I wanted to make sure he'd made it to his hotel okay. It had been dangerously close to Transition when the cops had arrived, and it was possible they'd detained him for questioning. But really what I wanted was to hear the familiar and comforting sound of his voice.

The call was answered on the second ring, but not by Luke. My blood turned to pure ice when Aleric's voice said, "Hello, Becket."

I couldn't speak. I could hardly remember how to breathe.

"You've been making things very difficult for me," Aleric said in an incongruously cheerful voice. "I'm rather annoyed with you right now."

My hands started to shake with a combination of rage and

243

fear, and I managed to squeeze a few words out of my throat. "What have you done with Luke?"

"Nothing yet. Well, he's a little banged up from when we grabbed him, but other than that he's in reasonably good shape. Still worth saving."

I put my hand in my pocket and touched the gun like it was some kind of talisman. I wanted to shoot Aleric dead, and I wouldn't feel a bit bad about it afterward. Unfortunately, I'd already established that bullets went right through him, so shooting him dead wasn't an option.

"Let him go," I said, just because the words needed to be said, not because I had any hope he'd do it.

"I'd be happy to. He's really not my type, you know?" He laughed at his own bad imitation of a joke. If he was trying to get under my skin, it was working. "All you have to do is come get him."

It was no surprise what he wanted in return for Luke, and if I thought he might honor an agreement, I'd have given serious thought into turning myself over to him. However . . .

"I know you too well, Aleric," I said. I was pleased to find that my voice came out a whole lot firmer than I felt. My hands were still shaking, but at least I was hiding *some* of my distress. It wasn't much as victories go, but it was all I had. "It's not in your nature to honor agreements."

He laughed. "True enough. Not unless it's to my benefit to do so. But it's not so much *you* I want—if you'll recall, I've already had you, and I regret to inform you that you're not all that."

My face went hot at the reminder, and my stomach twisted uncomfortably. In an intellectual way, I could admit that Luke was right and I wasn't responsible for the decisions I'd made while I was Nightstruck, but it still didn't *feel* that way. The thought of just *touching* Aleric made me feel dirty.

"What I really want," Aleric continued, "is your blood, willingly spilled. It's the 'willingly' part that should give you some reason to believe me. I can hardly expect you to give your blood willingly if I haven't released your boyfriend, now, can I?"

His reasoning made a certain amount of sense, but that didn't mean I trusted it. Not for a second, especially when I knew how loosely "willingly" could be interpreted. What if I handed myself over and Aleric started torturing Luke? I'd do just about anything "willingly" to stop that from happening. But again, I knew Aleric too well. Once he got what he wanted out of me, there would be nothing to stop him from hurting Luke. No, he would probably torture Luke to death right in front of my eyes just to punish me for being difficult.

Handing myself over to Aleric was not going to save Luke, and I was certain he'd find a way to twist my arm into opening another gate. Probably *many* other gates. So obviously handing myself over was out of the question.

The only problem? *Not* turning myself over was just as bad. I couldn't just abandon Luke.

"I know you don't trust my word," Aleric said, "and I don't blame you. But you can have it anyway. I give you my word that if you come to me and open a single new gate for me, I will release your would-be hero unharmed."

Aleric's word meant nothing. We both knew that. But oh how I wanted to believe him, how I wanted to believe it was in my power to save Luke. Just like I'd wanted to believe Aleric when he'd claimed my dad was still alive.

"I guess you've abandoned the thing about how my dad isn't dead and you'll free him if I just do one little thing for you."

I could almost hear his shrug. "I didn't have any real leverage then. This time, I do."

I closed my eyes, frantically searching for another option,

some other way to force Aleric to keep his word. I fingered the gun again, remembering that for whatever reason, Aleric wanted me alive. He said he only wanted me to open a single gate for him, but obviously that was just another one of his lies. He wanted me to keep giving blood until the whole world was covered with gates and condemned to darkness. Maybe if I threatened to shoot myself and could sound like I really meant it . . .

There was a fundamental flaw in that plan, I realized. Shooting myself would mean voluntarily spilling my own blood, and that was exactly what Aleric wanted from me. Maybe he'd rather have me as a renewable resource, but there was too high a chance he would call my bluff. I could threaten to blow my brains out right here inside this house, where the night magic couldn't get to me, but I doubted I could convince him I really meant it.

If only I were some kind of superspy, I could probably use an insta-kill suicide pill that would take me out without spilling my blood. That might make a more convincing threat.

The idea came into my head fully formed, and it resonated somewhere deep inside me. The only way I could force Aleric to keep his word was to make him genuinely fear that I would die without spilling my blood. And I knew how to make that happen.

"Give me proof that Luke is alive," I said, my heart hammering.

The sound became tinny, and I realized Aleric had put me on speaker. "She wants to know that you're alive," he said, presumably to Luke.

I waited for the sound of Luke's voice, but it didn't come. Aleric sighed dramatically.

"Look, sport," he said, "I can give her proof of life by making you scream, but I don't think she would like that very much, and I guarantee *you* wouldn't enjoy it. So just talk so we can move this thing along."

There was another moment of silence, but Luke apparently realized there was no point in suffering just for the hell of it. "I'm alive," he said resignedly. "But don't you dare hand yourself over. He's going to kill me anyway, and—" His voice cut out when Aleric turned the speaker off.

"Don't listen to your white knight," Aleric said. "It's all very tragically heroic of him to tell you not to come, but I guarantee I can make him change his tune if you don't give me what I want."

"I'll give myself up," I said, shivering as I tried not to think too much about what I was saying. "But I'll do it on my own terms."

"And what might those terms be?" he asked, sounding amused.

I sucked in a deep breath to still my shaking. "Meet me tomorrow at five o'clock P.M. on the Market Street Bridge. Bring Luke with you so I can see him and confirm that he's whole."

"Tomorrow?" He didn't sound so amused this time. More annoyed—and puzzled. "You're going to leave your love to my tender mercies all of tonight and all of the day tomorrow?"

I shuddered, but it couldn't be helped. If I set foot outside during the night, his creatures would see me and drag me to him in chains if need be. "I'm not stupid enough to go strolling through the city at night. I'll meet you tomorrow, and I'll get to the bridge during the daytime. I presume you'll have Luke in the square during the day and that the two of you can get to the bridge in about fifteen minutes on foot."

"We can put this off until tomorrow if you want," Aleric said, "but I can't promise your hero will be in quite as good shape tomorrow as he is now."

My hand clenched around the phone. "If you want a willing blood donor, then he'd better be in mint condition. Like I said, we're doing this on my terms, or we're not doing it at all."

"Oh, very well," Aleric said. "We'll do it your way. But I have a condition of my own: bring Piper with you. She and I have a score to settle."

"I don't know where she is," I lied, smoothly I thought. "I made her let me out of the car because I didn't trust her."

"All I can say is you'd better find her. I'll concede to your other terms and keep your boy intact until the meeting, but only if I have your word you will deliver Piper to me."

"Fine. You have my word I will bring Piper to you if it's at all humanly possible."

Of course under the circumstances, my word was about as reliable as his.

"Then I'll look forward to our touching reunion," Aleric said. "Tomorrow night."

I could almost see the unsavory gleam is his evil green eyes.

CHAPTER TWENTY-FOUR

As soon as the dawn Transition hit, I borrowed Piper's car and drove it out to the bridge to plot out my strategy for tonight's meeting with Aleric. I parked on Market Street, then proceeded on foot to the bridge. I leaned against the railing in what I hoped looked like a casual pose, looking down to figure out which way the water was flowing, then staring at the banks downriver in search of someplace I could climb out.

It didn't look super promising. The reinforced banks of the river didn't look too high from where I was standing, but I imagined they'd look pretty damn high if I were in the water. Too high to have a hope of climbing. The only likely spot downriver was a small pier that jutted into the river and had a couple of boats tethered to it. If I could get to the boats, I might be able to climb out.

Assuming I survived falling off the bridge and swimming in icy water for that long. I'm a pretty good swimmer, but that pier was a long way away, and I had no idea how hard the current was going to be. And of course assuming the pier didn't turn into something monstrous at night that would kill me instead of affording me a nice, safe exit.

Still, it wasn't impossible to imagine I could make it there and pull myself out of the water. I would have to park Piper's car somewhere close by, which would be kind of tricky given the lack of parking lots or public roads in the area, but no one was going to tow a car for a parking violation that close to Transition, so if I made it out of the water, I'd have a getaway vehicle handy.

Whether I had a reasonable chance of making a safe getaway driving a highly conspicuous car through the city streets at night was another question. Wherever I went for shelter, Aleric's constructs would surely see me and let him know my location. So wherever it was, it would have to be able to withstand an onslaught of Nightstruck and constructs until morning Transition.

After a thorough scouting mission that lasted till almost noon, I picked up some Chinese takeout and brought it back to our borrowed house. Piper was still bound up tightly in the basement, and when I offered to feed her the orange beef I'd bought just for her, Mr. Hyde glared at me so fiercely I felt it like a physical blow and jerked back.

Piper blinked the expression away and replaced it with a pleading look that hurt almost as much. "Please, Becket," she said. "You can't just leave me tied up in this basement forever. Either kill me, or set me free."

I snorted and stabbed at my cashew chicken with my chopsticks. "No freaking way."

"Then what are you going to do with me?"

That was a good question. Aleric had demanded I bring Piper to our meeting, but even if my conscience could have handled handing over another human being—one who still mattered to me despite everything, and who in her own half-assed way had saved me last night—the logistics were impossible. Piper might want to die, but not by Aleric's cruel hands. I had to be on the bridge before Transition hit, and there was no way I could get Piper there by force without well-meaning passersby interfering.

"Where did you go all morning?" she asked when she realized I was not about to answer her first question.

I hadn't yet told her about my talk with Aleric, and I didn't expect her to be especially helpful, but if nothing else, perhaps talking about my plan out loud would help me spot any glaring flaws I had missed.

The look of incredulity on her face when I told her what I had in mind was . . . disconcerting. When a person who admitted she probably should have been institutionalized looks at you like you're the one who's crazy, it's hard to maintain an aura of confidence.

"You're going to get yourself and Luke killed," was her oh-so-helpful feedback when I'd finished. Just what I needed to hear when my confidence was at an all-time low.

"I'm open to suggestions," I snapped. "Have you figured out any way I can hurt Aleric short of killing myself?"

"I told you I didn't mean that," she snapped back. "I don't want you to kill yourself, and that's what it sounds like you're planning to do."

I guess I hadn't managed to make my escape plan sound terribly plausible when I'd explained it to her. But at some point, any plan was better than no plan. And there was no way I was letting Aleric keep Luke.

"If you come up with anything constructive to say," I told Piper, "give me a holler. Otherwise, keep your opinions to yourself."

I stormed out of the basement as Piper went into full Mr. Hyde mode and started ranting and screaming at me. Most of what she said made little to no sense, although somewhere in there she did wonder what would happen to her if I left her tied up in the basement while I went out to get myself killed.

My faith in my ability to escape the situation I was about to put myself in wasn't exactly at an all-time high, but I didn't think it was as improbable as Piper made it sound. Sure, it would be hard, and there were a lot of things that could go wrong. But there was still a chance it could succeed. If I managed to get back to this house in one piece, I could barricade myself in the basement, call for help, and hope enough police would come to chase off whatever Nightstruck and constructs Aleric sent after me.

My odds might not be all that high, but I figured *Luke* would stand a much better chance of surviving, and if I got him away from Aleric, that would make tonight's adventure at least a partial win. No matter what else happened afterward.

For all Piper's foaming at the mouth, she had raised a legitimate question when she'd asked what would happen to her if I got killed. I hoped like hell that wouldn't happen, but as the endless—and yet simultaneously way-too-short—afternoon dragged on, I decided the only decent thing to do was to make a contingency plan.

As I walked from my illegal parking place near the pier to the Market Street Bridge, I put the battery back in my phone and composed a text to Sam, letting him know where Piper was and asking him to get her back to her parents—or to an institution, if that was truly where she belonged. I waited until I reached the bridge to send it, then took out the battery again. There was nothing to do now but wait.

There were only about ten minutes left until sunset when I got to the middle of the bridge, so there was barely anyone in sight. Thirtieth Street Station, which in the old days would have been bustling at this hour, was quiet and deserted on the other side of the river. Those few people I saw were either driving at warp speed or moving at a brisk pace just short of a sprint, hurrying to get indoors before things went to hell. A couple of people gave me worried glances as they raced past, but luckily no one tried to drag me to safety.

I crept to the stone railing on the side of the bridge and peeked over. The water seemed a very long way down, but not far enough down for the fall to kill me. I realized that if it were high enough to kill me, there'd probably be safety fences around the edges to prevent jumpers.

No, if I was going to die here tonight, it was most likely going to be from drowning or hypothermia. Piper's cheerful red car looked depressingly far away, and I wondered if my heavy winter coat was going to drag me down to a watery grave.

At about five minutes before Transition, the street around me was completely empty, no cars or pedestrians anywhere in sight. It was like I had entered a ghost town or was the star of some bleak post-apocalyptic movie. Shaking a little with cold and fear, I climbed up onto the stone railing, which was easily wide enough to stand on.

A gust of cold wind hit me, and I almost lost my balance and went plunging into the water too early. Adrenaline spiked in my system, my heart leaping into my throat. It was really hard not to climb right back down to safety. I hoped that when the time came, I'd have the courage to do what I had to do.

The sun kept sinking lower and lower on the horizon. I took out my gun, hoping I'd be able to discourage any of Aleric's entourage of Nightstruck from making an immediate grab for me.

I looked down at the railing beneath my feet and had another burst of adrenaline as I recognized a potential pitfall that

I hadn't even considered: what was this railing going to be after Transition hit? It likely wasn't going to be just a plain stone railing. But it was far too late to change the plan now, so I had to hope it would remain something I could stand on—and wouldn't turn into something that would eat me.

Transition began, and I watched the familiar city morph before my eyes into something strange and terrible. A few feet to my right on a raised section of the railing was a large, treelike lamp with several globes that would be lit at night. As I watched, those globes sprouted wicked metal spikes. The sconces they were sitting on changed into rusty chains, and the spiked balls dropped downward with a loud metallic clank that made me jump and almost lose my footing for the second time.

On the sidewalk across from me sat an ordinary metal trash can, which opened like a giant mouth and sprouted teeth. It kept expanding outward until its outside edges hit the pavement, at which point the teeth pressed flat. When full dark hit, it would be barely visible, but I knew those teeth would snap shut like a bear trap if anyone should accidentally set foot on it.

Beneath my feet, the stone railing rippled and shuddered. I held my arms out to both sides to keep my balance as the stone narrowed until it was barely wide enough to stand on. Ridges and curves formed, and the gray stone turned yellowish ivory. When it stopped changing, I saw that I was standing on a pair of impossibly large vertebrae and that the entire railing had turned into a long, curving spine.

I readjusted my stance, trying to find a steady balance on the uneven surface. The wind kicked up again, tugging at the ends of my coat and adding an extra degree of difficulty. It wasn't exactly a secure and comfortable position, but it could have been a lot worse. I hoped I hadn't made any other bad assumptions that were going to come back and bite me.

The Nightstruck seemed to appear out of thin air, blinking and looking momentarily confused. I remembered what it felt like to be in their shoes. They didn't remember how they'd gotten there, nor did they necessarily know where they were. Their last memory would be of whatever they'd been doing right before dawn. It was disorienting, but it's amazing what you get used to.

There were three of them on the bridge, two guys and a girl, all of whom focused on me the moment they got their bearings. I raised my gun, trying not to disturb my balance, and shouted, "None of you come any closer."

The guys both raised their hands in gestures of surrender, but the girl—woman, actually, now that I got a better look at her and realized that despite her classic teenage Goth gear, she was probably pushing fifty—looked shifty-eyed in a way that made me instantly watchful. I aimed my gun directly at the center of her chest and tried again.

"Aleric is coming for me," I said, and was proud of myself for not shivering or shuddering at the thought. "He won't be happy with you if anything happens to me before he gets here."

The woman considered my words for a moment, then shrugged. Her expression as she watched me wasn't what I'd call wholesome, but at least she no longer looked like she was contemplating eating me for breakfast.

"Fine. Let's wait for Al." She laughed. "This is going to be fun."

She and her two friends fanned out, presumably blocking off my escape routes in case I decided I'd rather cut and run. I fervently wished running away were one of my options. I lowered the gun, because there was only so long I could hold it up before my arms started getting tired, and because it was easier to balance if I wasn't trying to aim at someone, but I didn't put it away.

It would take a few minutes for Aleric and Luke to get to the bridge from the square, and the Nightstruck quickly grew bored with just standing there watching me. The two men decided it would be fun to have an explicit and inventively detailed discussion about what they would do to me when Aleric was through with me. I tried not to listen, I really did, but not listening is not the same as not hearing.

I glanced at the water below and reminded myself I had a very different endgame planned. It shows how ugly my situation had become that the thought of throwing myself off the bridge into freezing water was comforting.

A couple more Nightstruck wandered onto the bridge, then a few more after that, trickling in by ones and twos, until I had a substantial crowd gathered around my location. They entertained themselves by trying to make me flinch, each newcomer being challenged to describe their horrifying plans for me. I was pleasantly surprised that after a few minutes, their words started bouncing off me with little effect, to the point where when yet another Nightstruck man joined the group and opened his mouth to start, I rolled my eyes and said, "Yeah, yeah, rape, torture, horrible death. Got it."

He was completely dumbstruck by my blasé response, and I laughed at the look on his face. It wasn't that I wasn't scared anymore—I was terrified. But there was a certain ease that came with knowing it would all be over soon, one way or the other. As dusk turned to dark, I came to the conclusion that I was now more or less at peace with the prospect of my own death, and for the first time, I understood why Piper was so desperate for me to kill her.

Guilt and grief and terror are utterly exhausting to live with, and I was more than eager to shrug those burdens off my shoulders. I still had every intention of fighting for my life, but losing that fight no longer seemed like the worst thing that could possibly happen.

It was almost full dark by the time Aleric arrived. I wasn't a bit surprised to find that he'd brought not just an entourage, but a veritable army of Nightstruck, as well as both Billy and Leo. Luke was sitting backward on Leo's back, the snakes of Leo's mane wrapped around his arms and neck, holding him trapped. It was too dark to make out many details, but I was pretty sure there were bruises on his face. He was not the sort to let himself be taken peacefully.

I cried out his name when I saw him. Leo had him too wrapped up to allow much movement, but he tilted his head in my direction, and our eyes met.

"I'm okay," he yelled at me, his voice hoarse, but the look in his eyes said that was a lie. "Please don't—"

His voice cut out and his back arched as the snake around his throat tightened its grip and Aleric sneered at him.

"You don't have a speaking role in this little drama," Aleric said, putting himself between me and Luke. He looked me up and down with a proprietary eye. Several of the men who'd been so enthusiastically discussing my rape and torture shifted uncomfortably, like they hadn't considered that Aleric might consider me his property and were worried that he'd take offense at what they'd said.

"I've abided by your terms," he said, cocking his head at me. "Just what is it you hoped to accomplish by having me meet you here?"

Aleric had many faults, but stupidity wasn't one of them. I was certain he'd taken one look at the situation and instantly realized what I had in mind. Hell, he probably figured that out last night when I named a bridge as our rendezvous point.

I'd had plenty of time to think about exactly how I wanted to do this, how I could create the best chance to keep Luke alive. Even so, it took a few long, uncomfortable moments before I could unstick my tongue from the roof of my mouth to speak. Leo's mane of snakes hissed and writhed, and occasionally one would snap its fangs millimeters from Luke's face. The scorpion tail coiled and loosened, a pearl of venom forming on its tip.

I tore my eyes away from Luke with an effort and tried to sound like I was in full control of the situation.

"Let him go," I ordered Aleric. My voice shook, and I told myself it was just with cold. I willed Aleric to draw the same conclusion, to somehow overlook the terror I was certain showed in my eyes.

I'd had a long speech prepared in my mind, but the words fled now that I needed them.

Aleric smiled at me with a look in his eyes that said he was curious to see what I looked like without my skin. "Now why would I want to do a silly thing like that?" he inquired, rubbing his chin in a mockery of a meditative gesture. "Leo seems to have grown rather fond of his new toy."

Leo made a sound like he was gargling with rocks and nails, the rumble so low it made my bones and teeth vibrate.

"You can either let Leo have his toy," I said, "or you can have me. You can't have both."

He laughed. "I can have anything I want, foolish child. You could have, too, if only you'd been willing to take it."

I gestured toward the dark water waiting below without taking my eyes off of Aleric. "If you let Luke go, I'll come quietly and open one and only one gate for you. If you don't, I'm jumping and you'll never have me."

Luke tried to say something, but a snake strangled the words before more than a blurt of sound came out.

"Come now," Aleric cajoled, "you don't expect me to believe you're willing to die for some teenage Romeo, do you?"

Out of the corner of my eye, I saw one of the Nightstruck edging closer to me. I whirled and turned my gun on him. "Not another step. I will shoot you."

I held my breath, because I knew Aleric didn't give a damn whether his Nightstruck lived or died. If he ordered them to grab me, they would, regardless of my threat, and I would have no choice but to jump to avoid being captured. If I had to die, it would be a lot easier to swallow if I knew my death would save Luke's life.

To my relief, Aleric waved his minion off. I purposely let myself wobble and was gratified to see the flash of alarm in Aleric's eyes. He was trying to play it cool, but he didn't much like having me standing on that ledge. I told myself that was a good and hopeful sign. I needed him to care enough not to call my bluff.

"Luke risked his life to save me," I said to Aleric. "It seems only fair I should do the same for him."

Aleric's mouth twisted into an ugly sneer. "He didn't save you. He made you once again a victim to pain and grief when you had finally shrugged them off. By all rights, you should hate him, just as Piper hates you." The sneer turned into a mock frown. "Speaking of Piper, I remember giving you very clear instructions to bring her with you this evening, but I don't see her anywhere. Perhaps you're not so eager to save Romeo after all."

"I told you last night I don't know where she is. I don't care if you believe me or not. It's the truth."

"I can make you care."

"And I can go for a swim."

Neither patience nor subtlety was among Aleric's strong

suits, and though he was trying to project an image of confidence and nonchalance, his expressions were growing ever more brittle, his tone developing sharp edges.

"Touché," he said with what I'm sure was supposed to be a jaunty smile. It looked more like a snarl.

"Here's what you're going to do if you don't want me to jump," I said. "You're going to let Luke go and make sure he gets back to his hotel safely. When he's in his room with his mom—just the two of them—he's going to give me a call. When I can see on FaceTime that he and his mom are both safe and alone, I'll toss the gun and come down."

He raised his eyebrows. "And I'm supposed to believe you'll just come quietly and open a gate for me?"

"Yes." I glanced down at the water for the millionth time. "I'm willing to die if I have to. But I'd really rather not." I hoped Aleric couldn't see Piper's car sitting there in the distance waiting for me. If only the damn thing weren't so . . . red. If he had any inkling what I was planning, all he'd have to do was send someone to hang out by my car, and my escape route would be history.

The Nightstruck were looking back and forth between the two of us as we spoke, fascinated spectators at a verbal tennis match. I kept careful watch on them out of my peripheral vision, trying to ensure that no one could sneak up on me. Cold wind bit my cheeks and numbed my hands until I could barely feel the gun I held. There was a long, tense silence, and then Aleric heaved a sigh.

"You know, I'm actually interested to see what you're going to do," he said. "I don't believe you're going to come quietly, but I also don't believe you're going to martyr yourself for the greater good. You are not so unselfish as you'd like to believe."

I have to admit that that stung, no matter how unreliable the source, or how supremely unqualified he was to judge. Maybe it was because I doubted my own ability to follow through with my plan. There was a very real possibility that I was going to die if I jumped off that bridge, escape plan or not. I was telling the truth when I said I didn't want to die, but I knew that if it came down to a choice of dying or letting Aleric use me to let the Night Makers take over our world, there was only one right thing to do. I believed I was a good person, but was I that good? Was I as good as my dad, who had been badly outnumbered by the Nightstruck and yet had left the safety of our house to try to save a helpless victim? He'd paid for that bravery with his life, but I'd seen from the grimness in his eyes when he headed for the door that he'd known exactly what he was risking. He'd been willing to give his life in the effort to save one anonymous stranger. How could I hesitate to give my own when so many more lives were at stake?

I knew that Aleric wasn't trying to get under my skin, that he really believed I couldn't do the right thing when push came to shove, because he suddenly turned to Leo and said, "Put him down."

Leo made an unhappy sound, but when Aleric narrowed his eyes, the snakes in his mane uncoiled from Luke's arms and throat. Barely conscious, he slid off Leo's back and collapsed onto the pavement, sucking in great lungfuls of air. I winced and resisted the urge to rub my own throat in sympathy. The snakes hissed at him, and the giant scorpion tail twitched menacingly.

Aleric pointed to a couple of his Nightstruck. "You and you, help him get back to his hotel. Let no one else near him."

I hoped Dr. Gilliam hadn't changed hotels again, but she and Luke hadn't been planning to, and I doubted she would change her mind when Luke was missing.

"If for some reason Luke's mom isn't at the hotel," I said, "you have to call to find out where she is. I'm not doing anything until I know they're both safe."

"Understood," Aleric agreed.

The two guys Aleric selected moved forward, each grabbing one of Luke's arms and hauling him up to his feet. Still struggling for breath, Luke raised his head until our eyes met.

"Don't do it," Luke said, but his voice came out so choked and soft I could only make out what he said by reading his lips. He tried in vain to shake free of the two bruisers. I could see the anguished expression on his face in the moonlight, but he couldn't seem to find his voice. I hoped the snakes hadn't crushed his vocal cords or otherwise done permanent damage to his throat.

I couldn't be sure if he was telling me not to open a gate or not to throw myself off the bridge. Maybe both, though I hoped he knew me better than to think I was actually planning to do what Aleric wanted. I might doubt my ability to make the leap when the time came, but it was certainly what I *intended* to do.

I couldn't afford to stare longingly after Luke as Aleric's minions dragged him away, so I quickly averted my gaze and made sure everyone else was still where I left them.

It looked like Aleric was serious. He was going to call my bluff. Let Luke go, and then see if I would actually jump. He was that sure I wasn't going to do it. I only wished I were equally sure that I would.

Time passed in excruciatingly slow motion as I balanced precariously on that bony spine and waited for the call from Luke to tell me he was all right. I reasoned that it would be infinitely easier to make the jump if I could do it knowing I had saved him, that my sacrifice meant something. But the minutes ticked on and on and on, and my phone was silent.

There was only so long I could menace the gathered Nightstruck with my gun, and I was eventually forced to drop my arm to my side to relieve my screaming muscles. The movement sparked unsavory glints in many of the Nightstruck's eyes, but when one had the temerity to take a step toward me, Aleric stopped him with a barked command before I could get the gun back up.

"I intend to keep my bargain," he said with what was supposed to be a gallant smile. I ignored him, but the Nightstruck obeyed unquestioningly. They continued to watch me like starving wolves would watch a sheep, but they held their places.

Never in my life had time moved so slowly. I checked the time on my phone when I felt that at least ten or fifteen minutes had gone by to find that it was only five. I shivered with cold, though inside my coat I was drenched in sweat.

How long would it take Luke to get to the hotel? It was between this bridge and the square, so it should take less time to get there than it had to get here. Since Aleric and company had made it here about fifteen minutes after sunset, I figured the Nightstruck should get Luke to the hotel in about ten. There might be some issues getting security to open the doors at night, but Luke's eyes weren't Nightstruck green, so they would eventually let him in as long as his escorts kept their distance.

The ten-minute mark passed, and the fifteen-minute one followed suit, with still no phone call. I'd thought Aleric was letting Luke go in a show of supreme arrogance, but maybe I'd been wrong. Maybe he was just delighting in giving me false hope.

When a full thirty minutes had passed with no word, my gun hand rose of its own accord. My eyes were too dry from the biting wind to conjure any tears, but grief threatened to consume me as my hopes slowly died.

Aleric held his hands up and gave me innocent eyes. "Your boyfriend is a wannabe hero," he said. "I'll wager he's decided not to call to make sure you have no motivation to cooperate with me."

"I don't believe you," I said as I aimed my gun more or less at his head. It would have been hard to get a good aim on a barn door when my hands were shaking so hard. I wouldn't put it past Luke to stay silent for just that reason, but it seemed much more likely the Nightstruck had done no more than take him out of sight. I didn't think he was dead—Aleric would have too much fun using him to torment me—but he might as well be.

I had failed. I squeezed off a couple of wild shots, mostly for the purpose of causing confusion. I already knew the bullets couldn't harm Aleric, even if my aim were steady enough to hit him. The Nightstruck started yelling, and one of them went down in a spray of blood. Aleric stood there in the center of it all, smirking and unaffected.

I wished I could have done more. My hopes that I could swim to the car and drive to safety felt so far-fetched as to be almost ridiculous, and I was suddenly sure that if I jumped off that bridge, it would be to my death. I wished I could have saved Luke and that I didn't have to leave my city in the grips of the night magic. But I was out of options.

When push came to shove, it was surprisingly easy to take that first fatal step off the bridge.

CHAPTER TWENTY-FIVE

Stepping off the railing into empty air might have been surprisingly easy, but my body told me in no uncertain terms that it was not into this whole heroic sacrifice thing I had going on. Despite my willingness and determination, my arms started windmilling the instant I began to fall. The gun went flying from my hand as my fingers scrabbled at the air, frantically grabbing for a purchase that wasn't there.

A scream tore from my throat as I looked up at the rapidly receding bridge, and my body refused to give up the futile struggle, arms and legs flailing away without any hint of conscious control.

In the faint glow of the city lights, I saw a dark blot moving rapidly toward me through the air. At first I thought Aleric had sent someone jumping after me to try to rescue me, and I vowed to fight that person tooth and claw before I'd let him drag me to shore. Then I realized it was much too big to be a person, and that it wasn't falling—it was flying.

During the day, there's a stone eagle perched at each end of the railing. Long ago, when the magic got its first roots dug into the soil of Philadelphia, I had noticed one of those eagles changing slightly after sunset, though at the time I'd thought I was imagining things.

When the sun had set tonight, I'd been too busy trying to keep my balance on the shifting railing to notice how the eagles had changed, but I got an unfortunate look at the one that was swooping toward me and belatedly noticed the other three all hovering over the water under the bridge. While I'd been waiting around for Luke's call, Aleric had somehow signaled his creatures to lurk out of sight until they were needed.

It was too dark to make out any details of the eagle that was coming for me, but I could see metal spikes along the edges of its feathers, and I could see the scythe-like blades where talons should have been as it reached for me. I lifted my arm in a vain attempt to fend the creature off. And that's when I hit the water.

I knew it was water, of course, but it felt more like I had smashed into a slab of concrete. Thanks to all my frantic flailing, I took the brunt of the landing on my backside, quickly followed by my back, head, and legs. All the air was forced out of my lungs, and the pain whited out my mind for an instant. The bridge might not be high enough for a fatal fall, but it was still too high for anything like a safe jump.

The nonexistent concrete slab cracked on impact, and I was soon introduced to a whole new level of pain as the ice-cold water closed over me.

It felt like I sank about a mile deep, my lungs already empty of air from the force of the impact. My body's primal instincts demanded that I fight for life, just as they had while I was falling. I opened my eyes in the freezing water and could see nothing, not even a hint of light from where the surface had to be.

I thrashed with my arms and kicked with my legs, clawing in a direction I hoped was upward. It was hard to kick with my pants and shoes weighing me down, and even harder to move my arms thanks to the heavy coat. I kept fighting anyway, my lungs burning, my chest aching as the cold stabbed through my flesh.

It hurt. Oh God, how it hurt.

I kept fighting, though my fingers and toes and ears were already going numb and the cold tried to lock my muscles in place.

It wasn't fair that this was happening to me. I was carrying a shitload of guilt on my shoulders, blaming myself—even hating myself sometimes—for letting this magic into our world. But as Luke had pointed out more than once, I hadn't done anything wrong. I didn't deserve to die!

I tried to use this realization to motivate myself, to fuel my desperate struggle for life, but I was so, so cold, and it was getting harder and harder to fight my body's reflexive effort to breathe.

I discovered my hands weren't completely numb yet when I felt the tips of my fingers break the surface to be met with an icy breeze. Only a few more inches, and I would be able to get some precious, life-giving air into my lungs. I'd been crazy to think I could swim to shore in this paralyzing cold, with the weight of my soaked clothes and coat dragging me down, but I couldn't just give up and die.

Hold on, I willed my aching lungs. *Just a few more inches.*

But the need to breathe was too overwhelming, and no matter how hard I willed myself to hold my breath, I drew ice water into my lungs milliseconds before my head broke the surface.

Little known fact: it's hard to cough water out of your lungs when you don't have any air in them. My body tried to cough and inhale simultaneously, accomplishing neither. I knew my head was above the surface, because I could see little bits of light here and there, but the lack of oxygen meant that there were black spots all over my vision. My sodden coat dragged at me, an anchor determined to reach the river bottom.

I couldn't breathe, I couldn't see, and the cold had mostly paralyzed my limbs. I could only pray I would soon lose consciousness so I could complete the process of dying without having to suffer anymore.

I gave in to the pull, too tired to fight anymore, secure in the knowledge that it would be over soon.

I felt my body start to sink and was almost grateful. But it turned out it wasn't going to be that easy after all.

Something hard and sharp scraped along the skin of my back, and if I hadn't been wearing such a thick coat, I would surely have bleeding gouges from the contact. Instead of dragging me downward, the coat now dragged me up, the fabric digging in under my arms, the collar half-strangling me. My whole body seemed to convulse, spewing out a stream of water, and then the coughing took me.

As I fought to breathe, I felt myself being lifted out of the water, buffeted by great gusts of air. I couldn't see a thing, but as I continued to rise and my coat continued to dig into me, I realized one of the eagles had me, its talons buried deep in the fabric of my coat.

A few minutes ago, I'd lamented my fate and determined that I didn't deserve to die. However, I deserved the fate Aleric had in mind for me even less. Perhaps once I was Nightstruck again, I wouldn't feel bad about my role in bringing darkness to the whole world one gate at a time, but I couldn't just let that happen. It was remotely possible that I'd be able to resist the pull of the night and remain my normal self at dawn, but I couldn't trust myself—and knew how awful Aleric's wrath would be if I did manage to resist.

I started clawing at the front of my coat, trying to yank down the zipper and free myself. The eagle might well set its talons into my flesh if I wriggled out of the coat, but in the state I was in I doubted I'd stay on the surface of the water long enough for it to get a grip.

Do stone eagles swim?

I'd deal with that possibility later. The problem was, my fingers were like icicles attached to numb hands, and the coat was pulling against my arms so hard I could barely move them. I couldn't even find the zipper, much less grasp it.

Soon, it was too late. The eagle released me from its talons, and I dropped in a sopping heap onto the pavement of the Market Street Bridge, right at Aleric's feet.

At first, I could do nothing but crouch on the pavement, coughing, gagging, and shivering. My sodden clothes and coat clung to me, and water dripped and ran on the pavement. My throat was raw from coughing, and my lungs ached as if I hadn't breathed for a week. Fingers of cold burrowed into my flesh, stealing the life and energy from my muscles and bones.

Never in my plans for this confrontation had I considered the possibility that Aleric might send a stone eagle to pluck me from the water and plunk me right back down at his feet. I was supposed to escape or die, not still be stuck in the middle of the nightmare.

With a choked scream of rage that tore at my raw throat, I surged to my feet and tried to throw myself toward the edge of the bridge, hoping to topple over the railing before anyone realized I was able-bodied enough to manage it.

Two problems with my plan. One, I *wasn't* able-bodied enough to manage it. And two, the eagle was perched on the railing right behind me.

I lurched forward with all the grace and athleticism of Frankenstein's monster, tripping over my own feet. I grasped at the railing, even though the eagle was blocking my way. Behind me, I heard Aleric and some of his Nightstruck laughing at my efforts, but what did I care if they found me amusing?

I stumbled to my knees, then propelled myself up and forward once more, heading straight toward the eagle. It made a hideous screeching sound and spread its stone wings, making a solid, spiky wall between me and the questionable safety of the water.

There was no way I was getting by the damn thing, but I kept blundering toward the edge anyway. Better to go down swinging than to curl up in the fetal position at Aleric's feet, which was the only other option I could imagine.

The eagle screeched again, and it might have been my imagination, but it sounded surprised. I guess it hadn't considered the possibility that I wouldn't back down. Its heavy wings flapped once as it hopped awkwardly into the air and slightly backward, as if trying to get away from me.

I had neither the time nor the inclination to ponder the eagle's puzzling behavior. Besides, I had too much forward momentum to stop myself and think.

There was maybe about a foot's worth of space between the eagle's talons and the spiny railing. If I were an acrobat, I might have been able to jump into a nimble dive right through that space, but I was not an acrobat, and instead I collided with the railing, and my flailing hand raked down the length of one of the eagle's wings.

I cried out in pain as blood immediately flooded my palm, dripping down my forearm. I jerked backward and fell on my butt, staring up at the eagle, which had come to rest on the railing once more and was now making a high-pitched keening sound that threatened to shatter my eardrums.

The eagle stood there on the spine-shaped railing, its wings still outspread, and I could see the bright splashes of my blood on the spikes that had slashed my hand. Then the wings started folding closed, the spikes smoothing out and the wicked talons shrinking.

My jaw dropped open with amazement as I watched the nightmare eagle slowly transform back into its daytime counterpart: smaller, with folded wings and a body made of inanimate stone, no spark of life in its beady eyes. I could still see spots of my blood on its left wing.

My hand was still bleeding pretty heavily, a pool of blood gathering on my palm. The wound throbbed, and the sight of my own blood—especially in that quantity—made my stomach churn. But it also made me start thinking.

Aleric had always told me that he couldn't use my blood to open gateways unless I shed the blood voluntarily. That was clearly a good reason why he didn't slice me open himself and take as much blood as he wanted. But what if there was more to it than that? What if my blood had a very different power when it was shed by the night magic's creatures? Luke had theorized that my bloody nose might have had something to do with the magic in the square finally letting me go, but that had hardly been as dramatic as what just happened to the eagle.

And then I recalled something I had entirely dismissed from my memory, something that had struck me at the time as strange but that I'd ultimately ignored as unimportant. When Aleric had taken my virginity, he'd used a condom. Doing so had made absolutely no sense, and when I'd questioned him about it, his answers had been deliberately evasive. He'd also never used one again—because he only expected me to bleed the first time.

I turned slowly toward Aleric and saw that his Nightstruck were all in full retreat and that he'd put a good bit of distance between us while keeping a wary eye on me. I looked back and forth between him and the blood that pooled in my palm and felt a slow, incongruous smile spread over my lips even as my teeth chattered in the bone-chilling cold.

"You *can't* draw my blood," I said, feeling the rightness of my words. "It's poisonous to you when you draw it yourself, whether it's voluntary or not."

I hadn't *meant* to cut myself on the eagle's spikes—just like I hadn't *meant* to prick myself with the pin that had been in the baby's blanket—but it was still my own actions that had caused the wound. The big difference between the two incidents was that with the baby, it had been a totally normal, nonmagical pin that had drawn my blood, not the spikes of a construct animated by the night magic.

Cupping my hand around the blood, no longer feeling the pain, I struggled to my feet and was pleased to see Aleric take a couple more steps back. The eagle had turned back to its daytime self when I'd bled on it. I wondered what would happen if Aleric got some of my blood on him. He had no daytime self to return to. Would he die? Would he be sent back to his own world? And if so, would he be able to come back?

I was eager to find out, especially given the way he was looking at me. Like I was something dangerous. Like he was *afraid*.

I advanced on him, staggering because my feet were numb with cold and my whole body was racked with shivers. He licked his lips and took a nervous step back away from me. The edges of the water I'd dripped all over the pavement were starting to freeze, and it occurred to me that it might not be such a good thing that my hand wasn't hurting anymore. I had never been so cold in all my life, and I wanted to huddle in upon myself to try to conserve what body heat I had left, but I would probably never have an opportunity like this again. I had to take advantage, whatever the cost.

I kept my feet shuffling forward, picking up enough speed that Aleric felt compelled to turn and run.

I ran after him, closing my fist around the little well of blood in my palm and pumping my arms and legs to try to get something that resembled speed. My headlong sprint was likely no faster than your average jog, and Aleric had had a head start. I could barely feel the impact of my feet against the pavement, and I feared I would lose some toes to frostbite if I somehow miraculously survived the night.

My mind felt slow and lazy with a combination of cold and exhaustion, but I forced myself to keep moving, to keep running, even though Aleric was pulling ahead. Logic said there was no chance I could catch him. I wasn't a fast runner even when in top condition, and I was in pretty bad shape right now. The bitter air bit at my cheeks and burned on its way down my lungs, and I longed to get inside somewhere, anywhere, where it was warm. To get out of my soaking wet clothes and wrap myself in layers of blankets while drinking a scalding hot cup of cocoa.

Aleric reached the end of the bridge and ran down Market Street. His stride looked effortless, well short of a sprint, and yet he had no trouble keeping well ahead of me. I pressed myself for more speed, hoping the effort I was pouring into my run would warm me up at least a little.

I felt like my legs might shatter like fallen icicles every time I took a step, and sucking air into my lungs was torture. So much of my body was numb, but my throat burned with every forced breath, and my chest ached. I stumbled over a crack in the sidewalk and almost went down. If I fell, I wasn't sure I'd ever be able to get up again.

I wanted to lie down and quit fighting, wanted everything to just be over, but that was not among my options. And so I kept running, kept chasing, even though I knew my efforts would be futile.

Aleric was gaining distance on me, and when he got to Twenty-Eighth Street, about half a block ahead of me, he turned right and was out of sight. Not seeing my quarry made the urge to quit even stronger. My head was spinning strangely now, and the pavement felt unsteady under my feet. I staggered and stumbled every few steps, and yet my feet still propelled me forward.

I was certain that by the time I reached the corner, Aleric would be out of my sight. I was getting slower and slower when I hadn't been all that fast to start with. Aleric could probably have made it to the next block and turned another corner without even breaking a sweat. But my body was moving on autopilot now, and what was left of my mind knew that if I stopped, I'd die.

I was shocked when I reached the corner and saw Aleric standing still only about halfway down the block. He looked startled when he saw me, and I realized he'd come to a stop because he'd been sure I couldn't make it this far.

With a snarl of determination, I staggered down Twenty-Eighth Street. I couldn't manage a run anymore, my gait more of a limping, jerky jog, but I kept moving, my eyes locked on Aleric. He had not turned to run again, was instead standing there with his arms folded over his chest and a look of condescending amusement on his face. I guessed he was sure I was going to collapse before I reached him—and if I got close enough to make him rethink his assessment, he could just turn to run again and I'd never be able to catch him.

I couldn't feel the lower part of my legs, much less feel my feet, but I still heard it when I stepped on something that wasn't pavement. I glanced down and saw that I had stepped on a large sheet of plywood, painted gray to make it blend with the side-walk in the dark. I probably wouldn't have noticed it until too late even if it had been painted neon orange.

I tried to stop, or at least change course to go around the ply-wood instead of over it, but my momentum carried me another couple of steps forward until I was square in the middle of the plywood. Only it seemed the plywood was about as thick as your average sheet of tissue paper. I tried to turn around, but the cold and the exhaustion had stolen the last of my coordination, and I fell instead. I landed on the plywood on my butt and heard an ominous cracking sound. I had just enough time to see Aleric's victorious smirk before the wood gave way beneath me.

CHAPTER TWENTY-SIX

I didn't fall for long—it wasn't a very deep pit—but the landing drew a tortured scream from my throat. It felt like someone had thrust a spear through my lower back and through my shoulder. My head banged against rock, and another spear pierced the palm of my uninjured hand.

It was true the pit wasn't deep, but then it didn't have to be. My body weight was more than enough to drive me onto the sharp spikes that had been hidden beneath that sheet of plywood.

I tried to move, but the spikes that pierced my flesh wouldn't let me, and the pain of trying was too much. Already, my skin felt hot and sticky with blood.

Aleric came to squat at the edge of the pit, his eyes alight with sadistic pleasure as I whimpered. He grinned at me, delighted with his handiwork.

"This was supposed to happen because *I* was chasing *you*," he said. "I had your escape attempt all planned out, with Billy and Leo waiting to help guide you in the right direction. But I think I like this way better.

"Neither I, nor any of the constructs, nor any of the Night-struck have spilled your blood," he gloated. He actually rubbed his hands together like some cartoon villain, milking the moment for all it was worth. "You may not have chosen to bleed for me, but you were not forced, and that's good enough for the night magic."

I had the vague notion that I should say something, offer some last words of defiance, but I couldn't have spoken if I'd wanted to. I coughed weakly and tasted blood on my tongue.

"I'd have liked to have you willing," he said with a careless shrug. "We could have taken the whole world together, you and I. One gate at a time, until it was all ours. If only you hadn't insisted on being so difficult about it."

Black spots danced in my vision, and the pain from my wounds seemed somehow distant, almost irrelevant. That was kind of nice, even if it was a really, really bad sign.

"If you were willing to throw yourself off a bridge to keep yourself from cooperating," Aleric continued, "then I realized you were a lost cause. Better to salvage what I can from you and be done with it." His smile broadened. "Look at all that lovely blood you're spilling for me. I should be able to open at least ten or twelve gates with it, large ones at that."

His smile disappeared behind one of the black spots, which were growing steadily larger. I closed my eyes so I could stop seeing them, stop seeing *him*. His was not the last face I wanted imprinted on my mind when I died. I tried to conjure up Luke's face, to imagine him here with me, holding my hand and telling me it was okay, that I'd done my best and it wasn't my fault I'd failed. But the image kept slipping away, and I soon forgot what I'd been trying to do.

I sensed something vast and dark opening up beneath me. And I sensed myself starting a long, slow slide downward.

"Poor little Becket," Aleric's voice said from very far away. "You so wanted to be the hero of this story. But I have a secret to share with you: the darkness always wins. Always."

I forced my eyes open, willing myself to find one last gesture of defiance before all was lost. My vision was so hazy all I could see was his vague silhouette as he leaned over the pit, watching me die.

I coughed weakly and once again tasted blood in my mouth. The coppery tang reminded me why I'd been chasing Aleric in the first place. The spike in my shoulder prevented my left arm from moving, but an exploratory wiggle told me my other arm was usable.

It hurt so much I almost blacked out, but I managed to lift my right arm enough to cover my mouth with my hand, making as if I was trying to stifle a cough. Instead, I licked my bloody palm. I hoped my saliva and the blood already in my mouth wouldn't rob it of its potency. There were little sparkles around the edges of my vision now, and nothing seemed to hurt anymore. I supposed that meant I was almost gone. I would have one shot, and one shot only.

I gathered every last shred of strength I could find and breathed deeply through my nose, fighting my need to cough. Then I spit the mouthful of blood I had gathered at Aleric, with as much oomph as I could manage.

He cursed and tried to flinch away, but he hadn't seen it coming and was too slow. My blood hit his cheek, and he screamed in shock and apparent pain. He clapped his hand over his cheek and stared down at me in horror, his eyes wide. Even in the darkness, I could see by the little puffs of steam that left his mouth that he was panting, and it wasn't from running.

From somewhere in the distance, I heard a shout, and Aleric quickly looked up, his green eyes blazing with both fury and fear as he snarled at whoever had dared to disturb him.

My vision was growing continually dimmer, and my eyes were starting to flutter, wanting to close, but I was curious who was doing all that shouting. I wanted to stay alive and conscious long enough to find out, especially considering how Aleric looked. He hadn't gone up and disappeared in a puff of smoke like I might have hoped, but he was clearly horror-stricken anyway, still covering the side of his face where my blood had hit.

There was an explosive crack, and Aleric cried out again, doubling over. My eyes closed, and I forced them open one more time. I *needed* to know what had happened.

Aleric put his free hand to his shoulder, and it came away bloody. He gave me one last malevolent glare before he turned and ran. I heard another gunshot, but I couldn't keep my eyes open a moment longer.

Who the hell was shooting at Aleric? And how come he was wounded? I had to think that had something to do with my blood.

I hoped that second shot had taken him out. It was hardly an unconditional victory while I lay broken and dying in the pit he had built to trap me, but it felt like a win for the home team anyway.

I died with a smile on my lips.

CHAPTER TWENTY-SEVEN

I woke up and had no idea where I was or what was happening. I groggily assumed I was in one of the many anonymous hotel rooms I'd shared with Dr. Gilliam while we were on the run. My eyes were all crusty, and my mouth was dry as ashes, and I wanted nothing more but to go back to sleep. Except now that I was awake, I realized how much my entire body hurt. I groaned and opened my eyes.

I wasn't in a hotel room. I was in a hospital. There was an IV stuck in the back of my hand, and I heard a beeping sound that corresponded with the beating of my heart.

I remembered falling into the spike-filled pit, and I remembered the sound of shouting voices and gunshots. I tried to sit up, but it hurt too much, and I cried out in pain.

I'd been too disoriented to notice my mom, sitting in a chair beside my bed. Her arms were folded on the bed beside me, pillowing her head as she slept. I swallowed hard and wondered how long I'd been out. I couldn't see a clock anywhere, and a glance out the window told me it was still dark out, but that was the most information I could glean.

"Mom?" I croaked, then grimaced. My throat was so sore it felt like someone had taken a sandblaster to it.

Mom must not have been sleeping very soundly. She instantly

jerked awake and raised her head. When she saw my open eyes, she burst into tears and reached for me, then pulled back.

"I don't know where it's safe to touch you," she said between hiccups, then settled for laying her hand over the back of mine.

I blinked, struggling to make sense of the unexpected reality that I was alive. I didn't want to test my voice again, so I settled for whispering. "What happened? Why am I not dead?"

Still crying, my mom reached out and brushed some hair back from my face. "You texted Sam to tell him where Piper was. He went and got her, and she told him what you were doing. He went after you and found you in that . . . that . . ." She shuddered and hugged herself.

It must have been Sam who'd shot Aleric. "Is Aleric dead?"

Mom's brow furrowed in puzzlement. "Who?"

"Aleric! The guy who was trying to kill me!"

"Sam said he chased off some Nightstruck guy who was standing by you, but I don't think he killed anyone."

That was a damn shame. Had it been wishful thinking on my part when I'd thought Aleric had been wounded?

No, I realized with certainty. If Aleric hadn't just discovered he was vulnerable to gunshot wounds, he never would have retreated, never would have let Sam rescue me from that pit.

"What time is it?" I asked, glancing at the darkness of the window once more. It felt like about a thousand hours must have passed since I'd almost died, and yet it was still nighttime.

Mom glanced at her watch. "It's three o'clock." She saw me staring at the window. "In the afternoon."

I shook my head in denial even as my heart sank. Aleric had lured me into that pit not because he was trying to kill me but because he was trying to "harvest" my blood. If I'd been conscious when Sam had come to my rescue, I could have told him how important it was to clean up my blood. Whether he would have believed me or not was anyone's guess. But as it was, he'd had no way to know how important that blood was to Aleric.

It was almost funny. Aleric had given up on using me as a re-newable resource and had planned my death, but thanks to Sam's rescue, he had his cake and could eat it, too. I wondered how many new gates he'd opened, but I didn't really want to know.

"This is all my fault," my mom said miserably, and tears shone in her eyes once more.

I was so used to thinking everything was all my fault that it felt really strange to hear those words come out of my mother's mouth. At first, I had no idea what she was talking about, but I suppose that was because I was drugged to the gills. It took until she claimed responsibility to remember that she had brought the police to the hotel, that because of her I had had to go on the run—and Aleric had gotten his hands on Luke.

"Luke!" I cried, forgetting about the sore throat until too late. I tried once again to sit up, but despite all the meds the pain prac-tically knocked me out, and my mom hurried to put her hands on her shoulders and keep me down.

"Shh, shh, easy honey," she said. "You've had a bunch of sur-geries and more stitches than I can count. You need to rest."

"Where's Luke?" I insisted, though I gave in to the pressure of her hands and didn't try again to sit up. "Is he safe?" My en-tire purpose in going to that bridge was to try to save Luke, and for a little while, I'd allowed myself to hope that I'd succeeded. But the look on my mom's face answered my question, and it wasn't the answer I was looking for.

"Why don't you just concentrate on getting better and let me worry about everything else for a while."

"Aleric was supposed to let him go," I whispered, wondering

what else I could possibly have done. Surely there was some way I could have saved Luke if only I'd been smart enough.

"We don't know where he is," my mom said. "I haven't spoken to Dr. Gilliam since early last night, but I'm sure if Luke had come home, she would have let me know—just so I could let you know. She asked me to tell you she doesn't blame you for what happened."

My eyes burned and I had to blink rapidly to stave off tears. Dr. Gilliam knew exactly how much of that blame rested on my shoulders. "Aleric never would have taken Luke if it weren't for me." I felt my lower lip quivering dangerously. "But you believe I'm having paranoid delusions and none of this has anything to do with me."

My mom sighed heavily. "I'll admit that's what I thought before. It just all sounds so . . . crazy. But after everything I've been told by Dr. Gilliam, and Piper, and Sam, it's getting harder to deny." She glanced at the window, at the darkness that reigned at three in the afternoon. That probably made my story sound a little more credible, too.

I closed my eyes, partly to help fight the tears, but also because our brief conversation had sapped what little energy I had. Sleep was tugging at me, and I wanted to give in. I didn't want to think about what Luke might be going through right now—assuming he was still alive. If Aleric thought I had died in that pit, then he wouldn't need his hostage anymore.

I was just going to have to hope that whatever magic linked us told him I was still alive, because no matter how many gates he had already opened, I was sure he would want to open more if he knew I had more blood to give him.

I was exhausted, in a lot of pain, and greatly troubled by the darkness. I was terrified for Luke, and worried about what my own future held. I wasn't handcuffed to the bed, and I saw no sign of the police looking over me, but I doubted they had changed their minds about arresting me, even if Piper had recanted her accusations. I could ask my mom about it, but I figured that particular conversation could wait.

"Try to get some rest, sweetheart," my mom said gently, once again stroking my hair.

I made a sound of murmured agreement, and was sure I would soon sink back down into sleep. But for all the doom and gloom, I was also nurturing a tiny spark of hope.

Aleric had bled. That meant he was no longer invulnerable. And one way or another, I was going to get to him, and I was going to kill him. Maybe that would banish the night magic, and maybe it wouldn't. But twice last night I'd almost died, and I hadn't fought and clawed my way back from the brink of death to let Aleric and the Night Makers win.

My blood was the key. And if I had to shed every remaining drop of it to put things right, then that was exactly what I would do.